The Daffodil Garden

Rosie Chapel

First printing 2019
ISBN: 978-0-6485283-1-9

Ulfire Pty. Ltd.
P.O. Box 1481
South Perth
WA 6951
Australia

www.rosiechapel.com

Cover Designed by Tina Adams
www.tina-adams.com

Dedication

For those who refuse to let their scars define them…
this book is dedicated to you

Acknowledgements

My abiding gratitude to…

Janet, Melanie, Paola, Amy, Julie, Lilly, Jackie, Maria, Jade,
and my amazing friends in the 'London' chat,
for their love, support, and occasional
well-deserved, thankfully – almost always virtual, kick up the
butt!

Nick for being a sounding board,
regarding the historical military details.

Graham from A Fading Street Publishing
for his editing wizardry.

My hubby – just because!
And last, but definitely not least…
Pepsi and Poppy – for their pawsome supawvision,
and crazy antics which never fail to make me laugh!

Chapter One

Swinging an oddly shaped bag, a tall woman, shoulders covered in a warm wrap and whose gown had seen better days, strode briskly along a wet street. Doing her best to avoid the muddy water splashed up by passing carriages, she exchanged cheerful greetings with several people, smiled and nodded to others. Finally, the sun was peeking through, a welcome change after days of chilly rain, one which prompted her to whistle as she marched along.

Lucy Truscott was on her way home from work. The bag she was carrying was full of books, the titles therein covering a variety of topics from fiction to folklore, history to politics. Lucy seized every opportunity to broaden her mind, to educate herself as much as she was able, given she had never been to school.

Born in a dingy room to an unwed mother, Lucy's start to life was humble and, had it not been for her loving parent, things might have turned out quite differently. Cecilia Truscott was determined her daughter would not be dragged into the seedier occupations of those living in their neighbourhood. Cecilia had once worked for nobility and, even though such positions were difficult to come by, a good education meant Lucy should be able to find decent employment in a shop or one of the museums, or even in a merchant's household as a maid.

Cecilia taught Lucy to read and write, and helped her understand basic arithmetic, as well as manners and deportment, sewing and cooking. To be fair, Lucy chafed at some of her lessons; she preferred to run wild through the parks or gardens, to find a good tree, up which she could climb, and from where she could watch the world go by. Almost by accident, Lucy began to mimic those she observed from her hidden perch; the graceful bearing of ladies when they walked, the way they spoke, and how they treated others. Lucy was fascinated by the difference in behaviour across the elite of society; some aloof and condescending, while others were friendly and kind.

Lucy studied everyone and everything, deciding the majority of the nobility were a rather rude and mean-spirited bunch. She knew how hard those of her class worked, so these people could live a life of luxury and, while she accepted it was a matter of luck whether you were born into riches or poverty, she did not think that gave those with, the right to deride those without.

"You must understand, most have no idea how we live," her mother had once tried to justify the attitude of some countess or other who was unconscionably rude to Lucy one afternoon when she had been walking with her mother through Hyde Park.

"That is no excuse, Mama. They should be setting the example, and she had no call to speak to me thus," Lucy groused, her expression mulish. "I apologised for stepping in front of her, I even curtsied, that should have been it. Instead she whacked me with her parasol and called me a ragamuffin." Lucy looked down at her clothes, which although faded and unfashionable were of reasonable quality and suited the wearer. "I don't think I look like a ragamuffin." Her mouth drooped and her pretty face morphed from vexed to doleful.

"No, that you don't, my pet. Some ladies are spoilt and impolite. They should be pitied, for have probably never known love or compassion, becoming cold and empty. Remember Lucy, always be polite, do not give them reason to belittle you, and retain your empathy, for without it you are nothing but a hollow shell."

Lucy, with all the righteous indignation of being ten and five, scowled and ignored her mother's words, still seething from the countess' unkind attitude. Later when she was lying in her narrow bed, the incident replayed itself over and over again, and Lucy conceded her mother was correct, they were to be pitied. How sad their lives were so restricted, they could not sing in the street, shout for joy or jump in puddles, activities Lucy continued to indulge in whenever possible — to her mother's chagrin.

She never forgot her mother's plea, however, and tried her best to treat everyone she met with the same courtesy regardless of their station. This is not to say she always succeeded, and if someone behaved in a dubious manner, they would feel the lash of her tongue. Growing up on the periphery of the rookeries, Lucy had amassed an impressive collection of expletives, which inevitably shocked the recipient of her ire because her usual demeanour was respectful and polite. For her mother's sake, Lucy made a concerted effort to curb the more volatile aspects of her nature, but her vibrant personality meant she would never curtail it entirely.

Her exuberance *did* win over Mr Abbot, the proprietor of The Wise Owl Bookstore in Old Compton Street, who found himself engaging her as an assistant despite being absolutely certain he had no need of help at all. Since then, she had proved her worth time and time again, and the store was flourishing. Lucy was a voracious reader and as such was always able to suggest a book to even the most discerning buyer. Moreover, she had the knack of knowing how to make the shop look inviting. A table neatly placed in each of the bay windows overlooking the busy street, scattered with a cleverly chosen selection of books, along with a plate of fresh jam tartlets or small slices of fruit cake, was bound to attract attention.

Not content with that, Lucy suggested the paper they used to wrap a purchase ought to be discreetly stamped in one corner with an owl, then between them, they came up with the idea of placing a slim bookmark inside each tome, imprinted with the same image, no words, just the image. Anyone reading had a way of marking the page they were at, and the owl would remind them where they bought the book. It was not long after this that a shingle with an owl perched on branch, a book in its claws, appeared over the doorway.

Mr Abbot had to admit Lucy was shrewd; business was booming and, although situated a little way from the usual haunts of the elite, his shop graced customers from every walk of life.

That was six years ago, and The Wise Owl had gone from strength to strength; Mr Abbot eventually expanding into the adjacent building. He was astonished Lucy still worked for him. She had never shown any desire to follow the example of her friends who had married, declaring she was not about to give up what little independence she had gained. At two and twenty, Lucy had grown into a strikingly attractive young woman, yet was wholly unaware of it, or the hordes of bachelors who frequented the shop, purely on the off-chance she might notice them.

Cecilia Truscott had died three years previously, and although Lucy was devastated, she refused to let her grief swamp her, knowing her mother would not want her to be unhappy.

"Go on, live your life for yourself, enjoy every minute and do not waste a single one worrying about me. I have no regrets, and although not everything happened in the manner I expected, the choices I made gave me you, and for that, I am thankful every day," Cecilia informed her daughter hoarsely, when in the last throes of the fever, which shortly thereafter carried her to her grave. It was a conversation Lucy often revisited, for her mother was surely referring to the lingering shadow of her father. A man whose identity Cecilia never revealed.

For the most part, Lucy did not care. If he had no interest in his daughter, his daughter *definitely* had no interest in him.

Occasionally, at night when she couldn't sleep, she found herself thinking about him. She believed she must take after him, for she did not resemble her mother. Cecilia Truscott was a petite woman, with brown eyes and straight, chestnut-coloured hair. Lucy's curly dark-blonde hair, scattered with sun-kissed streaks was almost untameable, her eyes were an arresting shade of bluish-grey, and, unless you were subject to her ire, her lips were nearly always curved into a bright smile. Lucy presumed these traits came from her father and in quiet moments when she pondered his existence — if indeed he was still alive — she wondered whether he was someone who lived in the neighbourhood, or much further afield. Her mother did not discuss him, he was taboo. Periodically, Lucy dared pose a question, but her mother refused to be drawn, and these were the only times Lucy could recall Cecilia ever becoming angry.

Today, her parents were the last thing on her mind, she was looking forward to getting home, enjoying a hot meal, and putting her feet up. The shop had been busy all day causing her to miss luncheon. She managed to gobble down a slice of cake mid-afternoon, but her stomach thought her throat had been cut, so hungry did she feel. As she walked, her unusual height, dignified bearing, and distinctive features, drew many an interested gaze but Lucy did not notice. Her head was full of the last book she read, what she might have for dinner, and whether she could afford a new gown.

Chapter Two

Approaching one of the crossroads along Shaftesbury Avenue — the road, which acted almost as a delineation between the more salubrious neighbourhoods and the outskirts of the slums — Lucy paused to make sure there were no carriages approaching. About to step out into the road, her attention was drawn to a heated debate happening alongside her. Four people — three men and a young lady, all fashionably attired, seemed in dispute about whether to walk and in which direction, or hail a hackney.

Lucy frowned, this was not the safest area for those unfamiliar with its... idiosyncrasies, to be taking a constitutional, why on earth were they in this locale in the first place. *Surely, they were conversant with the hazards taking the wrong street could present?* Shaking it off, it was not her concern, Lucy peered along the street and noticed a four-horse carriage careening towards them far more quickly than would be deemed prudent given the wet conditions. Judiciously, taking three steps backwards away from the spray of mud and water being kicked up, she turned to alert those arguing to the imminent likelihood of being thoroughly splattered.

When she thought about it later, Lucy could not put her finger on what prompted her to move closer, but as she did so, there was a sharp cry, and the young woman seemed to sort of trip over backwards — although on what Lucy was never certain. In slow motion and with arms flailing, she tumbled into the path of the oncoming carriage. The three men did nothing to prevent it, just stood there, mouths agape. Without stopping to think, Lucy dashed forward and, grabbing the woman around the waist, dragged her out of harm's way, the pair of them landing hard on the pavement in an ungainly tangle of limbs.

Winded, Lucy couldn't speak, but the three men suddenly found their voices and, while lifting the woman off the ground, berated Lucy for assaulting their companion. Ignoring, or maybe uncaring of the fact Lucy was now caked in mud, her dress ruined, and her skin scuffed from the unforgiving flagstones, they fussed over the other girl.

"Rodney, do hush," a clear treble begged, "she did not push me, she pulled me, out of the way. It was actually..." the woman stopped abruptly, turned to Lucy and put out a hand to help her up. "My dear, thank you for your quick action. I do believe I would be dead under the wheels if not for you."

Grudgingly, Lucy allowed herself to be righted and as she came face-to-face with the person behind the voice, her mouth fell open in shock. Except for a slight variation in height, hair, and eye colour, and acknowledging she was probably a couple of years older than the woman holding her hand, to Lucy it was like looking at her own reflection.

The young lady mirrored Lucy's expression, while the three men questioned whether they had lost their senses. While clearly from opposite walks of life, the two women were so alike they could have been sisters

"I-I... h-how... w-who..." Lucy clamped her mouth shut and inhaled a deep breath. Dropping a neat curtsy, she tried again. "It was my pleasure, my lady. I do hope you were not hurt by my incautious behaviour, but to let you fall was unconscionable."

The other woman wriggled her body, stretched her arms, and flexed her hands. "I am uninjured, just a trifle muddy." She grinned suddenly, and so infectious was it, Lucy found herself grinning back.

"I am glad. Might I be so bold as to suggest you do not tarry in this neighbourhood. Not everyone has benign intentions." Lucy curtsied a second time and turned to leave.

"Please, wait a moment. I should like to know your name if

you have no objection."

"Why?" Lucy asked bluntly.

"Well, for one thing, you saved my life. That will not go unrewarded. Furthermore, you look just like me, and I do not believe in coincidence. We were fated to meet on what you claim is a disreputable corner, and even though the reason why eludes me, I have no mind to overlook it. No..." she waved aside panicked splutters from the man she addressed as Rodney, "...do not be such an old fusspot. What makes you think I would abandon someone to struggle home after so selfless an act? The lady is dirty and wet, through no fault of her own." Bringing her penetrating gaze back to Lucy, she concluded with, "Might I ask your your name?"

"Lucy Truscott."

There was a hiss from one of the three men, immediately stifled, and Lucy stared at them, brow knitted. All looked politely indifferent, yet all studied her intently and, although she sensed undercurrents, presumed they were simply vexed at their companion's determined attitude, and dismissed the sound as fancy.

"I am Elspeth Gillingham, and please say you will come home with me. We can get your gown cleaned and enjoy some refreshments. Moreover, it is not every day you meet your double, and I should like very much to learn more about you."

Lucy glanced down at her grubby dress, then spied her books lying in a puddle after spilling from her bag which she dropped in her haste to reach the woman before she was crushed by the carriage. She closed her eyes, *oh no, Mr Abbot would be so upset*. Elspeth followed her gaze and gathered up the maltreated tomes, shaking off the water.

"Do not fret, I am sure these will be salvageable." She read the titles as she handed each book to one of her companions. "Shakespeare, Austin, Radcliffe, Greek Myths..." her voice died away as she registered the last two books were non-fiction. One bore the rather rambling title of *The History of the Decline and Fall of the Roman Empire: Volume III*, and the other appeared to relate to politics. "You have rather an eclectic choice of reading matter... politics?" her tone quizzical.

"I believe it is important to understand why parliament does what it does, as for Gibbons... well I love history." Lucy felt impelled to elaborate, blushing a little, as she reached out to retrieve the books from the impassive gentleman currently holding them.

"Mr Garrick will hold onto your books until 'tis time for you to return home. Now please do come with me. You will catch a chill standing around in those garments."

"Lady Elspeth." Everything about this young lady screamed nobility and Lucy erred on the side of caution in her term of address. "I live not far from here, you do not need to interrupt your afternoon any more than it has so far been. Thank you, sir." She turned to address Mr Garrick. "Might I take those from you?"

"Please, Miss Truscott, Lucy."

Something in Elspeth's tone made Lucy hesitate and she scanned the younger woman's features. Her lovely face was shadowed, and Lucy was beset by the oddest notion something worried her. Unsure what, if anything she could do to alleviate her apprehension, Lucy realised she wanted to try. Nodding her head slowly, she opened her palms in a gesture of acquiescence.

"As you wish." Taking the formality from her words with a friendly smile. Her agreement rewarded by Elspeth's beam of happiness. "Would you like me to hail a cab? I expect I shall have more success than you in this neighbourhood," Lucy offered wryly, as she scanned the streets. Putting her thumb and middle finger in her mouth, Lucy blew, her piercing whistle making the other four flinch.

A hackney came into view from around the corner, rumbling to a halt alongside the group. The driver hopped down and unfolded the step whereupon the aforementioned Mr Garrick, assisted the two ladies inside. Rodney — Lucy had no idea whether he was a Mr or a Lord — and the other gentleman, whom Elspeth introduced as Mr Lindsay, joined them, while Mr Garrick climbed up to sit alongside the driver.

Twenty minutes later they arrived in a quiet square, Elspeth pointing out all manner of interesting sights on the way. Many, Lucy had already seen; she was an inveterate explorer and walked for miles on her infrequent free days but, unwilling to quash her new acquaintance's enthusiasm, held her tongue.

"Welcome to Rycote House," Elspeth said as they walked up the steps to the front door, which opened as if by magic when they reached it. A smartly liveried butler admitted them, taking in her ladyship's state of dishevelment and an unknown woman similarly bedraggled, without so much as the blink of an eye.

"Lady Elspeth, madam." His welcome including Lucy, who was beginning to feel this whole thing was a mistake. "Do come into the parlour where it is warm." He took Elspeth's cloak and would have taken Lucy's wrap, but she shook her head, unwilling to let anyone see how threadbare her gown was.

"Thank you, Harris." Elspeth smiled at the butler, before taking Lucy's hand, and leading her across the immaculate hall to a charmingly apportioned parlour decorated in soft lemon and cream. Despite the sunshine, the day was cool, and a fire crackled merrily in the vast hearth. "You must allow me to have your clothes cleaned, Lucy." Elspeth entreated again. "We are almost the same size, doubtless one of my gowns will fit you."

Lucy swallowed a snort of laughter and shook her head. Elspeth was of slight build and at least half a head shorter than herself. "I do not think so, my lady, although I admire your optimism. If you permit me, I shall stand by the fire for a minute or so, and then be on my way."

Elspeth tutted in exasperation. Walking over to a dark-red

bell-rope hanging in the corner, she gave it a tug. Less than a minute later a young girl appeared and, after dropping a curtsy, listened to Elspeth's list of instructions.

"Please arrange for two hot baths, one for me and one for Miss Truscott… the one in Hyacinth, I think." Tapping her chin. "While our guest is bathing, see to the cleaning of her dress, and find something suitable for her to wear. One of my gowns, or maybe one of Mama's…" ignoring Lucy who was desperately trying to intercede, "…and please ask Alice to assist. Thank you, Penny." Elspeth grinned at the young maid who responded in kind, bobbed another curtsy, and hurried off to do her mistress' bidding.

Elspeth sat Lucy in one of the huge wing-backed chairs circling the roaring fire and engaged her in light conversation. A pleasant half hour passed, then Penny returned to advise both baths were ready. Tucking Lucy's hand under hers, Elspeth escorted her up the stairs, handing her off to another maid when they came to a room which had a flower painted on the door. *Ahhh*, thought Lucy, *Hyacinth, now I understand*, feeling gauche at not realising.

Allowing herself to be ushered into the room, she spent the next little while being bathed, and having her hair washed. Alice, Lucy presumed this was she, would have towelled her dry and smoothed in some lightly scented cream had Lucy permitted, but the latter was used to looking after herself, and was uncomfortable with such pampering. Gently, she extricated herself from Alice's ministrations, affirming she was quite capable of getting dry and dressed without help.

Chapter Three

To Lucy's chagrin, Alice had removed all her clothes, including her chemise, so she wrapped herself in one of the towels while she rubbed her hair dry with another, and took the time to study the room she was in. Decorated in delicate hues of blue and cream, with an enormous bed, dressing table, two ornate wardrobes, and a chest of drawers, not to mention a couple of chairs hugging the neat fireplace, it was quite the most magnificent bedchamber Lucy had ever seen, and she was awestruck.

It was the height of rudeness to gawk in such a manner, but she was alone, and anyway, was helpless to prevent her jaw dropping. *Oh, to be rich.* She let her mind wander to her dream. The one where she was rescued by a knight in shining armour and whisked off to a fairy tale castle. All her worries about how to pay the landlord, or whether she could afford a pair of boots or a winter cloak, forgotten.

For a moment Lucy pretended it was her bedchamber, so different from the tiny attic in which she lived; a single room, which served as both bedroom and kitchen. Besides her narrow bed, the only other furniture was a small table and three rickety chairs. No fireplace, no bath. Lucy's face flamed as she compared the two, imagining Elspeth's reaction if ever she saw it. She would be horrified.

Forcing her mortification aside, Lucy concentrated on the unexpected encounter. Elspeth's lovely face drifted through her mind. How alike they looked. A connection seemed undeniable yet, at the same time, impossible. Maybe they were very distant cousins? She discounted that immediately. If they were legitimate cousins, it was unlikely she would be living in a hovel. A disquieting thought began to nudge at Lucy's consciousness.

Was she the result of an illicit affair? Had her mother chosen to indulge in, or been an unwilling partner, in a liaison with a member of the *ton*? Someone in Elspeth's family, perchance?

Lucy wanted to leave. It would not be fair to humiliate Elspeth or her family by her presence in this elegant house. Muffling an oath, Lucy paced the floor willing Alice to return with some clothes. No, she needed her own back, that way she would not be required to return anything she had borrowed. Yanking her damp hair into a loose plait, she tried to calm her nerves. The ormolu clock on the mantlepiece ticked sonorously, and it seemed forever before Alice bustled in, her arms full of material.

"Here we are, miss. I have found some dresses which might fit. I think Lady Elspeth's will be too short, but one of these should do."

"Might it not be easier for me to just have my own clothes? I can change when I get home." Lucy pleaded, quietly. Alice saw the uncertainty on Lucy's face and sought to reassure.

"Your dress and chemise are wet and dirty, miss. You might catch a chill, and her ladyship would be that upset."

"Yes, but if I might still have them, and then maybe you could show me the back door and tell Lady Elspeth I left without you realising. I do not want to get you into trouble, but you must see I am not one who should wear such quality." Lucy's tones were desperate even as her fingers stroked the material. It felt sublime. Dark lashes swept hot cheeks as she imagined herself in one of these fine gowns.

Alice, years younger than Lucy, patted her arm in a maternal manner. "Come now, miss. Don't talk like that. Whatever your station, I hear you saved her ladyship's life today. That makes you a queen amongst us staff. She is a treasure that girl and we would be heartbroken if anything happened to her. Been a frequency of accidents lately, a bit concerning if you ask me, but it's not my place…" Alice let that thought trail off as she turned her attention to the dresses. Lifting this one and that, she decided on a simple day gown in a pale grey hue that on anyone else, would have looked drab, but on Lucy, it complemented her lightly tanned skin and enhanced her intriguing eyes.

Fastening the last button, Alice stepped back and studied Lucy, twitching the fabric a little, making sure it sat properly. Satisfied, she nodded, then untied the plait, and brushed the fair curls until they shone. Twisting and pinning, the maid fashioned a neat bun, a few tendrils left loose to frame Lucy's thin face.

"There you go, miss. You look lovely and no mistake."

"You are a miracle worker, Alice." Lucy stared at her reflection, astonished at what the maid had achieved with so little.

"Go on, miss." Alice blushed at the compliment and shooed Lucy down the stairs to the parlour where Elspeth was chatting to the three men who had accompanied them back to Rycote House.

As Lucy entered the room, all four turned and stared. The silence lengthened, and Lucy found herself shifting awkwardly from foot to foot, once again possessed with the urge to hitch her new skirts and run as though the devil himself was after her.

"Have I missed some mud?" Lucy ventured, rubbing her face self-consciously, feeling heat steal up her cheeks at their continued scrutiny.

"Beg pardon," Rodney spoke first. "'Tis only…" he couldn't formulate what he wanted to say, recalling rumours of a bygone romance, hushed up and forgotten. Prior to this moment, he and the other two men had almost persuaded themselves, Lucy's likeness to Elspeth was a coincidence, but no longer. Her height, her colouring, her features, were replicated in a painting which hung in the library. She was the dead set double of Elspeth's grandmother.

"Lucy, come with me." Elspeth found her tongue and

grasped Lucy's hand. Bewildered, Lucy allowed herself to be dragged through the house, the three men on their heels, their presence perplexing Lucy who was curious as to why Elspeth had no chaperone. Opening the third door along a cool hallway, Elspeth came to a halt and, with a flourish, flung her arm towards the portrait over the fireplace.

Lucy sucked in a shocked breath. It was like looking at herself, more so than when she first saw Elspeth. Seated on an ornate chair, a regally elegant woman — dressed in an exquisite gown of dove-grey silk, a dark red cloak draped carelessly over the arm of the chair acting as the perfect counterfoil — pinned the viewer with a perceptive gaze. Her lips curved ever so slightly, her countenance suggesting she was amused by something. Her hair and eye colour — identical to Lucy's.

"My grandmother," Elspeth said by way of explanation, while they admired the picture.

"I-I…" Lucy was unable to form a coherent sentence. The traitorous theory whispered at the periphery of her mind and would not be ignored. *Who **was** she?*

"Lucy, you and I *must* be related," Elspeth's words cut into her confusion. "I will speak to Papa."

"No!" Lucy spoke more sharply than she intended. "Mama, she… I cannot… your family…"

"Whatever happened, it was decades ago. You are not responsible for what your parents did. Moreover, if you had not been born you could not have saved me today." Elspeth's convoluted reasoning warmed Lucy's heart, which seemed to be cracking. Everything she knew, everything she believed was being eroded as she gazed at the painting of the woman before her. She bent her head as she blinked back pesky tears. No! Weeping was for children.

"Thank you, Elspeth. Your generous nature is a balm, but most are not as understanding or forgiving as you. I doubt any in your family wish to reawaken memories of a transgression which occurred so long ago. 'Tis cruel to remind them, they may not even know it happened. You have been kindness itself this afternoon. Now, it is best I slip away, forgotten before I reach the street. I will arrange for this gorgeous gown to be returned forthwith and none need to know of this business." Lucy held the eyes of each in the room. The three men smiled, rather sadly she thought, but Elspeth was not to be thwarted.

"'Tis clear you and I are related. How, is yet to be determined, but I do not want to lose you. If you go, that will be it. You will disappear as though we never met, and I shall not see you again. This is not something I am prepared to contemplate. Your parentage may surprise me, it may cause discomfort, even anger, but none of that is your fault. You exist, you cannot be denied. Oh, that you may be my cousin or better still, my half-sister, a boon I have long desired."

Lucy gaped at this self-possessed creature who blithely implied her family would, with open arms, welcome an interloper, one whom no one even knew existed until this day. Half of her felt a tingle of excitement at the possibility of knowing her heritage, even though it was clearly on the wrong side of the sheets, the other half was terrified of the repercussions such revelations would engender.

She raised her hands in defeat. She had no defence against Elspeth's determination, but she tried one more time to stop this madness. "Lady Elspeth, a word of warning. I appreciate your need to discover the truth, but it could cause more harm than good. Mayhap 'tis better to leave secrets where they are buried. When I walk out of your home today, my life will continue as before, as though we did not collide on a wet street. Your family remain none the wiser that one member behaved unwisely decades ago. No one is hurt, no one is called to account. My mother is dead, I have no idea whether my father lives for I do not even know his name. Mama refused to divulge any information about him even on her death bed. My only certainty is that she loved him and continued to do so until she drew her last breath."

The old hurt reared its ugly head. Her mother did her best but knowing her life had been altered out of all recognition because she bore a child, tore at Lucy. If she was honest, she wanted to know whether the man ever knew about her mother's pregnancy. Was he married? Was it a lengthy affair or a brief dalliance? Did she leave of her own volition or did he throw her out, reject her? Did he force himself on Cecilia? No — that could not be right; her mother always spoke of him with warmth, her voice gentling in remembrance. Whatever happened, their relationship had been so special, Cecilia protected his name to her own detriment.

Lucy recalled the name-calling, the slurs and the innuendo. Her mother did what she could to shield her daughter, but the people among whom they lived were inherently judgemental. A single mother — the story her husband died at the beginning of the French Revolutionary Wars, regarded with scepticism, although none could refute it — meant Cecilia was treated with suspicion. Her neighbours seemed to believe she wanted a husband to support her, and felt her a threat to their own marriages, even though she never showed one iota of interest in another man. Lucy sighed heavily unaware the four in the room were watching her intently.

Chapter Four

"Miss Truscott?" Rodney's voice brought Lucy back to the present.

"I beg your pardon, sir... or is it my lord? Did I miss something?"

"I asked whether you would mind providing your mother's name?" Ignoring her first question.

Lucy blinked. "I do not think so, not yet. You may know more than I, and I am not sure I can deal with your censure," she replied in undertones. "No, not yet..." she repeated, her words dwindling. Her head was beginning to ache. This was too much. Glancing out of the window, she realised evening was drawing in, the day was over, and she had to get home. Her dinner wouldn't cook itself, meagre though it was. "Lady Elspeth, whatever you decide, I must return home. I have a meal to prepare, and an early start on the morrow. Mayhap we will meet again. I shall leave you my address and you can take the time to reflect on the implications of staying in contact with me."

"No, Lucy, you ought to stay for..."

"No, I ought not. My dear, if what you are beginning to suspect is true, you need time to process it. By all means talk to your family, with these three gentlemen, at least one of whom seems aware of some dark secret." She arched a brow at Rodney who had the grace to blush. "Do not rush into something you cannot extricate yourself from, because once that which was hidden is exposed, nothing will be the same. Thank you for lending me this gown. With your permission I shall leave through the domestic entrance and arrange its return with Alice."

Lucy faced the three men and dipped a perfect curtsy, turning to repeat the gesture to Elspeth. Then, she said goodbye and in a shimmer of grey satin was gone.

The hush that fell over the room upon Lucy's departure was palpable. None could find a way to describe adequately what had unfolded during the preceding hours. Elspeth, as though released from a spell, rushed after Lucy, only to find she had departed — without leaving her address. One of the footmen was dispatched to track her footsteps, but upon his return reported no sign of her. Back in the library, Elspeth rang for drinks and sank onto one of the chairs, indicating the other three should do likewise. Once refreshments had been served and all were comfortable, they began to talk.

*****

A little under an hour after she stepped out into the gloom, Lucy was climbing the stairs to her lodgings. Locking the door behind her she lit the few candles, which made her humble abode seem cosy instead of miserable. Her appetite gone, she sat at the table, her mind whirling with the events of the day. Night fell, stars blinked into existence, and still, she sat.

It was only when the candles began to dim that Lucy dragged her thoughts back to the mundane and remembered the books last seen in the possession of Mr Garrick. *Dammit all, that was inconvenient.* Bringing her to the peculiar dynamic of why a young lady of the *ton* was apparently being chaperoned by three men with nary a woman in sight, and out of the blue recalled Alice's comment. A chapter of unexplained accidents! Who would want to hurt Elspeth? Rycote House… was that named after the title holder? Maybe Mr Abbot would know. He was well versed in the rules of Society. She would ask him.

Yawning, Lucy pushed all else aside, there was naught she could do this night. After getting undressed, she made sure the lovely gown was hung properly, and slipped into her nightdress.

As she snuggled under the blankets, images raced through her head; Elspeth, the parlour, the library, and the possibility of a maybe teased at her. It was very late before a fitful slumber claimed her.

*****

Three days later, Lucy was stacking a new delivery of books on one of the many shelves while chatting with Mrs Wrightson, a regular customer, about the availability of a recently published version of Chaucer's Canterbury Tales, when she heard mention of her name. Concluding her discussion, she headed over to the desk where Mr Abbot was deep in conversation with a familiar figure.

"Your lordship," she greeted the sombre gentleman with a curtsy and a title, still uncertain as to his status.

"Miss Truscott, I am here to beg your attendance at Rycote House."

"Why?" she demanded, but without heat. "I cannot see how my presence will be beneficial to any at the residence."

"There has been a... development," diplomatically stated. "I do believe you are the only person in a position to... err... smooth the ruffles."

"This is not my home. How did you find me?" Lucy quizzed, a little truculently. Rodney gestured to the books he was holding. They were the ones she inadvertently left at Elspeth's.

"The address of the shop is stamped inside. I took a chance." Shrugging carelessly.

"You will have to wait 'til day's end. I cannot abandon Mr Abbot at the whim of the nobility."

Her employer interposed. "Go on with you, Lucy, I can manage. 'Tis quiet today and you have baked enough cakes and tartlets to feed a small army." He flipped his hand at her, waving her off to the rear of the shop where her reticule and warm woollen wrap were tucked into a drawer. Acquiescing, Lucy did as she was bid, and in less than a minute was stepping out into the spring afternoon with her taciturn companion.

"Please will you tell me whether I ought to address you as sir or Lord Something-or-other." She asked, politely as they crossed the path to the waiting carriage.

"I am Rodney Tyndall, Viscount Westbrook." He supplied, with a trace of a smile.

"Thank you," she said with a sigh of relief. "Now, what has everyone in such a bother, you need me?" she continued, once they were in the carriage and trundling through the streets.

"Wait and see." Was all she could get out of him, and with that, she had to be content. Thus, she ignored him and enjoyed the ride.

Arriving at Rycote House, Rodney helped Lucy down and offered her his arm, smiling when she hesitated. Suddenly, without knowing why, she trusted him. Smiling in return, she hooked her arm through his, her slim fingers resting on the fine wool of his coat and let him lead her into her destiny.

Walking into the parlour, Lucy was sorely tempted to turn tail and run. Instead of the three she was expecting to see, she was confronted by an extremely tall and hawk-like man wearing an expensive suit; his expression bleak. It was only the reassuring pressure of her escort's hand over hers that gave her the courage to advance further into the room.

"Miss Truscott, I presume?" the gravelly voice demanded attention. For the second time in under an hour, Lucy dropped a curtsy.

"My lord."

"Do you know why I have summoned you?"

"Apparently I am the only one who can solve your problem." She raised clear blue-grey eyes to his and heard a sharply inhaled breath.

"Cecilia…" It was murmured with such pain but so quietly, Lucy wasn't sure she had actually heard it. Her brow creased, she did not resemble her mother at all, or so she thought.

"I am Lucy. Cecilia was my mother."

"Was?"

"She died." Baldly. The man bent his head and Lucy saw a tremor run through him. "My lord, are you quite well?" Her solicitous tones brought his gaze back to hers, and the agony reflected therein made Lucy gasp. She turned to Rodney who was leaning on a window ledge seemingly at ease in this house. He inclined his head towards the figure in the chair. Lucy vacillated for less than a minute, then took two steps forward, and sank onto her knees in front of the man whom her news had clearly shattered.

"My lord, I am sorry to bring you such sad tidings. Mama died three years ago during the fever epidemic. In truth, I think she was tired. She had been alone for so long, since before I was born, and I believe she simply lost the will to fight." Lucy felt tears threatening and made a determined effort to swallow them. "She never married." She heard a groan; a hand lifted and then fell back. "She loved him, the man who was my father, and there was never anyone else for her. She did not impart his name, or how they met, or any details relating to him at all. I confess to feeling as though part of my life is missing, but I respected her reasons for concealing his identity. I presume it was to preserve his name or that of his family. Then by happenstance, yesterday I… errr… met Lady Elspeth, about which I suppose you were informed. I imagine that is why I am here."

Lucy reached out and touched her hand to his, currently resting on his knee. "My lord…" she took a breath and prayed for courage, "… my lord, might I be so bold as to suggest that you summoned me here to see whether the Lucy Truscott who helped Lady Elspeth yesterday, and who is reminiscent of her grandmother, is really the daughter of Cecilia Truscott whom I believe, perhaps, once upon a time you loved."

She was trembling. Despite her desire to know everything about her father, now it seemed within her grasp, Lucy could feel her nerve seeping away like the rain through the cobblestones. Of course, her sentiment might be erroneous. He could just be a member of the family who knew Cecilia, but his pale countenance and rigid demeanour spoke volumes. Whoever this man was, he definitely cared about her mother. She rocked back onto her heels and studied him.

He exuded power and charisma, from his impeccable clothes to his angular features. Iron grey hair, receding at the temples, enhanced rather than detracted from the prominent brow, and high cheekbones. His aristocratic nose, thin lips, and hooded eyes were at first glance, forbidding, yet Lucy saw laughter lines at the corner of his eyes and a mouth that seemed predisposed to smiling.

Sadness, his face was wreathed by sadness, his body language defeated. Lucy wanted him to smile, his visage was making her heart ache.

"My lord…"

He raised his eyes, they were the same hue as her own and mirrored those of the woman in the portrait. Lucy risked a tentative smile.

"Mayhap I should leave you to your thoughts. Again, I am sorry to be the bearer of such news. Doubtless, 'tis rather a shock." Lucy stood and shook out her skirts, smoothing non-existent fluff from the thin material. She really must get a new gown, which reminded her of the one she had borrowed and needed to return. "Good day to you, my lord." She dipped a curtsy then, rather at a loss, glanced at Rodney for guidance. The viscount was standing as though carved from stone, his face inscrutable. Shaking her head, Lucy turned and walked towards the door.

She was halfway across the room, when the older man

spoke.

"Miss Truscott."

She spun around and, meeting his gaze, waited.

"I would recognise you anywhere. You may be different in feature, but you are undeniably Cecilia's daughter. She is…" he paused, his throat working, "… was… also very beautiful. I must talk with you, learn what happened since she… since I… since she left, but I find myself struggling to digest what you have told me."

"Which is why I should go. If you wish to meet again, Lord Westbrook here seems well versed in tracking people down. He knows where I work, and I presume has already ascertained my home address." Lucy shot a wicked grin over her shoulder, startling Rodney into a grin of his own, the gesture lighting his face.

"Please, do not leave. Take a walk in the garden, I just need a little time to organise my thoughts then we will talk if you are agreeable." The man rose from his chair, looming over her from his imposing height.

Lucy angled her head to look up at him, and for an interminable moment, there was absolute silence. Then, she nodded and, seeing relief flood his face, was glad of her decision. In truth, she too needed to talk about this. Lucy was under no illusions about becoming the long-lost daughter, being welcomed with open arms; she was a side-slip, and nothing could change that, but she just wanted to know.

Chapter Five

Alice was summoned to escort Lucy to the garden. Once outside, Alice led Lucy along a path coming to a halt by a wrought iron gate which, she explained, delineated the formal gardens, from those accessible only by the Rycote family and their invited guests.

"Just wander as you will, miss. There's a summerhouse and, on so lovely an afternoon, it will be a pleasant place to sit. I will fetch you when his lordship requests your presence, but if you get cold, come back here and I'll take you to the library."

Thanking the helpful maid, Lucy sauntered through the garden. Neatly trimmed hedges were starting to sprout new, bright green leaves; here and there late snowdrops clung to sheltered spots, and bright crocuses circled the bases of a variety of trees still bare from the long winter.

Her head a jumble of chaotic thoughts, Lucy walked aimlessly, vaguely aware of, but not really seeing, the verdant new growth and promise of spring. This part of the garden was not enclosed, and without realising, she strayed into the adjacent park. Hugging her wrap, of which no-one had thought to relieve her, Lucy wandered, eventually coming upon a large area strewn with an abundance of flowers. Most she did not recognise, but they were so pretty and cheerful, their little heads bobbing in the breeze, she could not help but drop to the grass the better to admire them.

Had she known it, Lucy was gazing onto a profusion of primroses, celandine, and violet, among yet more snowdrops and crocuses. Subtle perfumes wafted around her, calming and soothing. This was a garden she could enjoy forever. Scrambling to her feet, her gown damp from the wet ground, she pottered around the numerous beds, bending occasionally to stroke a flower, or sniff a bloom. To one side, under a cluster of dormant trees which Lucy hazarded might possibly be wild cherry, a patch of earth was randomly scattered with long, slender shoots. Intrigued, Lucy made her way over and crouched to study them. The sunny corner had stimulated faster growth and several of the plants sported a broad green stalk topped with a bud.

Leaning closer and about touch the delicate floret, her hand was stayed by a barked order from somewhere over her left shoulder. Surprised, she had not seen anyone else — although being preoccupied, acknowledged this wasn't necessarily unexpected — Lucy rose to her full height and surveyed her surrounds.

A figure was stalking towards her, his attire leading her to presume he was probably a gardener. His demeanour was forbidding, irate even, and for a split-second Lucy felt a trickle of fear. Then she shook it off. She was used to the mean back streets of London; a gardener was no threat. As he approached, she noticed the hood of his cloak was sliding back to reveal a prominent and angry scar deforming the right side of his face. To her admittedly limited knowledge, she thought it might be a burn and, his daunting attitude notwithstanding, had the most peculiar desire to stroke the tortured skin, as though a mere caress would heal the ravaged flesh.

Banishing the sentiment as preposterous, Lucy folded her arms and watched him approach, somewhat confused by his behaviour. He reached her side, broad-shouldered and exceedingly tall — he was the second man that day to tower over her, which given her own height was most unusual — but she refused to be cowed.

"What gives you the right to come into my garden? Worse, touch my flowers?" he demanded, his mouth twisted derisively. He scanned her gown, and it was all Lucy could do not to cover the threadbare garment with her wrap. "Are you so bored, Lady Elspeth, you have taken to playing at serving wenches with your giddy friends?"

Lucy contemplated him with cool eyes. "My goodness me, what a *delightful* greeting. That you think I am Lady Elspeth is flattering, but we really look nothing alike." Her imperious tone making him pause to study her properly.

"'Pon my word, neither you are." The man raked his eyes over her tall, willowy figure, his expression nothing short of insolent, yet Lucy thought she discerned an inkling of something, something at any other time she would describe as vulnerable, flicker in their blue depths. "Who the hell are you, trespassing in Lord Blackthorne's grounds?"

"None of your business," she retorted with heat.

"You are in his garden, that makes it my business," he growled.

Lucy inhaled a calming breath; she was being impolite, and it was not like her. Modulating her tones, she explained. "I beg your pardon, sir. I did not realise I had strayed onto another's land. I was captivated by this splendid garden." She swung her arm around. "If 'tis your handiwork, you are to be congratulated."

He executed a sweeping bow. "Why thank you, good lady, I shall sleep better tonight knowing you are impressed." Sarcasm lending an edge to his tones.

Lucy glared. *What was **wrong** with this man? Even accepting she was intruding, she had apologised and did not think her remark patronising. Mayhap he was having a bad day.*

"I have said I am sorry; my intent was not to sound condescending. I love gardens, to have one on your doorstep must be marvellous," not quite able to prevent the wistful note creeping into her voice, "and this one is truly glorious." She indicated the buds which had prompted her closer inspection. "I was interested in these about to bloom, they seem familiar, yet I cannot place them. I would not have damaged them." Cautiously, she skirted around him and in three strides was back on the grass. She bobbed a curtsy and began to retrace her steps.

"You did not tell me your name." His voice caused her to turn.

"No, I did not." She agreed and was gone.

*****

William Harcourt, Marquis of Blackthorne, stood motionless for several minutes after the woman disappeared through the park. *Who was she? Why had he been so churlish?* He was normally much more reserved, but when he first spotted the person crouched under the tree, presumed it was a street urchin come to steal his precious flowers. This was the first year he had tried to cultivate daffodils and was not sure how well they would flourish here in what was a relatively sunny spot.

Her spirited response fascinated him, and he knew she had seen his scar, but she did not cringe or stare at him in disgust or horror as did most women, most people for that matter. Involuntarily his hand went to his face as though to cover the blemish. Forcing it back to his side, he ruminated over who she was. She resembled Lady Elspeth closely enough for him to mistake her identity, yet on closer inspection, she was taller and definitely thinner, her skin lightly tanned and her eyes were neither blue nor grey, something in between.

Dismissing a curiously unsettling feeling, William knelt on the soft earth and all but forgot the encounter, engrossed in tending to his beloved plants.

*****

Lucy hastened back to Rycote House, thankful she recognised the way. Meeting the gardener, or whoever he was, served to remind her of the yawning difference between those with status and those without. Scanning the hallway, she spotted the baize door leading to the domestic quarters. Pushing it open she followed the passageway coming into the bright kitchen, sun streaming in through several windows. To her relief, Alice was there, loading up a tray with three tall glass beakers of hot coffee and a plate of freshly baked biscuits. The aroma made Lucy's mouth water.

Willing her stomach not to rumble, she said. "I cannot stay, Alice, my coming here was a mistake. Whatever Lord Rycote thinks, or believes or questions about me, cannot change who and what I am. This is not my world. I know I am being cowardly, but 'tis better I leave now. Please apologise on my behalf."

Before the girl could reply, Lucy had fled through the kitchens and out into the mews at the rear of the property. Dashing away unexpected tears, she all but ran into the street, immediately swallowed into the crowds of people milling about.

Alice knocked on the door of the study, waiting for his lordship's invite before she entered. Placing the tray on a small table between two leather chairs, she curtsied, then hesitated.

"What is it, Alice?" Lord Rycote, who was slouched in his seat his mind elsewhere, flicked a glance at her, then seeing the maid's face, straightened. Rodney, who acted as his secretary and man of business, heard an odd note in his employer's voice and came around to perch on the edge of the desk.

"'Tis Miss Lucy, my lord."

"What about Miss Lucy?"

"She's gone." The words were stark, but it was too late to retract them. Alice bit her lip in chagrin.

Christopher Gillingham, eighth Earl of Rycote, stared at the young girl but he did not see her. All he saw was Lucy kneeling beside him, trying to soften the blow she had just delivered. He had no doubt who she was, and he suspected she had also figured it out. He ought to be the one to tell her, he should not have waited. Selfishly, he wanted time to wallow in the sadness of knowing he would never see Cecilia again, never hear her sweet voice, or feel the press of her lips to his. His distress at her loss, even though they had been apart for over two decades, blinding him to what was truly important.

Lucy — she was the child he never knew he had, born to the only woman he ever loved. He did have an affection for Elspeth's mother — who died around the same time as Cecilia, the irony of that not lost on him — but theirs was an arranged marriage. They muddled along together quite amicably, but there was no real ardour, no earth-shattering passion.

With Cecilia it was as though a fire blazed between them. When they were apart, he felt bereft, cold, despondent, all of which were obliterated the next time he saw her. When she was in his arms, he forgot everything bar her. Even now, so many years later, the memory of her touch was enough to send his heart rate through the ceiling and blood rushing to his loins. He swallowed a groan.

Now Cecilia was dead, and Lucy had gone.

"I know where Miss Truscott lives, my lord. I am sure I can persuade her to return." Rodney's voice jolted him back to the present.

Thanking and dismissing Alice, Lord Rycote reached for one of the coffees. While he sipped the rich brew, he registered Rodney's words. "You know her address?" His secretary nodded. "How long have you known this?" Dreading the answer. If Westbrook had been aware of Lucy's existence for longer than a couple of days, he would fire him summarily.

Rodney raised his palms. "Only since the day before yesterday, my lord. Miss Truscott forgot her books when she… err… left, the day she saved Lady Elspeth. The flyleaf was stamped with the name of the book store. It did not take much persuasion to wheedle her address from the store owner."

Choosing not to mention Mr Abbot's dire threats should it come to light Rodney's reasons for asking were less than appropriate.

"And?"

"She lives in rooms, or rather a room, on Litchfield St."

The earl shuddered. Litchfield St was off Charing Cross Road on the edge of Seven Dials, an area synonymous with degradation. Lucy was not representative of the usual inhabitants of the neighbourhood. She was neither unkempt nor dirty and, although too thin, was fortunate to be endowed with a thick mane of glossy hair, sparkling eyes, and her skin, albeit tanned, glowed with health. "She cannot stay there."

"I understand your concern, my lord, but I am given to understand she is quite independently minded and would require some convincing to relinquish even a morsel of it." Rodney had suffered an earwigging from Mr Abbot on how Lucy had been looking after herself since her mother died, and how she valued her autonomy.

"She cannot continue to live there. She is my daughter..." There, he had said it out loud. Oddly, the admission felt liberating and, unbidden, Christopher Gillingham was possessed by the most irreverent urge to shout it from the treetops. He contented himself with repeating the words. "She is my daughter."

"Something of which you have yet to apprise the lady in question." Rodney interposed.

Lord Rycote sighed. "Yes, yes, that minor detail. Nothing for it, man, you'll have to prevail upon her to return. Take Elspeth, she could talk the birds down from the trees given half a chance. I hear she even made young William next door smile, a feat I believed impossible."

His secretary gave a bark of laughter at this. 'Young' William was, in fact, nearing thirty years old, a veteran of the recent wars and now managing the Blackthorne estates, following the death of his father while William was in France. Elspeth had known him since childhood and regarded him rather like an older brother. They used to spend hours in his garden before he joined his regiment. In the wake of his return, a little over a year ago, he had become a recluse and Elspeth had only managed to coax him into her company half a dozen times.

Rodney knew all about the injury marring William's once handsome face and assumed, correctly as it happened, the retired soldier preferred not to deal with pitying glances and hushed whispers about his drastically changed appearance. Moreover, the *ton* did not wish to face the horrors of war. War was something that happened far away, on foreign shores, and to confront its aftermath in the guise of those, nobility or otherwise, wounded in body or soul gave it an immediacy which undermined their faith that England remained unconquerable.

"I will see what I can do. I make no promises, for I cannot force her to accompany me. This may be a meeting you need to undertake yourself."

Seeing the sense in this, Lord Rycote nodded, and the two settled back to business for the time being, while at the back of both of their minds, plans began to kindle.

Chapter Six

A week passed and, with no further contact, Lucy began to hope her brush with the Rycote family was just that, a brush. Deep down, she yearned to experience, if only for a brief moment, what it was like to be pampered, not to worry about choosing between buying food or a desperately needed pair of shoes, or whether you would be warm throughout the next winter. Even as she thought it, Lucy knew it to be futile; her life was here, split between the Wise Owl and her attic. To taste luxury would spoil her for reality, and likely leave her adrift between both worlds. What was the use of pretending it could work? Such things only happened in the contes de fées and they were called fairy tales for a reason.

She should stick to dreaming, but even that had changed. Her knight had taken on the aspect of a grumpy gardener and try as she might she could not rid her mind of him. Her slumber was disturbed further by a niggling worry surrounding Elspeth and those inexplicable accidents. While she tossed, trying to get comfortable under the inadequate coverlet, all manner of scenarios presented themselves. If she did not get a decent night's sleep soon, she would have to stop reading, for surely this insomnia was because tales of greedy villains or ancient political rivalries were playing on her mind — Elspeth, simply the catalyst.

*****

Another week flew by. Then, one evening, as she was locking up The Wise Owl — Mr Abbot had departed mid-afternoon to visit with an old acquaintance who wished to offload some of his books — Lucy was startled to see Viscount Westbrook... whom she always thought of as Rodney... leaning against the window frame, presumably waiting for her. The sun was setting, the pristine windows of the various shops along the street reflecting the flaming orange sky.

"You should not lurk in the shadows," she scolded. "If you had knocked on the door, I would have let you come and sit in the warmth." Disregarding how this might look. Society's rules did not apply to her.

The viscount gave a perfunctory shrug. "I was content to wait outside and watch the world go by. This is a busy street."

"Which, I suspect is why Mr Abbot thought opening a shop here might be a shrewd move." She countered with a sly grin. Rodney chuckled at her gentle taunt and levered himself off the wall.

"I am here to beg you to come with me to Rycote House for dinner," he said, and although his tones were dispassionate Lucy sensed her refusal would be... unwelcome. "Elspeth has been asking after you, she has been... discomfited of late, and I thought your company might cheer her up." His brow was furrowed, and Lucy saw a series of emotions flicker across his grave face. Light dawned.

Rodney was in love with Elspeth.

Lucy, keenly aware this was probably a mistake, was also astute enough to recognise it might provide a splendid opportunity to glean further information about these so-called incidents which had befallen her... what was Elspeth...? a relation of some kind...? Lucy still did not know for sure. An evening among the Gillinghams might prove interesting. Without thinking, she pressed her hand on his arm.

"I am pleased to accept your invitation."

His relieved smile was enough to quell Lucy's moment of indecision. She recalled her last visit and her precipitous departure, conceding she would have to face Lord Rycote eventually. Sooner was perhaps better than later. She could have her say, assure him he need not worry about her, and that would be that. Nevertheless, she would like to get to the bottom of those troubling mishaps. Alice didn't sound like someone with a flighty imagination, and Lucy mulled over the possibility of a chat with the maid, as well as some of the other staff to see whether there was a pattern. Mayhap, they would be amenable to talking with her, her status being somewhere below the kitchen cats, and therefore no threat.

All this ran through Lucy's mind as she allowed Rodney to assist her into the waiting carriage. The journey to Rycote House took less than twenty minutes and Lucy found conversation with her escort to be surprisingly relaxed. He was intelligent, amusing, and clearly besotted with Elspeth, although, Lucy suspected he believed himself unworthy of the earl's daughter.

Arriving at their destination, Lucy was helped down by the groom, and she tried to steady a sudden onset of nerves by smoothing her skirts. Unfortunately, this only served to remind her that her gown, while clean and neat, was faded and not even close to current fashion. Hours earlier when she set out to work, the morning was mild with a promise of warmth as the day progressed, thus she forewent a cloak in favour of a wrap and had no gloves. Tutting, she lifted her head to see Rodney grinning down at her.

"'Tis of no matter, Miss Truscott. No one here cares whether you are dressed as a pauper or a queen."

"Hah, all very well for you to say, dressed in an outfit that would cost me seven years wages." She waved her hand at his attire. Beautifully tailored trousers and jacket, under which she spied a cream cotton shirt, dark green waistcoat, and matching cravat. The epitome of elegant refinement. Lucy felt a wild urge to flee again, and it took all her self-control to climb the steps to the front door. Her companion must have sensed her panic, for repeating his gesture of her previous visit, offered his arm. She took it gratefully, unaware he could feel her trembling.

"Lucy, my dear," deliberately using her given name. "This is not the lion's den, nor the judge's chambers. 'Tis just dinner, and Elspeth will be so glad to see you."

Lucy grumbled something unintelligible then shook herself. She was perfectly capable of behaving in a manner of which her mother would approve, for one evening. Honestly, she was not usually so timorous. Unbidden, she recalled her mother's words after the upsetting encounter in the park all those years ago. Straightening her shoulders, she pinned on a smile and nodded.

"Come on then, let's do it."

The door was opened by the butler whose name, Lucy fortuitously recalled. "Thank you, Mr Harris, sir," she greeted the elderly man who took her wrap.

"It is my pleasure and welcome back, Miss Truscott," he replied, his lips twitching at being called sir. "They are in the parlour, my Lord." This last to the viscount.

Rodney grinned his thanks and ushered Lucy into the parlour. Candles glimmered in the several candelabras scattered about the room and a fire blazed in the hearth. When the two entered, three men stood to greet her and there was a flurry of silk as Elspeth flew across the room to envelop Lucy in a warm hug.

"Oh, I have missed you. Why did you leave so suddenly? Papa wanted to talk to you. We have so much to tell you. Oh, do sit with me. You know these two, and here's Papa." Elspeth waved her hand in the direction of her father and when she paused to draw breath, Lord Rycote stepped forward.

"Elspeth my dear, let Lucy come into the room before you swamp her with questions. Good evening, Lucy. I am so glad you decided to join us. My daughter is correct, we have much to discuss and just having you here has made her smile, something we have missed the past few days."

Lucy flushed, bridling at the trace of censorship threading through Lord Rycote's tones. She dipped the requisite curtsy and fixed him with a cool gaze, her eyes darkening to the colour of pewter. "Forgive me, my lord, it was never my intent to cause upset. However, I fail to see what prolonging our acquaintance achieves. Whatever happened was a long time ago and probably best forgotten. When last I was here, I realised this," she flicked her hand between them, "was a mistake, nothing has changed my opinion. It can only lead to sadness." Her tones as remote as her eyes and, in the same way as she had done on her previous visit, Lucy turned to leave.

This time her flight was arrested by Lord Rycote's next words.

"You are my daughter."

There was no vacillation in the earl's voice, his words rang bell-clear, reverberating around the room. Neither was there now, any denying it.

Blanching, Lucy spun slowly on her heel. All evidence to the contrary, she had managed to ignore the persistent voice in her head telling her she *must* be related to Elspeth. The divide was too great to cross, and members of the nobility did not tend to acknowledge their illegitimate offspring. "Might you be so kind as to repeat that…" her voice was barely a croak. She swallowed and cleared her throat, "my lord?"

"Lucy, you are my daughter. A daughter I had no idea existed. Please, sit by me and I shall tell you everything."

Lucy glanced at Elspeth, expecting a look of antipathy or shock, surprised when she saw only eager anticipation on the girl's… her half-sister's face. *Goodness me, she had a half-sister, one who, oddly, looked really happy about it. She had a father, and although not quite ready to acknowledge this newly discovered family,* a tiny thrill ran through her. *Was there any chance they might reach an accord?* She walked across the room and sank into the chair, Lord… her father, indicated and folding her hands neatly on her lap, waited.

His chest pinching just a little, Christopher Gillingham watched Lucy compose herself, witnessed the myriad of emotions chasing over her pale face which smoothed to bland when she sat down. She was correct, her features did not resemble those of Cecilia, but her mannerisms and her expressions were entirely her mother. A series of pictures from those carefree days when they believed they could be together for always floated through his mind and it took nearly all he had not to break down. Cecilia… just her name was enough to cause a torrent of sensations. He forced the memories aside and steadied himself. He had to get this right or he would lose his daughter, and *that* he could not countenance.

He eased into his seat, faced Lucy, and sending up a quick prayer for guidance — and coherence, began his tale. "Cecilia Truscott was employed as a governess to my youngest sister, your aunt Margaret. She arrived one spring morning, this time of the year in fact, for an interview with my mother. You need to understand, at twelve years old, Margaret hated the idea of a governess, and declared to anyone who would listen she was too old to need one. She could ride a horse and talk about the weather — in her mind the two most important things a young woman of the nobility should ever require." Christopher's lips curved in fond remembrance.

"Mama told us later, she was halfway through the interview, when Margaret stomped into the room and, very rudely, instructed your mother to leave. Before Mama could remonstrate, Cecilia asked my sister why. No one had ever requested her opinion about anything, and apparently, she just gaped at Cecilia." Christopher went on to recount what his mother had relayed about the day of Cecilia's interview, amusement warming his tones as he recalled his sister's ongoing disgust at the very idea of a governess.

The room fell silent as Cecilia Truscott came alive to those listening.

*****

Spring 1788 ~ twenty-eight years previously...

"What do you mean, why?" Margaret demanded.

"Why do you think I should leave?" Cecilia replied.

"Because I have no need of you. What could someone like *you* teach someone like me?" Her lip curled in distaste at the unfashionable attire the visitor was wearing.

"If you are able to provide a suitable answer to three questions, I will gladly leave," Cecilia bargained.

Beginning to splutter, Lady Rycote started up from her chair, pausing when Cecilia glanced over and, almost imperceptibly, shook her head, the gesture going unnoticed by Margaret. With an understanding smile, Lady Rycote settled back in her chair and observed.

Margaret came closer and stared into Cecilia's face which was open, inviting her trust. Grudgingly, she nodded and plonked herself on a nearby ottoman, her expression truculent. Cecilia bit back a smile and posed her first question.

Chapter Seven

"What is the capital of France?"

"Who cares?" Was Margaret's careless response.

"'Tis important to learn something of the world beyond our shores. Do you know France is so close to England, that from Dover, on a clear day, you can see her coastline? Her current monarch is struggling to deal with a terrible financial crisis, which is spawning rumours of instability and possible revolution. Even though women generally do not discuss politics when in large gatherings, in private things can be quite different. What if the gentleman who comes to court you, sits on a parliamentary committee overseeing foreign policy? What if he is a soldier? While we are not at war, we cannot discount the likelihood of being so in the future. What help would you be if you did not take the time to understand something of his daily activities, or what he might have experienced. I do not mean battles and injuries," Cecilia sought to placate before Lady Rycote could intervene, "but the reasons he decided to fight for our country in the first place. While a gruesome occupation, 'tis also an honourable one."

Margaret mulled that over, recalling her Papa and older brothers often talked about a king called Louis and his wife, Marie something or other — whom they considered a hindrance. She screwed up her face in concentration, desperately trying to recall whether anyone ever mentioned the name of the capital city. To no avail. She shook her head.

"I cannot tell you."

"It is Paris. A grand city which would be a perfect place for a husband to take his wife. It is often called the most romantic city in the world," Cecilia informed the child.

"Have you seen it?"

Cecilia nodded and, diverted for a moment, Margaret peppered the young woman with questions, which Cecilia answered as best she could.

"Next question. Can you play an instrument?"

Again, Margaret shook her head. "Why should I bother? It is boring."

"Oh, my dear, how can you say that if you cannot play? To hear music coming from underneath your fingertips is very special. It can soothe a troubled mind, cheer a saddened heart, gives joy to the listener, and can even encourage them to dance."

Margaret's face lit up, she did enjoy dancing and had mastered a number of those popular at balls. Her brothers were very patient with her, suffering bruised toes while they taught her the steps. "I love to dance." She stood up and executed a perfect pirouette. "Does that mean you can teach me to play?"

"I would be glad to teach you," Cecilia assured her, "but you still have one question left. Do you want me to ask it or do you think we might be able to come to an agreement?"

Margaret tilted her head to one side and studied Cecilia. She seemed pleasant enough, if *terribly* old-fashioned in her choice of gown.

"How old are you?" she piped up.

"Margaret! It is very impolite to ask a lady her age," her mother expostulated.

"*She* isn't a lady," Margaret retorted, contemptuously, annoyance bubbling again.

"Sometimes, being a lady has nothing to do with her status and everything to do with her manners," Cecilia stated quietly, before Lady Rycote lost her temper. "I thought we might be reaching a rapport, but I can see my efforts here would be wasted. I have no desire to help a young lady who has no wish to be helped. As I have several other interviews to attend, I shall take up no more of your day. Thank you, Lady Rycote, for being kind enough to meet with me this morning. I shall take my leave.

There is no need to ring for a footman. I know the way out." Cecilia stood and, after dipping a flawless curtsy, picked up her valise and made to depart.

Cecilia had her hand on the doorknob when Margaret called her name, a tremor in her voice.

"You have not asked your final question."

Cecilia smiled to herself and, schooling her features, spun to face the child. "Is there any point?"

Margaret twisted her hands together, her face flushed. "I am interested to know what it is."

Cecilia grinned, she couldn't help it. "Can you read?"

"You mean, actual books?" Margaret's nose crinkled in distaste. Cecilia nodded. "No, they are old and smelly and heavy, and worse than the piano. Ugh, all those words with no pictures." Margaret made a dramatic gesture and pretended to be asleep, making a snoring sound.

"Margaret, really!" Lady Rycote was mortified at her daughter's behaviour. "Honestly, child, you are such a heathen. I should forbid you to mix with those stable hands, clearly they are a bad influence."

Cecilia caught an expression of shock flitting across Margaret's face. Filing it away for later, she hid another grin. "Books are remarkable things. All those words allow us to conjure up other worlds where you can lose yourself for hours. Yes, some might broaden your education, but so many are pure escapism. Oh dear, Lady Margaret, we have much to do. Mayhap I should stay for a short time, just to start you off? You might think of me as a companion rather than a governess if that sounds less... irksome." She left that dangling and, turning to Lady Rycote, asked her potential employer an innocuous question about the estate.

Minutes ticked by. Out of the corner of her eye, Cecilia could see Margaret arguing silently with herself, her feet swinging under the chair she had dropped into. Ignoring the child, the two adults conversed about this and that, only stopping when Margaret sidled up to her mother and whispered in her ear. A broad smile lit her ladyship's face and she drew her daughter into a warm hug.

"Miss Truscott. If you are willing to put up with my prickly daughter, I would very much like to offer you the role of gov... companion. To start immediately."

Cecilia pretended to ponder this offer.

Margaret squirmed and blurted out, "Please." Making the adults laugh.

"I should be delighted to accept."

Margaret crowed and clapped her hands, before rushing off to tell her Papa, who had deemed it prudent to stay out of negotiations, content to let his wife deal with such matters.

*****

Present day

Christopher, sighed and leaned back in the chair, running his fingers through his hair, which although neatly trimmed, retained vestiges of the unmanageable style of his youth.

"So that was that, Cecilia remained with us for five years, Margaret begged her to stay on even after it was clear she no longer required a tutor. I met her that first evening. Mama insisted she join the family for meals, and I can still picture her chestnut hair glimmering in the candlelight, her brown eyes dancing with laughter while she told us an amusing anecdote. She stole my heart the minute I laid eyes on her. I sought her out under the most ridiculous pretences, and within weeks we were spending all our free time together, although she never neglected her duties. Margaret thrived under Cecilia's care and became quite the scholar, much to her own surprise."

There was a long pause, and the earl heaved a tired sigh.

"Then my parents began to talk about marriage. As heir, I was of the opinion I could marry whomsoever I chose; unfortunately, that is not the way of the nobility. Papa had been in discussion with the Marquis of Segrave and it had been agreed I would marry his oldest daughter. She was perfectly lovely and eminently suitable, but I loved Cecilia. There were many, *many* arguments but Papa was adamant. The announcement was made, and I was torn. Aside from the obvious problem that Papa could be sued for breach of promise, I would either break Cecilia's heart or cause a rift by refusing to marry Susannah."

He dropped his head into his hands.

"I took Cecilia on a picnic and, far away from prying eyes, explained what was about to happen. She was quiet for an age, and I waited for her to rebuke me, to yell at me, even hit me — she would have been justified — but she was remarkable. She took my hand, and said it was only to be expected. However much we hoped to be together, the son of an earl, his heir no less, would never be allowed to marry a commoner. I felt like a cad and promised we would find a way. I would persuade my parents she was perfect for me. They knew how much we cared about each other but, to them an agreement between gentlemen was binding, and duty, far more important than love.

"We had two months before the betrothal announcement. I knew it was not right or fair to continue seeing Cecilia, it would only make the separation harder, but neither did I want to miss a single moment with her. It seemed we were of like mind... we always were. 'I have no regrets, Christopher. The feel of your lips on mine, the way your hands stroke my skin, your tender words, all these things will keep me warm for a lifetime. Show me how much you love me.' Yes, we were reckless, but I had no defence against her, and no desire to fight her allure. Our lovemaking was passionate as always, if not tinged with desperation — the knowledge this heaven was not forever, circling our consciousness. I tried everything I could think of to get out of the marriage, but it was hopeless.

"Two nights before the betrothal ball, she slipped out to meet me. We came together with an almost savage hunger, then hours later, she kissed me and said she had to go, she could not watch me commit my life to another, and moreover, did not think it was fair to Susannah. I begged her to stay, knowing all I could offer was that she become my mistress, but she refused. 'If I was your wife, my love, and knew you sought another to pleasure your body, I would be heartbroken. We have been luckier than most, we found each other, however briefly. Even now, I harbour guilt because I allowed my love for you to push aside my sense. You must be true to Susannah, do not hurt her, she does not deserve it.' They were her last words to me, the next morning she was gone. A letter left for my mother explaining she had received news a family member was gravely ill, apologising that she had no choice but to depart immediately.

"My parents knew the real reason, they were not blind. For years, I tried to find her. I engaged a man to conduct a search, to no avail, it was as though she had vanished into thin air. In spite of this, I believe Susannah and I had a good marriage. We were well matched, and I hope I did not disappoint her, but I think she knew my heart was never hers. This is not unusual among the *ton*, most marriages are not based on love, but on my honour, I stayed true to her.

"Then two weeks ago, my daughter tells me of a young woman who saved her from falling under a carriage. A young woman whose features are so similar to her own, she is convinced they are related. Finally, we meet, and I know without a shadow of a doubt you are Cecilia's daughter. But your eyes, your hair, are pure Gillingham, and you look so like my mother, if you were the same age, you could be twins. Lucy, I am sorry I have missed out on your life but, with your permission, I would like to make that up to you. Had I known Cecilia was with child, I would have moved heaven and earth to find her, to help her.

At the very least, to provide for her. That she managed on her own is testament to her character, and determination to be independent.

"My dear, I have already talked for many hours with Elspeth. We understand each other and she is very excited at the thought of having a sister. Might you consider coming to live here with us with a view, if you feel comfortable, to becoming part of our family. I personally cannot think of anything that would make me happier."

It was a long speech, and as Christopher talked of Cecilia, he could feel the years receding, memories of halcyon days when life seemed less complicated, warming his weary heart. Lost in the past, he had spoken more openly than perhaps he ought, but he wanted those listening to understand the sheer depths of his love for Cecilia. He managed to move on, to do his duty, and his marriage had been amicable. Elspeth was the apple of his eye, and he believed he and Susannah had nurtured a well-rounded, vivacious child. He had mourned Susannah's death, realising he missed her undemanding companionship.

Now, here in front of him, sat a tangible connection to his beloved Cecilia — the woman who continued to haunt his dreams. He wished he had possessed the courage to deny his father's directive and marry Cecilia when he had the chance, regardless of the repercussions. Even as the thought crossed his mind, he knew Cecilia would never have allowed him to do so, she would not want to be responsible for, or the cause of, a rift in his family.

Chapter Eight

The room remained silent. Five people held spellbound by the tale of a love forfeited. One picturing her mother, maybe a similar age to her, before the elusive dream of a lifetime of happiness, and security, was snatched away, finally understanding why she never spoke of *him*. One beginning to appreciate, just how lucky she was to have so blessed a life. Two ruminating on what it would be like to find such love, and one believing he'd found it, if only she returned his feelings.

The quiet was disturbed when Harris knocked on the door to announce dinner would be served in ten minutes, shaking everyone from their respective reveries. Elspeth took the opportunity to ask Lucy whether she would like to freshen up. Lucy nodded and the two women left the room.

"Will you come?" Elspeth's first words when the door swung shut behind them.

Lucy shook her head, not in the negative, but in an attempt to clear the jumble of confusion in her head. "I have not made a decision, Lady Elspeth. However, I hear you have been beset by a worrying number of unexplained accidents recently. Mayhap we can come to an arrangement."

Elspeth frowned. "Who has been telling tales? Oh, doubtless it was Rodney, he's an old worrywart." Her tones vexed.

"He only has your best interests at heart," Lucy admonished, gently. "Do not belittle his concerns."

"I am not a baby in need of cosseting. I am capable of looking after myself." Conveniently forgetting scant days ago, she nearly ended up like squashed marrow under a carriage.

"Maybe so, but perhaps this is something we might solve together. I will come and stay here…" she held up a palm to stem Elspeth's crow of glee, "… *only*, if you agree to tell me everything that has happened, any peculiar occurrences or odd moments or strange feelings. Mayhap between us, we can unravel the mystery." Lucy could see Elspeth was thrilled by the idea when she agreed instantly. "Perhaps we ought not to apprise your Papa of our plans just yet, there is no point giving him anything extra to worry about." Lucy assumed Lord Rycote knew of the puzzling mishaps.

"He is your Papa too, Lucy." Elspeth, who had *not* informed her father, neatly changed the subject.

"That is something which will take some time, my lady. I have been without a father for two and twenty years and a mother for three, for anyone to assume the role of parent when they do not know the child is presumptuous and a tad arrogant."

Elspeth sucked in breath ready to do battle on behalf of her precious father, but Lucy forestalled her.

"I am not saying 'tis impossible, but you must remember this is very sudden, everything has shifted. Who I am is not who I thought I was and will take some adjustment." She smiled and tucked her arm through Elspeth's. "Now, come along, dinner must be about on the table, and I have no idea where the dining room is."

After Lord Rycote's revelations, dinner might have been a strained affair, but all at the table made an effort to keep the atmosphere light. As the meal drew to a close, however, the conversation wound its way back to Cecilia, and an amiable interrogation began. Suggesting they would more comfortable in the drawing room, the earl offered another glass of wine or a digestif, while the men lit pipes or cigars. Once everyone was settled, he answered their questions truthfully, aware Lucy was quietly absorbing everything without really taking part in the discussion.

As far as Lucy was concerned, there really wasn't much to discuss. It was obvious the earl and her mother had been besotted with each other and, had their courtship been approved, her life would have turned out very differently. A small kernel of unadulterated joy began to flourish. A father, an actual father — she would have to lay down some ground rules; there was no way she would be dictated to or be constrained by the ridiculous rules to which Society ladies were bound. She had been living her own life since the death of her mother and no one was going to take that from her.

Content to observe the interactions between this curious group of people, Lucy sipped her port and let her thoughts stray. Drawing on cigars, pungent smoke coiling around their heads, Mr Garrick and Rodney had begun a conversation about how long it took to travel to the East Indies and the numerous opportunities opening up there. Mr Garrick, especially, seemed enamoured of the prospects now available, and Lucy caught mention of untold wealth and the influence of the nobility. Lucy, sceptical of such promises, glanced across to where Elspeth, her father, and Mr Lindsay were embroiled in a lively debate about whether Napoleon should have been executed rather than exiled. Lucy smiled to herself, clearly Cecilia's views on education had influenced Christopher; Elspeth, holding her own against the two men.

Something made her gaze linger on Mr Lindsay. His expression was a mix of longing and a much darker emotion, almost akin to hatred, but that could not be right. Dismissing it as a trick of the light, Lucy put down her glass and walked over to the piano, which had been calling to her since she entered the room.

It was a beautiful instrument, the mahogany housing with its fine rosewood inlay, polished until you could see your reflection. Quietly, Lucy lifted the lid, the pale ivories begging to be stroked. She could play after a fashion, just a handful of pieces. When Lucy was ten and four, Cecilia had been employed as governess to a young boy whose mother often hosted musical evenings.

Cecilia was granted permission to teach Lucy twice a week, providing it did not interfere with her duties, the general running of the household or any of the soirees.

It was Lucy's first and, until recently, only experience of how the other half lived, and even then, she met no one other than the domestic staff. She did, however, learn to appreciate the wonder of music, and always looked forward to her lessons.

They stopped a little over a year after they started when the son was dispatched to boarding school — Cecilia's services no longer required. Since then, the opportunity to play hovered between infrequent and non-existent, but Lucy's fingers remembered, and they itched to touch the keys.

"Do you play, Miss Truscott?" Rodney, glancing up, had seen her hands reach out then drop back to her sides.

She shrugged. "Not very well. Pianos are not an item most folk I know can afford." With wry humour.

"Lady Rycote, Elspeth's grandmama, used to play. Mayhap you have inherited her talent."

"I sincerely doubt it."

"Play for us?" he invited.

Lucy bit her lip and stared at the handsome young viscount. "Do you think anyone would mind?"

"They would be glad. No one bothers anymore, they have a whole music room neglected since Lady Rycote passed. Elspeth is the most unmusical person I know, and his lordship has no time."

Lucy needed no second bidding and sank onto the cushioned stool. Running her fingers experimentally over the keys, getting a feel for them, she pressed the soft pedal hoping to muffle the sound, and any mistakes — inevitable after a lengthy period without practising. She began with a serenade by Haydn, flowing into an aria by Mozart moving effortlessly into another, before sliding into a popular sonata by Beethoven.

While she was playing, Lucy let her thoughts wander and,

unbidden, the face of an angry gardener drifted across her vision. She had no idea why he kept popping into her head, usually at the most inopportune moments, but it did. Now there was a chance she would see him again, and an unknown emotion teased her at the prospect. Paying it no mind, she concentrated on the music. She was a little rusty, these were not uncomplicated pieces, but she loved them and had played them many times. When her fingers stilled, she was surprised by the round of applause from her audience.

"Lucy, you play with skill." Lord Rycote praised.

Blushing, she bowed her head in acknowledgement. "Thank you, it is a forgiving instrument. 'Tis some time since I last practised, but it seems some things are ingrained." She smiled, the first spontaneous smile most in the room had seen, and it transformed her face. Christopher Gillingham saw an echo of Cecilia's vitality and sent up a prayer in hope his newly discovered daughter would be amenable to his proposal.

Lucy rose from the stool and walked directly to where the earl was sitting. While she played, her mind had cleared, all the nonsense bouncing around finally calmed, and she had her answer.

Bobbing a neat curtsy, she began, "Lord Rycote," he arched an eyebrow, "very well, F-father." Stumbling a little over the word. "If your offer holds, I would be glad to accept it should you agree to my terms."

"Terms?"

She nodded and, with no small amount of diffidence, laid out her conditions. Lord Rycote was hard pushed not to laugh at her earnestness and her determination to be excruciatingly polite. It sounded like a business transaction, and maybe to Lucy, it was. Perhaps she felt as though to consent without reserve would be to surrender her hard-won, albeit limited, independence.

Christopher listened attentively, and agreed with each one

of her terms, which turned out to be few. No stopping her from working at the book shop. No thinking he could start ruling her life and arranging a marriage. No chaperone. No preventing her from leaving the house at will.

They shook hands on the deal, at which point Elspeth clapped her hands and swung Lucy around by the waist.

"I have a sister, I have a sister. Oh Lucy, I am so happy."

The others added their congratulations and the remainder of the evening passed in a haze of good cheer.

*****

Lucy was caught up in a whirlwind of arrangements. Lord Rycote wanted her to relinquish her attic room, but she refused. She could afford to pay the rent and preferred to retain the room — just in case. Several staff accompanied her to Litchfield Street to assist with packing, ignoring Lucy's insistence it would take minutes for there was little she required. It was rather nice to have others take charge and within an hour they were heading back to Rycote House.

At the first opportunity, Lucy informed Mr Abbot of her change in circumstances. Her employer was stunned upon hearing she was the daughter of an earl, no less, and even more surprised when she affirmed she would be attending work as usual. He did suggest she might like to take a short break to adjust, but Lucy was adamant, preferring things to continue as they always had.

"I cannot swan about that house doing nothing all day, it would drive me to distraction. I am not one to sit idle and, if I am here, none of Elspeth's friends can call just to gawk at me." She grinned as she said this, having already borne an afternoon being badgered by a gaggle of women keen on scooping up every titillating morsel surrounding this newcomer.

"Well, you are always needed here, my dear. No one else

bakes ginger biscuits quite like you." Absent-mindedly patting her on the arm before wandering off to help a customer. Lucy chuckled, she loved her job and Mr Abbot was a sweetheart. Far more interesting than sitting in a parlour listening to gossip.

*****

A week flew by before Lucy had any time to herself. Not only did she have her job, but also it took her a little while to familiarise herself with the house. At four storeys high, it seemed never-ending to a young woman whose largest abode had been two rooms. She introduced herself to the domestic staff, apologising that her presence increased their workload, which they cheerfully denied, assuring her she was very welcome.

Then there was her bedchamber, Hyacinth, the room to which she was taken the day she met Elspeth. She found it was actually two rooms, as there was a dressing room attached, which made Lucy laugh. Her meagre collection of clothes and two pairs of shoes vanishing into the cavernous wardrobes. The bed was so comfortable it was like sleeping on a cloud, and she loved the crisp cotton of the sheets and the soft warmth of the quilt. The room was at the rear of the house, overlooking the garden with the park beyond, and Lucy spent hours sitting on the broad window ledge admiring the view, breathing in the clean fresh air.

Elspeth was kindness itself and generous to a fault, making sure Lucy lacked for nothing; explaining this and that, deflecting the more avid visitors, and dragging her half-sister to the modiste, after their father tactfully intimated Lucy might like to update her wardrobe.

As she had no intention of going to any of the social events the *ton* were enamoured of, Lucy tried to rein in Elspeth's enthusiasm, but her protests fell on deaf ears. Elspeth was in her element and after two days of standing on a box being prodded and poked, Lucy gave up. She did concede — when the modiste arrived at Rycote House accompanied by a veritable army of dressmakers, carrying what seemed a mountain of new gowns in various hues from soft pastels to more vibrant tones, new shoes, and all the accessories a girl could wish for — that to be pampered in this manner *was* rather wonderful.

Chapter Nine

Eventually, her new clothes were stored away, hung or folded into their rightful places. Her small collection of treasures brought from the attic room were arranged, and she was free to relax. It was a Sunday afternoon and Elspeth was at a picnic somewhere. Lucy had been included in the invitation but declined politely, saying she would appreciate an afternoon at home, grateful when Elspeth said she understood.

The day was warm for the time of year, it would soon be April, and spring had come to London. The air was redolent with sweet fragrance from early blossoms, and the trees were beginning to sprout bright, green foliage. Lucy ambled along neatly trimmed pathways and into the park behind Rycote House. Unconsciously, her steps took her to the daffodil garden. As she approached, she was halted in her tracks when she saw the mass of yellow flowers, their heads bobbing in the breeze. Some were bright yellow, some sported a paler petal with an orange centre, and others were creamy white. They reminded Lucy of the women at the market who gathered to gossip.

Unwilling to call down the wrath of the gardener again, she found a convenient tree where she could admire the flowers from a safe distance, and made herself comfortable. Sitting on the lush grass at its base, she rested her back against the trunk, and stretched out her legs. It was so peaceful; the only sounds the whisper of the leaves above and the twittering of the birds. The hectic pace of the previous week caught up with her, and within minutes Lucy was asleep.

Deep in thought, William Harcourt made his way between the flower beds. He was very pleased with the show of daffodils but one or two of the varieties he planted seemed to be struggling. He had discussed this with one of the gardeners at Kew Park, who suggested they might not be getting enough moisture, or that the soil might need bolstering with some rich organic matter. He was so caught up in his musings, he did not see Lucy until he tripped over her feet.

Lucy bolted awake, momentarily confused about where she was, to see someone lying in a heap in front of where she was sitting. Her instinctive reaction was to laugh; having a man literally fall at your feet was every girl's dream, but she tried to swallow it, acutely aware the person in question might not see the funny side.

"What the devil?" A grumble reached her, and as the man picked himself up and brushed bits of leaf and soil off his clothes, Lucy realised it was the grouchy gardener.

"My apologies, sir. I must have fallen asleep." She twinkled up at him.

"You!" Recognising the woman nestled against the tree, rather like a wood nymph. *What? Wait, where did that come from? Wood nymph?* That same unsettling feeling when first they met, rippled through him. *William get a hold of yourself.* "**Now,** what are you doing here? Come to pick more flowers?"

"Oh dear, do you not know how to be friendly or even smile? 'Tis a shame, we seem to be forever at odds. I have not touched your precious flowers, I have not even breathed on them. I came for some peace and quiet which, apparently was a mistake… something I promise not to repeat." Her smile dwindled as her voice chilled, and William, cursing himself for his boorish behaviour — he was the one who tripped over her — unexpectedly, wanted to see her smile again.

He opened his palm placatingly. "No, Miss… errr…" Lucy saw no reason to help him out so just held his gaze. "Miss. 'Tis I who should apologise. I was not looking where I was going. I hope I did not hurt you." He did not smile so much as his face became less stern.

Taking pity on him, Lucy flexed her limbs. "No, I still have two legs in working order. Nothing to lose sleep over." An imp inside prompting her addendum, alluding to his comment the last time they met and, unable to help herself, she winked, a sly grin tugging on her lips.

William gaped at her. She was joking with him. He could not recall the last time anyone had done that. Mirth lurked, and before he could stop it, he guffawed.

Lucy's eyes widened, as she watched his whole countenance change. The scar gave one corner of his mouth an endearing quirk, and his eyes crinkled most attractively. She gulped. *Endearing? Attractive? Lucy, seriously.* His merriment was infectious however, and Lucy joined in.

"Good afternoon, sir. My name is Lucy Truscott and I am… errr… staying with the Gillinghams." Lucy introduced herself, standing so she was at less of a disadvantage height-wise.

"I am pleased to meet you, Miss Lucy Truscott, I am William Harcourt and I live next door."

Neither thought to clarify their true status, although William remained puzzled by Lucy's obvious similarity to Elspeth.

"Are you perchance a relative, a cousin of Elspeth's?" he dared to venture.

"Something like that." Was all Lucy was prepared to say. "Please, do tell me about these flowers. I have seen them, occasionally, gracing the flowerbeds in Hyde Park, and they are in abundance at the Covent Garden markets, but their name eludes me."

Seeing she was not going to elaborate on her connection to his neighbours, William let it go and launched into an enthusiastic monologue about daffodils and the propagation thereof.

Lucy listened, riveted by his expressive features. She barely noticed the scarring because his eyes held her captive, they were the bluest blue she had ever seen, like the sky on a summer's day, and were currently glowing with passion for his subject. His hair was somewhere between blond and brown, like molten sugar, and a little longer than current fashion — the unruly locks masking the burn somewhat, and she thought she could discern a smattering of grey at his temples. He was, Lucy concluded, cocking her head while she contemplated him, devilishly handsome; the scar adding to instead of detracting from his tanned good looks, quite piratical in fact.

His attire was worn and comfortable looking. A kind of leather tabard protected a faded cream linen shirt — turned up at the sleeves — and dark brown pants. She noticed some knotty skin under his forearms and presumed they, along with the damage to his face, were part and parcel of the same incident. His hands seemed unmarred, and they were large, powerful hands. An image of his long fingers stroking her neck popped into her head and she gulped, feeling heat wash up her cheeks. Banishing it, she forced her brain to focus on what he was saying, but that brought her gaze to his mouth. To those perfectly formed lips, all save that appealing irregularity at one corner… *oh, so they are appealing now? Lucy Truscott, you are a brazen hussy.*

By sheer effort of will, Lucy managed to drag her attention back to William until he wound up and offered to show her the different plants. She nodded, and happily tucked her arm through his when it was offered.

For his part, William continued to be intrigued by Miss Lucy Truscott. There was definitely more to her than met the eye, and he had an urge to find out what. She was not conventionally beautiful, by that he meant beautiful in the way the *ton* measured it. She was too tall, and too slender — angular almost — but she had an aura about her, something intangible yet compelling drew him to her. Her head was currently tilted to one side, her fair hair, sprinkled with golden-blonde highlights was beginning to unravel from its neat style, pale strands curling around her lightly tanned, heart-shaped face.

Lips, not too thin, not too plump and she was biting the bottom one in concentration. Quashing the desire to smooth his thumb over the maltreated flesh, he let his gaze travel upwards, following the line of her pert nose, which led inexorably to her eyes. They were a piercing grey-blue, their hue changing with her emotions. He had been pinned by cool silver, yet now they were a tranquil blue, like the sun reflecting on a lake. *Silver? Reflections on a lake? William what is **wrong** with you, man?* Even as he chastised himself for his poetic thoughts, William Harcourt sensed that whoever this Miss Truscott was, she would leave an indelible mark on him.

Time flew by, the two chattering as though they had known each other for an age, not the hour or so they had actually been acquainted. It was only when the shadows lengthened, and the air cooled that Lucy registered the day was nearly over.

"Oh, sir, I do beg your pardon, I have monopolised your afternoon."

"It has been my pleasure, Miss Truscott, and might I be so bold as to ask you to call me William? I fell over your feet, we have just been on our knees in the soil, we even rubbed shoulders while we discussed plants and books and history. Maybe we could chance to be less formal?"

Lucy leaned back on her heels and studied him. He was so easy to talk with and she was surprised how much they had in common. Although she did not know how to cultivate plants, she was always eager to learn new things and was fascinated by his breadth of knowledge. She also discovered they shared a love of ancient history, and that to read a book by the fire was their idea of the perfect evening's relaxation. Slowly, she nodded.

"I do believe I am amenable to your suggestion, on the understanding you call me Lucy."

William looked as though he might protest, but Lucy raised

her eyebrows and he yielded.

"Very well… Lucy. I repeat, I have enjoyed our conversation and look forward to meeting you again soon."

"I do like an afternoon's promenade," she said, artlessly as she allowed him to pull her to her feet. She bent her head tutting at the smudges on her dress. "Oh dear, I keep forgetting to be careful of my gowns," flicking at the marks, unaware her comment gave William even more food for thought.

While she was speaking, William heard a sharp crack, immediately preceding a high-pitched sound, like a cross between a whine and a whistle. He knew that sound, he had heard it too many times to ignore it or presume it was his imagination. Without thinking, he flung himself at Lucy, knocking her backwards onto the grass and shielded her with his body.

Too shocked to yell, and her breath knocked out of her, Lucy lay motionless for seconds, then, sucking air into her lungs, she bellowed. "***Mr Harcourt!*** What the devil do you think you are doing?"

"Shhhhh… stay still." His urgent tones penetrated Lucy's fury and, tentatively, she raised her head trying to see what prompted such rash behaviour. A second *thunk* shattered the quiet of the garden and they were showered with splinters as a flock of birds lifted from the surrounding trees, squawking in alarm.

"William?" Striving for composure. "What is going on?"

"Keep your head down. Someone is shooting at us."

"***At us***?" she squeaked, her voice pitched so high, William half expected a pack of starving dogs to materialise.

"Hush, yes, and they may still be out there. Lie still, you are safe.

"Safe? I am currently being squashed by a great lummox,

not sure I would define that as safe." Lucy groused into his lapels.

William felt a rumble of laughter build. This woman was a breath of fresh air. He had just told her they were in someone's sights and she was making quips. His voice quivering with amusement he replied. "Just a moment longer, and then I shall unsquash you."

Lucy grinned at William's reply and sliding one arm out from between them, gave his shoulder a light punch. "Just make sure you do not take advantage, good sir."

"The thought never crossed my mind, good lady, I am more interested in keeping my head, in us both keeping our heads."

"What a sha—" Lucy bit off the rest of the sentence. *What had got into her today?* She blamed the fright of the moment. William's body was warm, she could feel his hair brushing her face. Greatly daring, she drew in a slow deep breath, inhaling his scent — a tantalising blend of sandalwood and lemon, and something else, something with exotic overtones, but so faint she could not pinpoint it. The heat coiling through her was unidentifiable, but undoubtedly delicious, prompting her to wriggle, partly to banish it, partly to get more comfortable.

William groaned.

"Oh, I beg your pardon, I did not mean to hurt you."

"You did not hurt me." His voice was a little strangled. Lucy squirmed, worried now, eliciting a sort of wheeze.

"William? You are in pain. Oh no, are you shot?" Her hands swept over his back, checking for what, he had no idea, but her gestures and the way her body shimmied against his sent William's blood rushing to places he would rather it didn't.

"Lucy, stop moving, please." His request more abrupt than he intended.

She stilled and seemed almost to deflate. Even without looking at her, William knew her expression would be one of puzzled confusion.

Inching himself up and shifting to one side, he leaned on one elbow, his keen hearing discerning no rustling in the undergrowth — suggestive of someone creeping up on them, or the sound of a gun being cocked.

"Lucy," he spoke gently, "I am not in pain, at least not the way you think." She stared at him, her enchanting eyes — reflecting the pinkish tint in the sky above them — bewildered. Feeling an unaccustomed flush warm his face, he continued. "Your... errr... gyrations caused a reaction I... umm... did not expect."

His words hung in the air, then Lucy's bright red cheeks told William she had grasped his meaning. As she opened her mouth to respond, he did what he had been wanting to do all afternoon — he traced his thumb over her bottom lip and, unable to stop himself, followed his thumb with a kiss.

Featherlight, he barely even grazed her lips. It was Lucy's first kiss and she really was not sure how it worked, but lordy, she wanted to do it again. While her head supposed she ought to be outraged by his audacity, her heart fluttered, and her spine tingled.

Silence fell between them as she looked up at William, seeing his wary gaze.

"God, Lucy, that was unconscionable of me. Please, I b—"

Before he could finish his sentence, Lucy shuffled until she too was resting on one elbow, and they faced each other. With deliberation, she stroked her free hand over his distorted cheek, and on around his ear until she was cupping the back of his neck. She brought his face to hers and their lips met.

Chapter Ten

They were lying on the grass in the dappled shade of a larch tree, bright daffodils dancing around their heads, on the edge of a park frequented by the inhabitants of the surrounding houses, yet neither William nor Lucy gave a thought to any of this because the spark of something utterly irresistible was beginning to smoulder. Innocent in matters of the heart, not to mention the lips, instinct overrode Lucy's inexperience.

The kiss deepened.

Hands explored.

Fingers teased.

His head screaming at him to stop — they had just been shot at for goodness sake, a lunatic could be stalking them — William was powerless against the rush of emotions, kissing Lucy was evoking. Just when ardour was about to override sense, the caw of a raven in the tree above them broke through the haze and, reluctantly, William lifted his head.

"Why, Miss Truscott, I do believe I have reneged on my promise." William smiled a little crookedly.

Lucy arched a quizzical brow.

"Not to take advantage of you."

Lucy tapped her lip, as though pondering that. "I do believe you have, Mr Harcourt. What a to do. Perhaps a forfeit is in order."

William's expression mirrored hers.

She placed a hand lightly on his chest. "If you promise to kiss me again, I will forgive your transgression." Her tone — pure innocence, her eyes — sparkling with mischief.

William's slow smile did peculiar things to Lucy's heart rate, and she was pleased to feel the rapid tattoo of his under her hand.

At least she was not alone in this state of... *what* would *you call it?* She was tempted to label it bliss, but to term it thus seemed... hasty.

"It would be my greatest pleasure."

William helped Lucy to her feet, risking a quick kiss on her nose as he did so. For a man who hated being the centre of attention, who had closeted himself away since his return home a little over a year ago, from the moment he heard the whizz of the first bullet, William had been hounded by the most radical notion. He wanted to be the centre of Lucy's attention for the rest of his life.

Less than a month ago, nay, less than a week ago, such an earth-shattering revelation would have seen him haring off to his country estate until common sense prevailed, but now all he cared about was whether Lucy wanted that too. As quickly as the thought manifested, doubts reared. Was it fair to subject someone he loved to his flaws? *Love? Where did that come from?* They did not know each other, their acquaintance was not long enough even to be deemed brief, never mind loving, and he bore more scars than those visible.

Even as he tried to repress the sentiment, William recognised he was deluding himself. He *was* falling in love with Lucy.

As her heartbeat settled back into a steady rhythm, the desire coiling through Lucy began to dissipate, to be replaced by something akin to melancholy. She was sensible enough to acknowledge that the man holding her hand... *he was still holding her hand...* might possibly be one of those reprobates she heard women gossiping about over a cup of tea in the bookshop, but William did not seem the dissolute type. Moreover, it was unlikely he would risk his presumably envied position for a dalliance. The chance the kiss might lead to something more tangible sent a ribbon of heat so fierce through Lucy, she had to bite back a moan.

William's quick ears caught the stifled whimper and a wave of panic hit him.

"Lucy, were you struck by splinters? Please do not tell me a bullet grazed you." Appalled he might have missed something so fundamental, William relinquished his grip on Lucy's hand and carefully spun her around, checking for any sign of injury.

Lucy giggled at the panic in his face. "William, I am fine, 'twas naught to do with splinters or bullets. Just a vaguely disconcerting thought. I apologise for giving you a scare."

Huffing a sigh of relief, William sought her hand once more, the gesture more telling than any words. Together they hunted for the bullets, finding one — rather too close for comfort, in the tree under which they had been lying, the other embedded in the soil several feet away.

"Perhaps someone was just practising." Lucy posited, not knowing whether William was aware of Elspeth's chapter of accidents.

"Perhaps," William allowed, "although I understand Lady Elspeth has suffered more than her fair share of misfortune lately."

Lucy twisted to face him, her brow creased. "You know about that?"

"I overheard two of the maids discussing it," he stared at Lucy, "and you look just like her."

"You think they mistook me for Elspeth?"

William was surprised at her calm tones. "I cannot see any other explanation."

"Well, that rather changes things does it not? The occasional minor mishap can be attributed to clumsiness, or coincidence. Being shot at is no accident. Someone, although why eludes me, seems determined to harm Elspeth and I refuse to let anything happen to her."

William grimaced. Quite how this slip of a woman thought

she could thwart someone with malicious intent was anyone's guess.

Taking the opportunity to pluck the odd twig and a couple of leaves from her hair, he said. "Allow me to escort you home, Miss Truscott. I would like to be certain you are not ambushed on your way through the park. Moreover, it means I get to spend a few more moments in your company."

Lucy beamed her thanks and William experienced an odd hiccup in his chest.

They strolled back to Rycote House chattering about this and that. William scanned the area constantly, listening for any untoward noises, but the park remained quiet save the chirping of the birds. Upon reaching the gate, Lucy unhooked her arm from William's and put her hand on the latch. After pushing it open, she turned and dipped a curtsy.

"Thank you for a most interesting afternoon, Mr Harcourt. I should very much like to repeat it, without the extra... errr... entertainment."

"I made a promise, one I have every intention of fulfilling." He lifted her hand and brushed his lips over her knuckles. "I am usually in the garden of an afternoon. I would be exceedingly glad if you found the time to join me."

Lucy grinned. "My afternoons are often free. I prefer not to accompany Elspeth, when she goes calling. I look forward to our next rendezvous."

"Not as much as I." Throwing caution to the winds, William drew Lucy against him and kissed her as though he never wanted to let her go.

Startled — such an overt display of affection was unexpected, but then nothing about this afternoon had been expected — Lucy stiffened and then relaxed as warmth infused her body. Her arms went around his waist as he held her close with one hand and tangled the other through her dishevelled locks. She could feel the thud of his heart, its chaotic beat matching hers, and she smiled against his mouth. How was it possible to fall in love with someone in less than an afternoon? *Had she fallen in love or was it just her imagination running riot?* Lucy knew later she would need to examine this with calm reason but right now she did not care and abandoned herself to the delectable sensations, William's lips and hands were creating.

Eventually, rational thought managed to regain a modicum of dominance and they broke apart, breathing heavily.

"You bewitch me." William husked. "I am counting the hours 'til next we meet." Watching a becoming pink colour Lucy's cheeks. He turned her around and ushered her through the gate, pulling it closed behind her. She pressed his hand where it rested on the wrought iron, "Lucy," his voice became serious. "Please take every care." He did not elaborate, it was obvious to what he referred.

"Worry not, William, I am going to speak with Lord Rycote. Mayhap he can coax Elspeth to go to the country. She should be safe there." Lucy assured him. William handed her the two bullets saying Lord Rycote might need more than just her word. Pocketing them, she said, "I hope to see you again soon." Then smiled and swirled around, disappearing up the path and into the house, the need to tell her father what had occurred, to warn him his daughter might be in danger, adding urgency to her steps.

William stood at the gate until she was out of sight, ruminating over the events of the afternoon. Never in his wildest dreams could he have imagined meeting someone who affected him so profoundly in so short a span of time. Yet she had. He remained curious as to her connection to the Rycote family. She spoke of Elspeth in a familiar manner, no honorific. That suggested she was a relation, but he had never seen or heard of her before, which was unusual — Elspeth and he had been friends for many years.

Making mental note to ask Lucy when he felt it appropriate, William headed home.

Lucy dashed into the kitchen to find Alice, Mr Harris, and cook sitting around the huge table engrossed in a discussion about the menu for a dinner Lord Rycote was in the process of arranging.

"Please excuse me for interrupting," which gained her three matching grins, "is his lordship home?" Lucy asked.

Mr Harris nodded. "He is in his study." Standing to show her through.

"Stay here, sir. I do not need announcing."

"Lord Westbrook is with him."

"He should hear this too." At their quizzical looks she added, "Something happened, I will tell you later, but Lord Rycote should be the first to know."

They nodded sagely and Lucy was gone, hurrying through the house to the study. Rapping loudly, she hopped about waiting for the summons to enter. At the sound of her father's deep voice, she shoved open the door with more haste than care and all but ran into the room.

Her father gaped at his new-found daughter, who looked as though she had challenged a haystack to a fight and lost. Her dress was rumpled and grubby, bits of dried mud, grass and — were they cobwebs? — clung to her hair, and her hands were dusty. Where on earth had she been? A question he posed in startled tones.

"Lord Ry... P-papa." Lucy still struggled to call him this. Catching the quickly rectified curl of his lip, she glanced down and, embarrassed at her unkempt state, sought to clarify. "I can explain. I was shot at today. I was in the park, well actually in the daffodil garden, and someone shot at me... us... twice. I... well... I was talking with the gardener at the time, and he saved my life. He pulled me down and I landed on the dirt, hence my… errr…." Waving one hand at her dress. "The bullets went over our heads. He thinks I might have been the target, which seems logical. I resemble Elspeth, and he is the gardener. No one can be angry enough to shoot a gardener." Lucy ground to a halt as the two men continued to stare at her, flabbergasted by her words.

"Are you sure it was gunfire?" her father eventually managed to ask, stupefied, ignoring her comment about talking to the gardener.

Lucy nodded. "We found the bullets." She dug in her pocket and withdrew the two mangled bits of lead.

She heard a double intake of breath and Rodney came to where she stood. She tipped the bullets into his hand. He rolled them around, studying them.

"Where were you again, precisely?"

Lucy described where they had been standing. The men listened attentively, then Lucy asked what else had happened to Elspeth.

"What does Elspeth have to do with this?" her father queried, suddenly recalling Lucy's previous comment about her resemblance to her half-sister. Lucy frowned and glanced at the younger nobleman who looked pained.

"Do you mean to tell me you do not know?" she squeaked, and in that moment, recalled Elspeth's deflection the evening she agreed to move here. "How could you keep this from him?" Lucy accused the younger man.

"Elspeth did not want to worry his lordship, she said there was nothing really to tell."

"Tell me what?" Christopher Gillingham demanded, testily.

"About the mishaps." Lucy was floored they had kept this from the earl. "I do not know the details, but apparently your daughter has been plagued by a number of incidents. They sounded suspicious to me when I heard about them, but Elspeth assured me they were nothing to worry about. The day we met I thought it odd, she almost fell into the path of a carriage when she was not standing close to the edge of the footpath. She did not trip or lose her balance, she seemed to lurch forward, as though shov..."

Abruptly, Lucy stopped speaking as the enormity of what she had just said hit her. The only people standing with Elspeth that day were her three guardians. Raising her eyes to Rodney, she glared at him, fury mounting. "Is this why you have not spoken to my father of it? You three are involved? *You wish my sister harm*?" she shrieked this last and hurled herself at the viscount, outraged that the man she assumed to be in love with Elspeth might be deliberately hurting her.

Chapter Eleven

Rodney grabbed Lucy's hands, his superior size and strength easily subduing her. "Of course, I do not wish her harm." Exasperated. "We did not inform his lordship because Elspeth insisted, she had no mind to upset him. I disagreed but she was adamant." He released Lucy, then stepped back and lifted his palms in a conciliatory manner.

Lord Rycote observed this interaction, struck by two things, no if he was honest, three. Lucy referred to him as her father and called Elspeth her sister. This was the first time she had done so in his hearing, and that maybe she had begun to think in these terms warmed his heart. Secondly, that she would go to battle for them, and by the way she threw herself at Westbrook, likely to her own detriment. The third, and the one which almost passed unnoticed in the drama of the moment, was how Westbrook spoke of Elspeth. He did not use her title. It was a telling slip.

"When you two have quite finished." He stood from behind his desk and approached the pair, who continued to glower at each other. His movements reminded Lucy of a cat stalking a mouse and she shivered. She would not want to be on the receiving end of his ire.

"Pray tell me," his tone silky, "what are these *incidents* to which Lucy refers?"

Rodney swung his eyes between the two, again struck by their likeness. Lucy was still too thin, but her delicately feminine features were simply a softer, more winsome version of her father's and currently they both wore the same expression — infuriated with a side order of asperity. Under their gimlet gazes, he capitulated. Sinking into the nearest chair he detailed the several instances which, until today, they attributed to bad luck, wrong place wrong time or coincidence.

"Thank you, Westbrook. Now how long have you been in love with Elspeth?"

Lucy saw the young man's jaw fall open in surprise and swallowed a wild giggle. A smile twitched at the corners of her father's mouth, and in that instant, the tension in the room lightened perceptibly.

"Errr… hmmm…"

"Shall I ask Elspeth?" The earl lifted an eyebrow.

"Perhaps five years, eight months, three weeks, five days, and about nine hours." The words growled from reluctant lips.

"That sounds to be…"

"… about as long as I have known her. Yes, it does, funny that." A tinge of sarcasm in his response.

"Does she reciprocate your affection?"

By now Rodney's face was puce. He stammered and stuttered but failed to find the words.

"I hazard she does." Lucy interposed, taking pity on the viscount. "Their behaviour when they think no one is paying attention is revealing, but only if you know what to look for. However, whether his lordship is in love with Elspeth is immaterial, save I acknowledge he is one less suspect. What is important is that we get her out of the city. Do you have a country estate to where she could remove until we have unearthed the culprit?"

"I do and there is no 'we' in this situation. Do you suppose I am about to place another of my children at risk?" Christopher Gillingham's steely gaze bore into Lucy.

"You need my help."

"How exactly?"

"I look enough like Elspeth to fool people from a distance. My presence might draw out whoever is behind these attacks. It is different now. Before you did not even know what was going on, and the four of them," artlessly waving her hand at Rodney, "did not mount a concerted inquiry, probably presuming it was simply a run of bad luck. Now you *know* someone is definitely tracking her, but *they* do not know *we* know, so the tables are turning. We continue to behave as though unaware. I will 'become' my sister and do whatever it is Elspeth does," Lucy's perplexed grimace indicating she had no idea what that entailed, "thus, with discretion, vigilance and a bit more coordination we should be able to uncover the perpetrator." She beamed at her father, confident he would fall in with her suggestion.

Lord Rycote, however, never did anything without weighing up every angle. Resuming his seat, he leaned back, steepled his fingers together and studied Lucy. Her idea had potential, but he did not want to put her at risk any more than Elspeth. He rang for a maid and within seconds, Nell — Alice's younger sister — appeared.

"Nell, please find Lady Elspeth and ask her to come to my study." Nell curtsied and fled, returning less than five minutes later with Elspeth; Messrs Lindsay and Garrick on her heels.

Lucy watched when her sister's gaze alighted on Rodney; they gleamed, and she knew her supposition was correct. Catching her father's eye, she gave him a knowing smile, glad to see the responding quirk of his lips. Straightening his face, he said.

"Elspeth, did you think me so far into my dotage I am the one in need of protection? I fought in wars, my dear, and am quite capable of taking care of you for a little while yet. Thank you for trying not to worry me, but I am afraid this has taken a serious turn. Your sister was shot at this afternoon."

Elspeth blanched and gave a sort of choked squawk. "Lucy, no."

"I am not harmed, Elspeth. The gardener saved my life. I did get a tad… errr… grimy, but naught a good clean and brush up cannot cure. Papa is correct, however, this needs to be addressed by people who know what to look for. Someone is intent on hurting you. They must be stopped." Lucy paused, another thought coming to her, oblivious to the fact she had commandeered the discussion. "Who would wish you harm? Have you denied a gentleman's suit? Disfigured someone?" As she said this, William's face floated into her head; her eyes glowed with a dreamy light, and her countenance softened. The others in the room were intrigued by the sudden change, but none felt it wise to interrupt. "Err… what was I saying? Oh yes, disfigured someone? Failed to repay a debt or wager?" Unaware, among the *ton*, the latter two were generally restricted to men.

"As far as I am aware, none of those things. Certainly, I do not gamble or attack people."

"Then maybe you are being targeted to get to Papa." Lucy turned to Christopher. "What have you done that might cause offence? Business disagreement? Did you dismiss someone who may be holding a grudge? Kill someone, a duel maybe?"

"Lucy. Really, as though Papa could kill anyone?"

"He fought in the wars, Elspeth, he will likely have killed several of the enemy." Lucy's tones were practical, unemotional. "Come on people, we need to work this out. Make a list, anything is feasible at this point. All we have, so far, is that the person can handle a gun, quite well as it happens. He, or she, must have been standing some distance away or we would have seen them, but the bullets only just missed us. Whoever it is, is practised in stealth, we neither heard nor saw him, or her, leave."

Those in the room listened to Lucy as she talked, somewhat taken aback at her comprehension of the situation and its possible causes. Noticing their bemusement, she chuckled, adding.

"I live near Seven Dials; my world is far removed from yours and I rub shoulders with scoundrels. Granted, most would not act with subterfuge. A fist fight, or a knife used in the heat of the moment, a murder over an unpaid debt or because they have been wronged, is the most likely form of retaliation. To stalk their victim for weeks prior would be rare; it involves too much planning, and most do not have the time or inclination to hound their quarry on a prolonged basis."

"You live here, Lucy," Christopher interjected, quietly and without censure, "and I agree. We need to start from the beginning, from the first incident and see whether there are any commonalities, like the time it happened, the place, who was with you, where you were going, all those things. Rodney," turning to his secretary, "please check through the ledgers to see who I have dismissed and why. That should keep us busy for a couple of days. Might I suggest we meet here again the day after tomorrow at eleven?" The three men nodded. The question did not really rate an answer, as all were in the employ of the earl and, thus at his beck and call.

After Lucy said her piece, she moved over to the side of the room and studied the four men. Elspeth, she rejected as being in any way involved. Regardless of the fact it was too complicated to inflict a mishap on yourself, Lucy did not believe her sister had the cunning to orchestrate such a scheme, neither did she believe Elspeth would deliberately upset her father.

The mental picture of Elspeth falling on the day they first met still bothered Lucy. If she was pushed, it can only have been one of the three with her, there was no one else close enough. The only one she was prepared to discount was Rodney, he would never harm a hair on Elspeth's head. That left Mr Garrick and Mr Lindsay unless a passing pedestrian shoved into one of them, which meant it was either an unfortunate accident or planned beforehand with precision timing. Lucy puzzled over that while the men became engrossed in their discussion. Motioning for Elspeth to accompany her, Lucy left the room.

"Walk with me?" she invited. Elspeth grinned and hooked her arm through Lucy's.

"Where are we going?"

"Somewhere we cannot be overheard. I need to talk to you."

Lucy led her sister to a room at the rear of the ground floor, this was the music room. Another piano, much larger than the one in the drawing room, graced one corner; a viola and a flute lay in their respective cases on an ornate walnut cabinet, and two elegant stands, complete with sheet music stood near two high-backed chairs. Opposite the door, large bay windows overlooked the garden. It was one of Lucy's favourite rooms.

"Elspeth, if you have no objection, I would like to revisit the day we met."

"You wish to return to the street?" Elspeth looked perplexed.

"No, you goose. I want to talk about what happened prior to you falling. Was there anyone standing close to the four of you who might have tripped and shoved into say Mr Garrick, who then tumbled against you? Maybe someone you saw earlier in the afternoon who followed you?"

Elspeth mused on that but shook her head. "I cannot recall anyone behaving oddly, or following us, but neither was I looking for such things. I know Rodney said I should take more notice of what was going on around me, but I thought he was just being over cautious. I am quite clumsy you know."

"Yes, but you cannot say being clumsy gets you shot." Lucy contended drily.

"Are you sure it was deliberate?"

"There can be no doubt. Elspeth, whether you like it or not, this is real. It is not a story in a broadsheet, or some gossip easily ignored. This is happening and you are in danger. It was only by the quick actions of next door's gardener that I was not killed or at the very least wounded."

"A gardener, Lucy, really?" Elspeth did her best not to look down her nose at the news her sister had been consorting with the help.

"Yes, Elspeth, really. He is a lovely man and very interesting.

That is not the point, the point is had he not been there, I might well be dead or, at the very least, badly injured."

Elspeth paled, the reality of the situation beginning to sink in. She had managed to persuade herself that the peculiar mishaps were just that, mishaps, but Lucy's stark words did more to convince her than anything else. Icy fear tickled down her spine, and all of a sudden, she remembered something.

"I think I was pushed."

"So do I." Lucy held Elspeth's gaze; smokey grey on forget-me-not blue.

"Then…" Elspeth did not want to voice her suspicion.

"I am sorry, but I fear it can only have been one of those three." Lucy nodded as tacit understanding passed between them, and Lucy took Elspeth's hand, squeezing lightly. "I think you must go away for a while. Lo… Father says you have a country estate. I urge you to travel there, without ceremony and as soon as possible. You need to be somewhere safe until whoever is behind these attacks is caught."

Elspeth studied Lucy for a moment, then pulled out of her grasp and began to pace the room, ticking off what she would need on her fingers.

Lucy interrupted. "What did I say about no ceremony? Elspeth use your brain, you cannot draw attention to yourself by taking two carriages, numerous staff, and a mountain of luggage. You want whoever is stalking you to think you are here in London. *I* will be the one seen getting into the carriage. If the rumour mill is as fast as I imagine it to be, by now, everyone knows about Lord Rycote's illegitimate daughter. What better way to protect you from malicious gossips than by dispatching me off to the countryside? Out of sight, out of mind. I suspect many of your lot would think that decision the perfect answer." Not quite able to quench the disdain in her voice — past slights still rankled.

"Surely Papa…"

"No, Father has never suggested any such thing, but his peers would not think it untoward. It offers us a way to get *you* to safety without raising eyebrows. You would slip into the carriage before it leaves the stables, only take one valise, and maybe ask Penny to accompany you. Lord Westbrook cannot escort you, he will need to stay here and continue his life as normal."

"Why would I want to take Rodney?"

Lucy just stared at her. Elspeth blushed, whereupon Lucy gave her an impish grin. "Because I am not blind. Does he know how you feel?"

Elspeth shook her head. "I doubt it, I cannot think anyone as worldly as Rodney would even notice me."

"Tsk, Elspeth Gillingham do not undervalue yourself." Lucy's tones verged on exasperation. *Honestly, these people lived with their heads in the clouds. Did they never discuss anything other than the weather?* "You are a beautiful young woman, with plenty of spirit. Any man would be an idiot not to notice you. Talk to him, really talk to him, before you leave. I assure you he is very aware of you and has been for a long time."

"Do you think so?"

"I know so. Now come along, we should rejoin the others. Let me see whether I can wangle you two some private time together after dinner." Lucy gripped her sister's hand. "Do not, I repeat do not, mention your suspicions to anyone. We need to keep this between ourselves. Yes, you can tell your Rodney, he is not part of this, but no one else."

Chapter Twelve

In accord the two young women returned to the drawing room, to find the men still absorbed in their discussion. Lucy leaned close to Elspeth and murmured.

"You see, we are organised, our plans laid, yet these four are still clucking about who will do what."

Elspeth chuckled and interrupted what was clearly a very involved debate, saying, "Papa, Harris has just advised me dinner is about to be served. Mayhap you could postpone this until later?"

The men nodded, and the conversation during the meal was light, circling around upcoming events. The busiest period of the Season was almost upon them, bringing with it balls, picnics, soirees and goodness knows what. A chance for the ladies to show off their new wardrobe, and the men to ply their suit on the lady he, or his family, deemed most suitable.

Although cool, the evening was clear, the rising moon casting its subtle luminescence across the garden and, in the lull between the end of the meal and the serving of a digestif, Lucy suggested a stroll. All agreed it was just the thing after so sumptuous a repast. Lord Rycote offered Lucy his arm and they stepped out onto the terrace, along with Mr Lindsay and Mr Garrick. Dropping the briefest of nods in Elspeth's direction, Lucy hoped she understood her unspoken message. Fortuitously, Elspeth was familiar with obscure cues and distracted the viscount with an innocuous question.

Lucy contrived to keep the other three occupied by quizzing them about the various plants and trees, mentioning the gardener of the neighbouring property had managed to cultivate daffodils, and would it not be excellent if they could grow some at Rycote House? Thus, it was quite some time before they returned to the drawing room, upon which it was clear to Lucy that Elspeth and Rodney had used their time alone to great advantage. Elspeth's radiant eyes, pink cheeks, and ever-so-slightly swollen lips telling their own tale. While their admissions would make the enforced separation taxing, they would also warm them when either felt lonely. Unbidden, William's face floated through Lucy's mind, actually to be fair, it had taken up residence there, a constant reminder of the afternoon and *that* kiss.

She wanted to see him again, but with all this talk of what was going on, it occurred to Lucy that to continue to meet might place him in danger. He had already overcome so much. Whatever had caused those scars, and she surmised it was most likely from the battlefield unless he had been burned in a house fire, was surely enough trauma for one lifetime. It was not fair to risk him being hurt again. More than this, Lucy was disquieted by the torrent of feelings his kiss had unleashed, acknowledging she was likely already halfway in love with him. While her status was unclear, there was no denying she would always be a by-blow. No self-respecting gentleman, gardener or otherwise, would be interested in anything more than a dalliance, and that she could not condone. She knew *precisely* how badly they ended.

Even as she elected to avoid any possibility of bumping into him, Lucy's heart ached with a sadness she could scarcely comprehend.

*****

Sometime later, after Mr Garrick and Mr Lindsay had departed, the remaining four were ensconced in the library, sipping hot chocolate, and ruminating about the day.

"Although this whole thing still seems far-fetched, Papa, I believe we already have the solution. Lucy told me of her idea to have it appear she has been sent to the country, but that *I* will be the one to go. You can put it about that you judge it the most prudent way to protect the family until the inevitable gossip has died down. Then, hopefully, while Lucy is being me, whoever is behind this might be tempted to show their hand."

Lord Rycote started to speak, stammering a little in his haste to stem his daughter's candid disregard for common sense. Even though Lucy's proposal had been circling his mind, he was not yet persuaded of its merit.

"Papa, it is the only way. I know you do not wish either of us in harm's way," Elspeth interrupted him, "but this cannot continue, I do not want to spend the rest of my life looking over my shoulder in case someone is pointing a gun or chasing me with a carriage. This fiasco needs to end sooner rather than later."

Lucy reiterated her opinion, as did Rodney who concurred with Elspeth. Acknowledging the sense in their argument did not mean the earl approved, but until they came up with a better idea, it was all they had.

"We must keep this between ourselves. Obviously, Mr Lindsay and Mr Garrick will know I am not Elspeth, but I think we should restrict her, or officially my, whereabouts to ourselves. If anyone asks, tell them she went to Scotland. Something…" she did not finish her sentence, unwilling to voice her concerns, but the expression she surprised on Mr Lindsay's face continued to niggle her.

Thus, it was agreed. Elspeth would depart three days hence and remain at Gillingham Park until it was safe to return. Lucy would assume the persona of her sister for anything which did not involve her being in close proximity with people Elspeth knew, and the three men would monitor her every move.

*****

While missives were dispatched, bags were packed, and

arrangements made, Lucy continued with her normal routine. She worked at The Wise Owl and spent time with Elspeth, but even though she longed to see William again, Lucy did not revisit the park. In quiet moments she pondered her reticence, worried he would think her shallow and that the reason she had not sought him out was because she was repelled by his scar.

*****

Mid-morning, four days after the shooting, an ornate carriage emblazoned with the Rycote family crest drew up at the front door of Rycote House, luggage neatly strapped to the back. Lucy, a defiant tilt to a head held high, descended the steps unhurriedly, taking the time to pause, turn, and hold the gaze of the man watching from the doorway. She allowed a look of antipathy to wash over her features, so if anyone else observed their interaction she appeared at odds with her recently discovered father.

Lord Westbrook, Misters Lindsay and Garrick emerged behind the earl, the four standing in silence while the carriage rumbled away. They waited until it had vanished around the corner then trooped back inside, the slam of the heavy door like the closure of a chapter.

Hidden from view inside the carriage, Lucy and Elspeth embraced.

"Please take care, Lucy. I would be devastated should anything happen to you."

"Nothing will happen to me. You must remember, I am used to watching my back, and sleeping with one eye open. While the majority of those I grew up amongst would never think to harm anyone, especially not a woman, there were also a healthy number of villains."

Elspeth shuddered. "Lucy…"

"It was all I knew, Elspeth. It was not as though one day I

was living in the lap of luxury and the next I was begging for food on the streets. The world beyond your doorstep is harsh and precarious. We work hard for little coin, and our treats are a fresh loaf of bread and maybe a new cloak for winter. That is just the way it is, nothing can change it, but because of that it is probable I would spot something out of place more easily than you." Blithely ignoring the fact, she had been unaware someone tracked her movements only days previously. "I am sure your beloved will hot-foot it to Gillingham Park the minute we have solved this mystery, but for now we must say goodbye." Lucy hugged her sister again, aware they were slowing down. "Now, do you remember what I taught you? Just in case."

During the last week, Lucy had demonstrated one or two techniques by which Elspeth ought to be able to incapacitate any prospective attacker long enough that she could flee, should the necessity arise. Elspeth had proven herself surprisingly adept and Lucy was fairly certain, provided she didn't panic, her sister would not be taken by force unless a weapon was involved.

Elspeth nodded.

"If you have the chance to practise while in the country, might I suggest you do so? The more you do it, the more instinctive it becomes. To react without overthinking is the most effective method. Now, 'tis time to say goodbye. Be on your guard." Lucy kissed Elspeth's cheek, grinned at Penny who was accompanying her mistress and, as the carriage rattled to a halt, opened the door.

Before Alfred, the groom, was able to drop the step, Lucy had hopped down, vanishing into the maze of streets. Fifteen minutes brisk walking brought her to a scarcely used path leading to one of the avenues adjacent to Albany Square where the Gillingham's lived. Once there, she paused to make sure there was no one about then casually sauntered across to the narrow alleyway, the far end of which was the mews at the rear of Rycote House.

Slipping in through the door normally frequented by tradesmen, Lucy greeted the domestic staff, busy in the kitchens and made her way to the library. Stepping into the cool of the room, she sank into the closest chair.

"Elspeth…"

"Is fine and safely on her way. As far as I can tell that went off exactly as we planned, and I am certain no one witnessed my return. Now we just have to hope I am able to fool whoever is behind this."

Her father and Rodney offered sober smiles, and the three began the business of plotting their strategy. Attending the social functions so beloved of Elspeth was out of the question because that would bring Lucy too close to her sister's friends and acquaintances, none of whom were easily deceived. A ride through the park on horseback or by open-topped carriage might fool some, especially if she was seen with one or more of Elspeth's self-appointed guardians. Lucy remained suspicious of Mr Lindsay, but as yet had nothing tangible with which to accuse, so refrained from voicing it.

They decided to use the rumour mill to their advantage. Hints would be dropped, and they would ask the domestic staff to 'let slip' that Elspeth required some time to adjust to the recent revelations and thought it wise to avoid social gatherings until she was at peace with what her father had done. Thus, the occasional sojourn would not be untoward and her absence at balls and picnics entirely understandable. Such discoveries, while not unusual among the *ton*, were the least sensational when handled with the utmost discretion.

*****

The days sped by. In spite of keeping herself occupied, to her annoyance, Lucy found sleep eluded her. Too many things crowded her mind and, when she finally did doze off, her dreams were convoluted. One evening, not quite a week after Elspeth departed, and after a particularly busy day at The Wise Owl, she announced her intention to walk home, much to the consternation of Rodney and Mr Garrick. It took all their powers of persuasion to coax her into the carriage, and only then on the proviso she could take a constitutional in the park behind Rycote House — unchaperoned.

"I know Elspeth would be happy for you to tag along, but I am not accustomed to having someone overseeing my every move." Her guardians were always within earshot when she left Rycote House and it was becoming… wearisome. Accustomed to walking between her attic room and the book shop, being transported in a carriage every day, while convenient, meant she was not getting the exercise she enjoyed. The rides themselves were pleasant enough, at least two of the three men escorted her, and Lucy could not deny she found their company congenial. They passed the time chatting about this and that. Mostly it was mundane matters, but occasionally they touched on more personal topics, and although they managed to conceal it, Lucy was pretty certain she shocked them with some of the anecdotes from her childhood.

It was more that she valued her privacy and chafed at the current lack thereof.

After calling a perfunctory greeting to her father, she ran up to her bedchamber, shrugged out of her cloak, dropped her bag of books on the bed and grabbed her favourite blue wrap. Tripping down the stairs she was soon through the garden and into the park. A light shower during the afternoon leant a crisp freshness to the air and everything seemed washed clean. Raindrops, clinging to the leaves, shimmered in the early evening sunshine. Lucy loved this time of year. When the brief interlude of balmy days, blue skies, refreshing rains and heady fragrances revitalised the senses, before the heat of summer sapped energy and made everything wilt.

She paused for a moment and breathed it in, admiring the shadows playing over the ground as the breeze soughed through the trees. Hugging her wrap around her shoulders, she meandered aimlessly through the park, her mind focused on the mysterious incidents.

"I was beginning to think you were a figment of my imagination."

Lucy jumped, the deep voice interrupting her deliberations. "Mr Harcourt. Is it your avowed intent to startle me? 'Tis becoming a habit," she enquired, teasingly.

"I beg your pardon." He bowed. "I had not realised you were so easily disconcerted. You barely flinch when shot at, yet with a simple question, I unnerve you." His tone derisive, his expression... contemptuous.

Lucy sighed and rubbed her forehead distractedly. Fair enough, she *had* been avoiding him, it was nearly two weeks since their encounter almost at this exact spot. "No, 'tis me who should apologise. I shied away from returning. I..."

"Spare me your excuses." William cut her off, anger and something akin to disappointment, chilling his words. "Doubtless, like all the others, you are repulsed by me but thought it easier to ignore my existence, to pretend we did not share a... moment rather than hurt my feelings," he jeered the last three words, "or admit it to my face. I thought... I believed you were different, that my impediment did not disgust you. My mistake."

He turned his back on her and began to walk away.

Chapter Thirteen

Lucy's mouth fell open, and her brow lowered during his bitter retort. Fine, she had not seen him for almost two weeks, but he did not know why, nor had she given him any reason to think she was revolted by his scar. Fatigued after a long day, her temper — borne of sleepless nights, worry about Elspeth, and, yes, a soupçon of guilt that she had neglected to account for her absence, spilt over.

"How **dare** you presume to know what I was thinking?" she challenged, her voice dangerously quiet. "You think I just kiss random strangers? That I allow them to kiss me? That I am so shallow, I would be repulsed by so inconsequential a blemish? That you know anything at all about me, and why I might have stayed away. You arrogant..." she paused, biting back some of the cruder expletives she usually opted for when the occasion demanded, choosing instead, "... twit. Did it *ever* occur to you, I was trying to protect you, keep you safe? Oh no, Mr 'I assume everyone pities me', that is far too radical a concept."

William twisted around, and to her unending mortification, Lucy felt tears threaten. She knew his reaction was her own fault. It had taken all her willpower not to rush into the garden every afternoon when she arrived home on the off-chance she might see him. That he might repeat that sublime kiss, the memory of it never far away. She should have sought him out and explained; he knew about the threats to Elspeth, but it was too late, she could not turn back the clock.

"Think what you like." Lucy spat the words, trembling, more with distress than anger. Her chest was tight, and a peculiar sensation ran through her as though she was being ripped into little pieces. It was an unfamiliar ache, but vaguely reminiscent of when she lost her mother, prompting her to question whether it might be grief.

Lucy stormed off through the park, needing to put some distance between William and herself. She did not want him to see her tears, crying was for babies, moreover, it just gave you a headache and never solved anything. She could not recall the last time she cried. Even when her mother died, she did not weep. She had maintained a veneer of cheerful optimism for so long, that when Cecilia finally relinquished her grasp on life, Lucy was unable to find release in tears – she still couldn't.

William was dumbfounded. *She was trying to* **protect** *him? What on earth from?* No one had ever wanted to protect him before, and in spite of the anger crackling between them, he could not prevent a smile curving his lips or the warmth coiling around his heart. Lucy cared.

He strode after her — muttered curses about beetle-headed ingrates and inconsiderate boors floating back to him on the breeze. Swallowing a chuckle, it probably wasn't prudent to laugh right now, he quickly caught up to her.

"Lucy." No response, not even a slowing of her steps. "Lucy, please wait." Heartened when she seemed to hesitate, then she shook her head and continued marching. "Dammit, woman, permit me a moment." He reached her side and, snaking his hand around her elbow, spun her to face him. She was walking so fast the momentum caused her head to collide with his chest.

"Humpnerf." Her exclamation muffled in the folds of his jacket. Steadying her against him, William risked running his fingers down her spine, to soothe not seduce.

"It seems I am fated to apologise to you, Miss Lucy Truscott."

Lips pressed together in a grim line, she leaned away, angled her head, and pinned him with a baleful glare, shuffling her position until she could fold her arms. William would not have been surprised had she tapped her foot also. He drew a weighty sigh.

"Lucy, I am sorry I accused you of spurning me because of my scar. I fear it has become an instinctive reaction since my return from the war. It was just I believed... and then... I still hoped... but..." he ran out of words, unable to articulate his concern that, what they seemed to be hovering on the brink of was only in his head, that he had imagined the connection, the attraction.

Lucy studied him for so long, William thought she was not going to dignify his plea with a response. Finally, after what felt like a lifetime, she growled as though dissatisfied with the outcome of an internal debate, while conceding it was the right answer.

"In truth, I should be the one to beg forgiveness. I am not usually so spineless." Her voice was harsh, raw, and her face reflected acute unhappiness, although about what he could not tell. "William, we scarcely know each other and there are things about me of which you are not aware. Things which would send any decent gentleman running as far in the opposite direction as he could go, make you regret kissing me, and wish you had never promised to repeat it."

He watched as her head drooped, then her shoulders straightened, and she raised her eyes back to his, her indecision palpable. A mask fell over her features and her voice lost all inflection. His heart clenched.

"William, the reason I am at Rycote House is because, owing to an unfortunate accident not far from Seven Dials, I met Elspeth. I still have no idea what she was doing there that day, but she fell, or rather I believe she was pushed, into the path of a speeding carriage. I... well... errr... anyway, suffice it to say she dragged me back here and showed me a painting of her grandmother, whom I resemble closely, declaring we must be related. Rather than bore you with all the details, plainly stated, it transpires my mother and Lord Rycote had an...

entanglement prior to his marriage to Elspeth's mother. When it became clear his family would never allow him to marry her, my mother I mean, she left. Apparently, he tried to find her, without success. He had no idea she was with child… I was the result." She shrugged with apparent indifference.

"Now, two and twenty years later, here I am, trying to fit into a world I know nothing about. My half-sister who, by the way thinks our meeting was destined, is being stalked by some madman bent on harming her. To top it off, I meet a man who turns my normally sensible and unromantic brain to pulp, only to realise it can never have a happy ending, because, discounting the fact any association with me probably places him in imminent danger, I am a bastard."

William stared at her, as with this last word she branded herself; declared she was, essentially, tainted by the actions of her parents. She began to speak again, but he gave her no chance to justify or defend. He bent his head and crushed his lips to hers. He heard a sound, like a cross between a moan and a sob and felt Lucy mould herself to him. His arms tightened, and he slid one hand around to cup the back of her head, his thumb resting on the pulse fluttering in her neck.

How long they kissed, Lucy would never remember, neither did she want it to end. She had shared her secret, confessed she was illegitimate, and he still kissed her. Was there *any* chance this was maybe, possibly, the beginning of something enduring? As her body began to melt, she truly hoped so.

Eventually, William lifted his head, his eyes glazed, his heart hammering, and his breathing erratic.

"Oh God, Lucy. You entrance me. I am not afraid to admit, this past week I have lingered in the garden hankering for a single glimpse of you, knowing my behaviour to be irrational. When I close my eyes your face is there, watchful eyes deciding whether to trust. You evoke the sirens of myth for the sound of your voice, even when you are vexed, captivates me. I want to hear that voice scream my name in the throes of passion, then sing me to sleep in the aftermath. I want to hear you laugh, cry, argue, praise, defend, question, tease, and cajole. I want to watch you dance, study you while you sleep, sit with you while you read, and most of all I want the chance to kiss you senseless every day for the rest of my life."

William drew a shuddering breath. Baring your soul, opening your heart was exhausting, especially for someone who had been a recluse for nigh on two years, but he wanted to tell her everything. He placed his hands on either side of her face, searching her eyes. She held his gaze without flinching, the blue-grey hue, unpredictable as quicksilver was unruffled, but she seemed to sense there was more and remained silent.

"I do not want us to have secrets. Secrets can destroy relationships. You have been honest with me regarding your heritage. I suspect you think me a gardener, and while I would be glad if that was my position, it is only one of my titles."

He felt Lucy stiffen at the mention of titles and rested his forehead to hers.

"Trust me, my love." The endearment rolled off his tongue unbidden, it was worth the risk, he could not lose her. He lifted his head and looked her straight in the eye. "I am William Harcourt, tenth Marquis of Blackthorne. I was wounded in battle; my scars go deeper than the mark on my face. My flaws are many and varied and I ought not to subject you to them, but in the brief time we have known each other I believe something is stirring, something worth pursuing and, while I accept 'tis precipitous, I would very much like to see where it might lead."

"Y-you are a m-marquis?" Lucy gawked at him, eyes round as saucers. This was turning into a most interesting walk. Her head insisted this was madness, any romance between them was doomed, in much the same way as that of her parents, but while William was stroking her face as though she was the finest china, her heart held sway. Wary eyes searched hers, as though he knew she was fighting the temptation to flee. "H-how…"

"My father was marquis, he died, the title is now mine."

"No." The ghost of a smile tugged at her mouth. "How can we make this work? Your family will not want you to court someone like me. So, my father is an earl, which I believe places me lower on the social scale even if I was legitimate, but I'm not, my status is beneath that of your servants. Do you not see? History is repeating itself and I refuse to fall in love with you only to watch when duty demands you wed another. I cannot. When I thought you were a gardener…" she trailed off. Lunacy, it was lunacy.

"Lucy, my darling Lucy…"

The timbre of his voice sent shivers along her spine, *dear lord, she could love him for his voice.*

"I am my family. My father was an only child, as was my mother. As far as I am aware, I am the last of the Harcourt line. Even if I was not I would relinquish everything for you. A title is hollow, a house merely a shell unless you are able to share them with the one you love." He stopped abruptly, aware he had declared his hand, *what an idiot, talk about precipitous, great, just great. Are you **trying** to scare her off? Again!* Inhaling a deep breath, William pinched the bridge of his nose between his finger and his thumb. He opened his mouth, closed it, then before coherence abandoned him completely, opened his mouth once more to say what, he did not know, when a light finger came to rest against his lips.

The candour in his tone persuaded Lucy to trust as nothing else could and, daring to dream, she murmured. "Do not retract your words, for if from your heart, they are the most wonderful

I have ever heard." She paused, collecting her thoughts. "Do you believe in fate? You said you were fated to apologise to me, but I do not think the apology is what is fated. Fate saw to it that we met, the rest is in our hands. Misunderstandings, jumping to conclusions without giving the other the opportunity to explain, is why we had to apologise, and I am as guilty as you." She leaned up and touched her lips to his. "Mayhap we should start afresh. No more secrets and we agree to tell each other if something seems amiss. Moreover, with that in mind, I should like to hear all about your life, including, no especially, when you went to war and how you were injured." Shyly asked, holding William's gaze and, gripping his hand, willing him to understand she yearned to know everything about him.

Chapter Fourteen

"That works both ways, Lucy, and are you certain? It was a…" William hesitated, searching for a less stark way of phrasing what he suffered, "deplorable episode and not a tale for ladies' ears."

"Ahhh, how quickly you forget. I am no lady, William, and although I have not witnessed the evils wrought by war, I have probably seen similarly heinous acts in the streets of St Giles. Life there is not so far removed from the battlefield, 'tis just the weapons are different. Don't you see, if you tell me, you have shared a burden you probably do not realise you carry. To know what happened helps me appreciate what you have been through and are still recovering from. I daresay you are debilitated by nightmares. Surely, it is better to talk about what happened until the horror is consigned to memory, not something you relive every time you close your eyes. If you keep it bottled up inside, you will never be at peace."

While she was speaking, Lucy noticed William lift his free hand to his scar as though to cover it. Lucy reached up, entwined her fingers in his and drew them away from his face.

"As for this…" with her other hand, she traced the puckered skin. "… 'tis not something to be ashamed of. You should not hide your face. You should walk with your head held high. This speaks of courage, of honour and integrity, more so than any medal. You fought for our country, you were prepared to give your life to protect its sovereignty. Yes, it is now part of you, but only a miniscule part of a whole that, to me, is perfect. You have experienced more in a year or two than most will experience in a lifetime, in ten lifetimes, yet you feel it somehow diminishes you. You spend your days here, in the garden and, while I agree tending to plants is a pleasing pastime, they cannot stroll arm-in-arm through a park on a sunny afternoon and are quite unable to discuss the current political upheaval, or laugh about the latest fashions, or debate what caused the downfall of the Roman Empire, or simply discuss their day."

Grasping his hands, she took one step back, held his gaze, and opened her heart.

"But mayhap, if I promise to sing you to sleep, you could do all of those... with me?"

William's head was swirling and he swallowed on a gulp. Lucy's words struck a chord. He had never looked upon his behaviour as hiding; more his reluctance to leave the haven of his home became second nature, a way to avoid pitying stares and tactless comments. Lucy was correct, he had nothing to be ashamed of. He recalled the endless weeks in hospital while he recovered, talking with other wounded soldiers, many of whom had sustained far worse injuries than he. All were glad to be alive, to be home and away from the horrors of war.

Somewhere along the line, he had forgotten how to be thankful, grateful, happy. He had his life, he had the use of all his limbs, and although the scars were ugly they would not prevent him from doing anything he wanted. He had a comfortable home, and it seemed as though he had found a woman who could see past all his insecurities to the man he once was.

Tucking her back against him, he rested his cheek on her hair. "Thank you, Lucy Truscott, for having the courage to say what I needed to hear. Over the past year many tried but I refused to listen. Mayhap I was not ready," he shrugged, "but you have reached something deep within my soul, your temerity has loosed the fetters in my mind which have imprisoned me as securely as when I was held captive by the French." He paused, tilting her chin with one finger, so he could look her in the eye.

"And I desire nothing more than to do all those things...

with you."

Then, with achingly sweet tenderness, he kissed her.

A shout not far from where they were standing jolted them back to reality and they broke apart, faces flushed.

"Heavens, that is probably Alice calling me for dinner. Time certainly flies when one is... talking..." Lucy rasped trying to steady her breathing.

"Well, it *was* rather an... engrossing conversation." William smiled, trailing a finger along her jawline. "Might you return on the morrow?"

"Wild horses would not keep me away. We have much to discuss, 'tis your fault for diverting me from more important matters." Mischief glittering in her eyes.

"That is because you are such a delicious distraction." William let her move out of his embrace, only to draw her arm through his. They soon reached the gate leading to the formal gardens of Rycote House, whereupon William pressed a chaste kiss to her cheek. "Until tomorrow."

"I'll be here." Lucy hoisted her skirts and dashed up the path, turning once to wave, making William grin like a moonstruck calf.

Alice, standing on the grass below the terrace looking puzzled, breathed a sigh of relief when Lucy appeared. "Oh, miss, I was getting worried, what with everything else going on."

"Do not fret about me, Alice. I know how to look after myself, but thank you, 'tis long since I have had anyone care about my welfare." The two women chatted, as they climbed the wide stone steps to the terrace, and through the library. "I shall change for dinner, if Lo— Papa asks, I will be back momentarily."

During the meal, Lucy confessed to her father that the man

who saved her was not in fact their neighbour's gardener, but William Harcourt, and despite the brevity of their acquaintance, perceived a depth of affection quite unanticipated. Christopher was hard pushed to keep a straight face — her explanation was far more convoluted than necessary — and declared himself pleased for both parties. The Marquis of Blackthorne had confined himself to his four walls for long enough, and it seemed Lucy had succeeded where Elspeth failed. Not that the latter had ever shown any romantic interest in their neighbour, but the earl was beginning to think if his exuberant daughter could not smash through William's reserve, no one could.

"I think William might be able to help us, Papa. He is another wise in the way of crafty schemes. Perhaps he and Lord Westbrook might work together for we know he cannot be behind the mishaps. He was with me when I was shot. Very difficult to shoot me from across the park when he is right beside me." She forbore to mention the kissing, for although she was passed the age of majority and he had agreed not to interfere in her life, her father might not view an intoxicating kiss on second meeting in too favourable a manner.

"I concur. Rodney will be here in the morning, I shall mention it to him. It will be good to see young Harcourt out and about again. Been shut up in that house far too long in my opinion."

"It cannot be easy facing people whose inability to see beneath the surface makes them recoil. Their behaviour is shallow and unwarranted, especially as it is something over which he had no control and the reason he remained in seclusion." Lucy's mouth twisted in scorn at such insensitivity.

"I doubt they meant anything malicious, Lucy. Many cannot cope with the horror of war turning up on their doorstep so to speak."

"I imagine William would prefer that too," she remarked, drily.

Christopher acknowledged the truth of her words, and adroitly moved the conversation to other topics, the rest of the evening spent in pleasant chatter.

*****

The following afternoon, after returning from a hectic shift at The Wise Owl, Lucy vanished into the park. Prior to leaving the house she had, for reasons she was inclined to ignore, taken a little extra effort with her appearance. It had been a warm day for the time of year, and she chose one of her new dresses, a gown of the finest lawn in a becoming shade of lemon, the lightweight fabric much cooler than the wool of her working attire. Gathering up a linen wrap — more for propriety than any other reason — she called her whereabouts to Mr Harris, as she sailed past the kitchens, confirming she would be back in time for dinner.

The staff chuckled at her lack of formality. Without trying, Lucy had won their abiding devotion with her unfailing politeness, ingenuous manners, and determination not to make their lives any more arduous by her presence. All behind the baize door knew of the strange goings on and, without her being aware, kept a watchful eye on Miss Truscott.

Skidding to a halt near the borders of William's garden, she scanned her surroundings. He was nowhere to be seen. Glancing at the sky, Lucy reckoned it was about half after four. She ruminated over where he might be, not confident enough to attempt to pick her way through his garden to his home. His staff did not know her, and she would be humiliated if they turned her away.

Suddenly she felt awkward and uncertain. *Did she look too eager? How was one supposed to behave in situations like this?* She had never been courted, but vaguely recalled her mother giving her a list of instructions on how to behave, and in the back of her mind she remembered something about it being up to the gentleman to do all the running. If a woman gave the impression of being too keen it would scare them off, or worse they might think her forward or brash — conveniently forgetting their intimate conversation of the previous day. She rubbed her nose. *How long should she dally, without looking like a fool?*

Currently out of Lucy's line of sight, William was hurrying to meet her. An appointment with his man of business had gone on longer than anticipated and he feared she would not wait. Rounding the dense bushes at the bottom of the garden path where the park began, he slowed his steps, the better to admire her unnoticed. He loved that Lucy was unusually tall, it made him feel less of a giant next to her. This afternoon her willowy frame was encased in an ankle length gown, her shoulders covered in a swathe of material, the blend of pale yellow and leaf-green evoking one of the daffodil varieties of which he was so enamoured. He watched as she rubbed her nose, her body language suggestive of indecision, and he knew he was just in time to stop her fleeing.

"Lucy," he murmured her name, and even from feet away she heard, her head swinging in his direction.

A beam lit her face and she took a hesitant step towards him. Then gave up being decorous and ran into his arms, lifting her face for his kiss, which, of course, he bestowed most satisfactorily.

"I was beginning to wonder whether you were coming," she tried to chide but couldn't because she was so happy, making William chuckle.

"I was held up in a business meeting and could not extricate myself," he explained. "I should have finished an hour ago, but there were one or two extra items on the agenda, which required immediate attention." He did not elaborate and Lucy did not care. He was here now that was enough.

"Do you have time to talk?"

"Of course. Would a bench in my garden be a suitable place

to discuss this matter?"

"That sounds most agreeable."

Taking her hand, William led Lucy back the way he had come, through an ornate gate reminiscent of a church lychgate and into the grounds of Harcourt House. Beyond the high hedge separating park and garden, was a large patch of lawn, at the centre of which grew a large, sprawling oak tree. Calf-high hedges of box and privet, neatly trimmed, enclosed beds full of plants, most yet to bloom. The edge of the garden had no formal layout and William, spying Lucy's interested gaze, explained it was a mix of several different plants, such as roses, lavender, delphinium, peony, and campanula. He hoped the combination would offer a colourful contrast to the green of the hedging. Under the tree was the aforementioned bench to which they headed, quickly settling themselves.

A maid, who William introduced as Megan, came to ask whether she could bring them some refreshments. William thanked her and she flew off to return almost immediately with a tray on which stood two glasses of cool lemonade and a plate of tiny cakes, leaving Lucy to suspect William had forewarned his staff.

"Were they expecting you to bring me here?" she ventured.

William grinned. "I may have mentioned it. I imagine they have been keeping an eye out. You are the first lady I have ever brought into my garden, and they may be a trifle... errr... enthusiastic."

Lucy tapped her lip, a mischievous twinkle in her eye. "In that case, mayhap we should give them a little something else to talk about." Leaning close, she slid one hand over his damaged cheek to curve around the back of his neck. Bringing his head to hers, she kissed him, her lips gliding over his, and she heard his intake of breath as their tongues met. She could taste the tang of lemonade and the sugary sweetness of the cakes mixed with

something else, something indefinable that was essentially theirs.
It was a heady blend.

Chapter Fifteen

Just when William began to forget where they were, Lucy broke their kiss. William's face was a picture.

"Well, that is unfair. I shall revisit this later, madam."

Lucy giggled and pretended to fan herself. "Oh, good sir, if you must."

"I really must. Now, before you distract me again with your feminine wiles, tell me about Elspeth."

Lucy spluttered with indignation and jabbed a finger into his leg.

William raised his palms. "You kissed me, my dear. I was just an innocent bystander. Fine," as he spied a warning glint in Lucy's eye, "mayhap not altogether innocent." He dropped a kiss on her nose. In accord they leaned back against the bench, admiring the garden in the late afternoon sunlight, while sipping the rest of their lemonade. Swallowing the last of her drink, Lucy placed the dainty glass on the tray and shared what she knew of the strange happenings.

"Until we were shot at," she concluded, "Elspeth had managed to convince herself they were all just accidents and coincidences, but when I asked her to recall the day we met, she admitted she felt as though she had been pushed." Lucy rubbed her nose, a gesture William was coming to recognise as an expression of confusion, then twisted to face him. "She has gone to Gillingham Park, and I am hoping to fool whoever is behind this into thinking I am Elspeth. I know we are not exactly alike but, from a distance, we could be mistaken for the other. You thought I was she when first we met."

"Lucy, you could be in grave danger."

She shrugged. "I think there is danger, regardless. At least this way one of us is safe. I do not relish being in someone's sights, but this needs to end. Papa cannot conceive who is behind this, or what their motive might be, but we cannot be held to ransom by another's actions. 'Tis as bizarre as it is ludicrous."

"Has Lord Rycote organised any kind of surveillance or come up with a way to catch the perpetrator?"

"I have at least two of the three men who seem to act as guardians for Elspeth with me every time I leave Rycote House. 'Tis a bit restrictive in all honesty, but I suppose I understand why Papa judges it necessary.

"Of *course.* it's necessary!" William expostulated. "The man, or woman, although I am inclined to go with the former, tried to shoot you." He was stunned at Lucy's apparent nonchalance.

"William, I appreciate his concern, but being under constant watch is uncomfortable." She wriggled on the seat. "I feel like a naughty child."

"Well then, the sooner he is caught the better. Might I accompany you back to Rycote House and beg an interview with your papa. Surely another head can only be beneficial?"

"You would do that for me?"

William nodded. Lucy gripped his hand.

"Thank you. I think that is a capital idea but let us tarry just a little longer here. I relish the peace of being alone with you."

"As do I, my love." William was gratified when Lucy snuggled against his side. He slung an arm along the bench behind her and, as they fell into mundane chatter about nothing very important at all, absently trailed his fingers up and down her arm, unaware he was sending delightful frissons right through her, all the way to her toes. For a little while they enjoyed the tranquillity of the garden and each other's company.

An hour or so later, they made their way to Rycote House to find the earl and the viscount relaxing in the library with a glass of whisky each. The French doors stood open, a light breeze wafting through a room lit by the dying rays of the setting sun and, unexpectedly, Lucy acknowledged it was beginning to feel like home. The tiny attic room with its bare walls and one cracked window becoming a dreary memory.

Lucy was about to make introductions, when her father jumped to his feet.

"Blackthorne! Good to see you, good to see you, about time you got out and about. No point locking yourself away, man. Elspeth missed you. I understand you and Lucy have become… acquainted?"

"Rycote, Westbrook," William greeted both men. All three shook hands, and then Christopher poured William a whisky and offered Lucy her choice. She opted for a glass of water — alcohol loosened her tongue causing her to speak first and think later, and the rare times she indulged had not ended well.

She listened while the three men began a comfortable conversation, realising they were well acquainted even though she knew William had scarcely left his home during the past year or so. Hopefully, there was an established trust which would make their working together much more straightforward.

William was invited to stay for dinner, which he accepted to Lucy's delight and, during the meal, the four began to make plans.

"I know Mr Lindsay and Mr Garrick are aware it was Elspeth who left for the country, and not I, but might I reiterate that we do not tell them where she went?" Lucy glanced around the table, seeing consternation on the faces of her father and Rodney.

"Surely you do not suspect either man, Lucy?" Rodney demanded, shocked at her request.

"My Lord…"

"Please, call me, Rodney," he begged. "I have been calling you Lucy for the past three weeks. All this formality is farcical when we are discussing attempted murder and the possibility one of our friends might be behind it."

'Thank you. Rodney, the day we met, Elspeth did not trip, she believes she was pushed. She cannot recall anyone barging into your group causing one of you to jar her. That leaves the three of you. If it was not you, it can only have been Edward or James," Lucy ignoring convention in her need to make things less complicated.

By the expression on the faces of those listening to her Lucy surmised this had not occurred to any of them.

"No, no, no! Lindsay and Garrick have been in my employ for years, since before Susannah died. What motive would they have?" Christopher argued.

Lucy shrugged. "I have no idea, but what other explanation is there?"

Her father looked at Rodney. "Surely it was more likely either a complete accident or someone who pursued you unnoticed, and who managed to get away unseen in the melee?"

Rodney swung his gaze between Lucy and Christopher, once again arrested by their uncanny resemblance. His mind flew back to the horror of the moment when he realised Elspeth was falling and he saw the hurtling carriage. All he had to do was reach out and grab her, but it was as though he was frozen, unable to stretch even one finger to save her. His whole focus had been on Elspeth, deaf and blind to everything else going on around him.

He shook his head. "I know what you want to hear, Rycote, but I cannot say one way or another. If Lucy had not..." he trailed off, unable to articulate what might have been.

"Yes, but I did, and she was unharmed save an assortment of bruises. I am almost certain there was no one close enough to barge into you. We must think again. How are James and Edward connected to you, Papa?"

"Edward is the nephew of Susannah's brother-in-law, a relation by marriage. James is the son of my best friend, Vernon

Garrick, who also happens to be my solicitor."

"Have either of them shown any antagonism towards you or Elspeth?" William, who was listening intently, interposed. Christopher was shaking his head when Lucy said quietly,

"Yes."

There was a long pause while plates were cleared, and a mouth-watering baked custard was served, the warm, yet light dessert, a perfect complement to the rich and numerous main courses. Lucy still ate little, but she loved this dessert and refused to say any more until she had eaten it, saying it would spoil if left to go cold.

"There's nothing wasting, while I enjoy this." Was her irreverent response when they pressed her to elaborate on her comment.

Dessert consumed, Christopher suggested they move to the drawing room, and once they made themselves comfortable, three sets of eyes bore into Lucy, who smiled, grimly.

"After dinner, on the evening you told us about Mama, you Papa, Elspeth, and Edward were debating something about Napoleon. It was fleeting, and in the moment, I thought I must have imagined it, but when I thought about it later, I knew I was not mistaken. Edward was staring at Elspeth as though he loved and hated her at the same time." She paused and, in quiet appeal, added. "Just consider the possibility. We cannot discount him. What if he is enamoured with Elspeth, knows how Rodney feels and does not wish to lose her to a rival?"

"Yes, but would not that prompt him to do away with Westbrook?" William contended.

"Logically, yes, however, it has come to my attention of late, that when people are in love, rational thinking is thrown out with the bath water." She held William's gaze, and he had the grace to blush, before grinning at her sheepishly. "Mayhap, his argument is that if he cannot have her no one can." She raised her hand placatingly as her father spluttered a denial. "I am not saying 'tis Edward behind the attacks, but neither can we say with any certainty he is not."

Rodney added. "I have not uncovered any employee with enough of an axe to grind to take it out on Elspeth, my Lord. The last person to be discharged was five years ago. Although displeased with his attitude, you noted it may have been a personality clash and thus, did not let him go without sufficient coin and a reasonable reference." He shrugged, "I cannot see him holding a grudge for five years, especially as you did not ruin his chances for further employment."

"Hmmm, all fingers seem to point to Lindsay." Christopher pursed his lips, letting his mind roam. Something was teasing at the edge of his consciousness, but it would not be pinned down. "There is something, but I cannot hold onto it. Doubtless it will come to me. It is probably trivial and entirely unconnected. Vigilance is the key, my friends, and daughter." He smiled at Lucy who responded in kind.

He spun in his chair to fix William with an uncompromising stare.

"Now that discussion is concluded, I would like to ask whether your intentions towards my daughter are honourable?"

"Papa!" Lucy exclaimed, her hands lifting to cover flaming cheeks. "We talked about this, you said you would not interfere. I am so sorry, William."

"I have changed my mind. Do you recall what I said about when I met your mother? I know how men think and, clearly, it is not usually with their brains. I will not have your heart broken."

Lucy was mortified. "Papa, *please* stop talking," she beseeched. "William, pay him no mind. Lord Rycote has no say in my personal life."

"I agreed not to arrange a marriage for you, Lucy, but I made no promises not to interrogate any and all suitors you bring into this house."

"How many suitors has she had?" William enquired, poker-faced. Lucy gaped at him, about to remonstrate, when she spotted the slight quirk of his lips and the devilish glint in his eyes. Taking pity on her, he continued. "Rycote, my intentions towards Lucy are genuine and of the highest honour. We may have met a mere handspan of time ago, but that does not mean my affection is any less profound. I will not rush your daughter into anything she is not comfortable with, but I believe my sentiment is reciprocated, and once all this trouble has been laid to rest, I will revisit this conversation." His eyes settled on Lucy while he spoke, their azure depths blazing.

She sucked in a breath and, forgetting they were not alone, reached for his hand.

"William…" she breathed, her heart thudding as he interlaced their fingers, and lifted them to his lips. A subtle cough reminded her where they were, but although she gave her attention back to her father, she did not let go of William's hand.

Chapter Sixteen

The days lengthened, new leaves and dizzying displays of blossoms sprouted on trees and plants. For a while everything was calm and life seemed to be returning to normal. Lucy and Elspeth exchanged letters which, while sporadic, were treasured, for they were about those years before they met. Through their words, the sisters came to know each other. No brief missives, these were lengthy epistles, detailed and candid.

Every day, since the evening William made his intentions clear, Lucy received a daffodil. Each one came with a card tied loosely around the tall green stem. On the card, William wrote a line from a piece by the prominent poet, Wordsworth. Although his works were oft criticised, William found Wordsworth's poetry soothing. Moreover, several mentioned a woman named Lucy, and as the poet and he shared the same given name, William was drawn to the parallels. As he anticipated, Lucy was familiar with Wordsworth, and to quote the remainder of the verse became something of a game when next she and William were together.

The couple met as often as possible, bearing in mind his reputation as a recluse and her role as Elspeth, and during these snatched interludes began to open up about their respective pasts. Both had suffered hardship in one form or another, and although Lucy had not witnessed the horrors of war, she had suffered privations all her life — growing up in the slums of London was its own battlefield. William had yet to disclose how he was injured but, to Lucy, it was enough he felt able to talk about the preceding months of conflict.

They *were* finding their brief encounters to be insufficient. Stolen kisses and murmured endearments were all well and good, but their underlying passion was becoming harder to deny.

In light of this and determined to spend more than an occasional half hour with Lucy, just over a week after he declared his hand, William invited her to his home for dinner which she accepted with alacrity. To prevent any suggestion of impropriety, Lucy was persuaded to allow Alice to accompany her. Lucy, who had never needed or wanted a chaperone, quickly discovered Alice knew all who worked at Harcourt House and thus shooed her off to enjoy an evening with them — the serving of the simple yet tasty meal requiring little attendance. Thereafter, Lucy assured anyone who enquired that she was quite capable of walking between neighbouring houses unescorted.

Before the meal William gave her a tour of the house, and Lucy was interested to see, in contrast to the bright, colourful garden, the interior decor and furnishings, while elegant, were sombre in tone. Curtains were drawn in many of the rooms ostensibly to protect the furniture, and even though there was not a speck of dust, their obvious lack of use lent an overall air of genteel abandonment. She also noted, but forbore to comment, the doors on most of those rooms currently in use had been removed.

"Do you ever open the windows?" Lucy asked, her mouth running ahead of her brain. "Oh, I do beg your pardon, that was uncalled for." Embarrassed by how rude she sounded.

To her relief, William chuckled. "Do not fret," he replied, taking her hand, and tucking it through his arm as they walked along a carpeted hallway. "For a long time, I tended to avoid the daylight, the sun seemed to irritate my scars. Then, I suppose it became easier to leave everything closed. The only time I ventured outside was to work in the garden and even then, I had to wear a straw hat. You would not credit how difficult it was to find one with a suitably broad brim. Eventually, I had no choice but to get one custom made by Lock's," naming the famous hatters, "in a style reminiscent of a fishmonger's boater. It may not be the most stylish accessory, but it serves a purpose and allows me to indulge one of my passions."

"I think it sounds very dapper, and what other passions do you have, pray tell?" Lucy queried artlessly.

"Why you, my dear." Which statement, of course, made Lucy blush furiously, and William's chuckle bloom into outright laughter. He kissed her hot cheek and ushered her into the library where shortly thereafter Mr Grantley, William's butler, came to announce dinner.

William's staff, though modest in number, were trusted and long-serving — more family than servant. Days earlier, when he had introduced them to Lucy, all reacted with polite astonishment that their master was hosting, nay, courting a lady; the last time such a thing happened, if ever, beyond their recall. Lucy endeavoured to learn their names, and soon she managed to commit them all to memory. Unusually for her, she found herself painfully shy in their presence, for, as when she was first invited into her father's home, Lucy was under no illusion that, in reality, they were all of a higher status, yet she was the one upon whom they waited. She tried to explain her diffidence to William while they were sipping hot chocolate in his library, after their second evening meal together.

"You need to understand having someone serve me my food, help me to dress, do my hair, all those little services you take for granted, is difficult. I have never had such pampering and regardless of who my father is, I am still a child of the slums. I am lucky in that Mama ensured I was educated to a certain degree; she taught me how to speak properly, how to enunciate my words, and how to modulate my accent. Thus, I have a respectable job but, had you met me in the street, you would have walked by without a second glance. The likes of me are so far beneath the likes of you as to be invisible. No," as William interrupted to refute this, "I know your behaviour is not deliberate or spiteful, it is simply the way of the world. Perhaps you have not weighed the repercussions a prolonged association with me might engender."

William's mind flew back to the day they met when he presumed her to be Elspeth playing a game. He had been appallingly discourteous, and Lucy was correct, his reaction *was* involuntary. It was not, however, born of any inherent disdain for those less fortunate, more that prior to meeting Lucy he had never given it any more than a fleeting thought. As Lucy asserted, it was just life. He believed himself to be a fair and kind employer. His staff were paid decent coin, they were clothed, housed, well fed, permitted one day off every week with seven days holiday a year. He had shut up most of the rooms at Harcourt House, so even though his staff was paltry in comparison with the number at Rycote House, their tasks were also less arduous. That said, and despite the cordial relationship he shared with all those who worked for him, it was clear, even if he didn't distinguish, they were not equals in the eyes of Society.

"Dash it all, Lucy, you are correct, I never gave it a moment's thought." He paused, reminded of his time in the military. "When I was in the army, the status of those who served alongside me was immaterial. Rank, of course, was a different matter, but I was more concerned with making sure we all made it out alive than whether they were a duke or a farmer. Moreover, I feel it necessary to point out that while I may be blind to those who move in a different circle, if I saw you in the street, even if you were dressed in a sack, I would notice you." He smiled, reaching over to trail the tips of his fingers along her arm. "You have an uncanny knack of touching a person's soul."

Lucy stared at William, seeing the candlelight mirrored in the dark blue depths of his eyes like stars in a midwinter sky.

Unable to stop herself, she put her drink on the table between them, got up from her chair, and in two steps was on his knee. Taking his cup, she placed it alongside its twin.

"I do not wish you to spill such delicious hot chocolate," she murmured, stroking his ravaged cheek. "'Tis... too... good... to... waste." Interspersing each word with a kiss, featherlight. She felt a tremor run through him as his arms enclosed her, one hand gliding up her back to caress her neck, his fingers entwining in her hair.

"I can find no fault with your argument," he concurred, huskily, "'twould be travesty. Lucy..." words failed him as Lucy untied his cravat, inquisitive fingers seeking under the neckline of his shirt. "Lucy," he repeated her name, and she raised her eyes.

He held her gaze.

Time stopped.

Then, with a groan, he captured her lips. She opened to him and their tongues met in sweet confusion; teasing, tasting, tantalising. Her uninhibited response encouraged William to deepen their kiss. Passion swirled, and heat flared, while hands searched. Lucy found being able to touch the tiny v of skin at William's throat was not enough. Pulling at the soft cotton she managed to free his shirt from his trousers and, with a sigh that could only be described as jubilant, slid her hands over the hardened planes of William's abdomen and upwards to his chest.

She heard him suck in a sharp breath when her fingers taunted his warm flesh, and she became aware he was scattering kisses along her neck to the hollow at the base of her throat.

William contemplated whether his heart would burst clear out of his chest with the sensations Lucy's innocent gestures elicited. This spirited young woman had revived a part of him he believed long dead, crumbled to ashes like the aftermath of the fire that almost stole his life. Nevertheless, despite their obvious ardour, and however much he might wish to ignore convention, William was determined not to take advantage of Lucy. She deserved more — she deserved his respect, she deserved everything. Thus, after blazing another trail along her shoulder, he lifted his head and caught her wandering hands.

"My love, I think it is time I took you home." Lucy stared at him; her hair tousled, her lips swollen, and her eyes glazed. *Heavens, she was bewitching. Damn his gentlemanly instincts!* Kissing her again, he sighed. "Lucy, if we don't stop, I know where this will lead and, while I yearn to make love to you right here, right now, I refuse to give in to my baser urges. There is no hurry. In fact, I am rather looking forward to taking my time, to indulge in a leisurely seduction. If we rush, we will be at the end before we have begun, missing everything in between, and although anxious to reach the destination, I would very much like to savour the journey."

His words had the same effect on Lucy's heart rate as did his lips and his hands. She cocked her head, and with one slender finger, tapped her lips. The seconds ticked by, the silence in the room broken only by the crackling of the fire. She studied his features, finding it preposterous, yet oddly felicitous that this man whom she had known for so short a time made her feel not only as though she was the most beautiful woman ever to have walked the earth, but also, that with him she had come home. She gave him her answer — one, which was never in any doubt.

"Hmmm… good sir, I am inclined to yield to your proposal, on the proviso that the journey is not too… errr… protracted."

William grinned at her pert reply and, after succumbing to one more heart-stopping kiss, informed Mr Grantley he would be escorting Miss Truscott home, the two slipping out through the garden as had become their habit.

Hushed conversation and several more kisses ensued, but Lucy was soon home and being helped into her nightdress by

Alice. Moments later she was fast asleep, her dreams proving most satisfactory.

Chapter Seventeen

Early the next morning, there came a knock at the front door of Rycote House. When Mr Harris opened it there was no one to be seen, but standing proudly on the step, a wide terracotta bowl, not too deep, not too shallow, filled with daffodils. Tucked between the leaves, a letter addressed to Miss Lucy Truscott.

Mr Harris, a knowing smile on his wrinkled face, went to find the recipient who was eating breakfast with her father.

"Excuse me, Miss Lucy, but you have a letter and a delivery." He held out the silver platter on which he had placed the missive.

"For me? Are you sure?" Lucy's nose crinkled in puzzlement as she plucked the folded sheet from the tray.

"Quite sure," he smiled, adding, "my lady."

"Pooh, my lady indeed." She grinned at the butler who winked and left the room. Lucy turned the letter over and over, expecting it to be from Elspeth, surprised when she recognised the writing as William's. *Well, how interesting.* A tingle ran through her as she imagined him sitting at the enormous desk in his study, penning her a missive.

"Oh, Lucy, open it, do. You are worse than Elspeth. She toys with her letters for so long, by the time she comes to read them, they are barely legible." Christopher chided.

Chuckling at his expression, Lucy broke the seal and unfolded the sheet. She scanned the page, then began to read it properly. It was another poem by Wordsworth, this one entitled *I wandered lonely as a cloud.* The words resonated with her, conjuring up the day they met, a sentiment shared by William who added a postscript.

My dearest Lucy,

Until very recently, a daffodil was just a flower, a very pretty flower, but a flower all the same. Now, it represents something infinitely more precious. Every time I see one, I think of you and, while I trust you know the strength of my devotion, this poem conveys the joy you brought into my life more eloquently than I ever could.

I may still wander but am lonely no longer.
Faithfully and forever yours,
William

Lucy stared at the words, her fingers smoothing over the paper. *Oh, be still my beating heart*, the phrase from a play by Mountfort, yet another William, floated through her mind. *What was it with these Williams and their silver tongues?*

"Lucy," her father's voice broke through her reverie.

"Hmmm…"

"Lucy, what does it say?"

"Here." Blushing, she passed the letter to the earl.

He read it, narrowed his eyes at his daughter then read it again. "Poetry?"

"Do not disparage his letter, Papa. To brave ridicule by writing in so romantic a fashion speaks volumes for his character." Lucy glared at her father who raised his palms in contrition.

"I was not disparaging, just asking. Blackthorne is not the first to display his heart in paper, I remember…" he trailed off as long forgotten memories surfaced. He came back to the present to see his daughter leaving the room. "Lucy?"

"Just a moment!" her lilting tones floated back to him. The door swung open again, and she staggered in obscured behind a great pot. "Look what he sent." She plonked it down on the table with little care for the polished surface. Christopher winced but bit his tongue, relieved when he saw there was a thick mat under the base.

Lucy stood, hands on hips, admiring the display, leaning in

to inhale the subtle fragrance. "My own daffodil garden, how thoughtful." And after asking Mr Standish, the footman, whether he would be so kind as to carry the pot upstairs to her bedchamber, disappeared into the study to compose a heartfelt reply.

*****

The days slipped by. Lucy was always busy at the book shop, but in her guise as Elspeth felt she ought to at least make the effort to embrace some of the leisure activities her sister enjoyed. Thus, and with no small amount of trepidation, Lucy decided to learn to ride. It was a pastime Elspeth adored, but Lucy had been on a horse, or rather a pony, a grand total of twice in her life. Every September, when she was a child, her mother took her to the Bartholomew Fair at Smithfield. It was a treat for her birthday and better than any gift. Famous for its exhibitions, multitude and variety of stalls, food-sellers — their wares, mouth-watering — animal pens, musicians, street performers, and displays, the list went on, it was a four-day veritable feast for the senses.

Two years running Lucy begged to be allowed a pony-ride. When she looked back on it now, and in light of the superlative care lavished on the horses in the Rycote stable, she realised the poor animals were sorely treated — undernourished and ill-groomed. Cecilia had been loath to pay good coin to a handler who cared little for his charges, but under her daughter's constant pestering, finally gave in. Neither time had Lucy shown any flair as an equestrian. In fact, halfway through her ride the second year, she slid off, landing ignominiously on her backside and, smarting with embarrassment, point blank refused to get back on. Pepper, Elspeth's roan mare was a stunning creature, but she was huge, and Lucy, who felt Goliath would be a better name, was more than a little guarded in her enthusiasm.

Her father suggested she trial Misty, a placid dapple grey who had been Susannah's horse. Although knowing who Misty's last owner was made Lucy uncomfortable, she had to concede the mare was far more suitable. Albert, the Rycote's head groom, took Lucy under his wing and spent hours schooling her. The park behind the house, rarely used at this time of year, proved a convenient place to practice unobserved.

She did admit to William — one afternoon while she fidgeted on the bench trying to find a comfortable position in which to sit, every muscle in her thighs and hips screaming — that maybe trying to keep up the ruse she was Elspeth was not the best idea after all.

"I am sure I could find a way to soothe the ache." William assured her with a roguish grin, sending fire up Lucy's cheeks, and heat coiling in her centre.

"Lord Blackthorne, you are quite the most audacious man." Lucy had swatted at him, to little effect — William simply kissed her into silence.

Now it was a week later, and Lucy was about to put her hard work to the test. She still refused to ride Pepper, and it was agreed, should anyone comment, they would be told the mare had thrown a shoe.

"I cannot countenance riding that monster," she declared. "There is a reason Elspeth named her Pepper." Ignoring her father's stifled laughter. Tossing her head, she stomped off to the stable to be met by Albert, Rodney and Mr Garrick — the latter two would be accompanying her.

"She'm be all ready, miss," Albert said, leading the gentle mare from her stable, and passing Lucy the reins. Using the mounting block, Lucy managed to clamber onto Misty with a fair degree of elegance and settled herself into the saddle.

"Oh, this was a mistake," she muttered, her stomach in knots.

"It will be fine, just relax, a horse can always sense nerves and, even the meekest will play up," the viscount, already mounted, countered with a grin. His stallion, Dante, was stamping in irritation, sensing a gallop, and chomping at the bit to get on with it.

"Just great, thank you for making me more nervous," Lucy groused as Mr Garrick trotted up on Mozart — brother of Misty, to join them.

"Come now, 'tis a perfect day for a short ride, we are early enough that not many of Elspeth's friends will be out and about. It's only an hour," Mr Garrick coaxed. Lucy shot him a rueful grimace.

"On your own heads, be it," she declared and took a deep breath, pushing aside her disquiet. "Lead on." She waved a gloved hand at Mr Garrick, who urged Mozart forward. Misty followed, with Rodney bringing up the rear. Once out of the mews, they kept to a sedate pace in the direction of Hyde Park, where, Lucy had been informed, their objective was a brisk trot along Rotten Row. The road widened, allowing them to ride abreast, chatting about nothing in particular.

It was a glorious spring day. London was basking in bright sunshine, the air was fresh, and there was only the slightest breeze. Birds dashed about gathering twigs and leaves from which to fashion their nests, catching a bug or two as they zipped by. While they rode, Lucy suddenly registered that, in spite of the shadow hanging over the Rycote family, she was happy.

There were very few other riders abroad, most waited until the afternoon when there was more chance of being seen by all the right people. The three were hailed by one or two, but, to Lucy's relief, no one approached them. She was aware her companions were constantly scanning their surrounds, but Lucy could not see how anyone could cause a problem in so open a space.

They had been trotting along for half an hour or so when

Lucy heard a familiar voice.

"Lady Elspeth, Westbrook, what a lovely morning for a ride. Mr Garrick!" William was riding towards them on a chestnut mare. Unbeknownst to Lucy, he was relishing this opportunity to admire her slim figure encased in a deep blue riding habit with its matching, wide-brimmed hat, currently tilted over one side of her face, deliberately obscuring her features.

Lucy hid a grin at his greeting, surprised he had ventured out. In the month or so that she had known him, this was the first time in her recall he had chosen to leave his home for anything other than a meal at Rycote House, or the most urgent business matters. He brought his horse alongside, and the four fell into easy conversation. They had been riding for perhaps ten minutes, when Misty began to sidestep, prancing in apparent agitation.

"William?" Lucy pleaded, gripping the reins. "What do I do?"

"Try not to panic." Biting down on a laugh when Lucy rolled her eyes at him. "Relax your grip, tightening the reins makes her want to run all the more." William turned his horse in an attempt to close the gap between them, but Misty kept one step clear, tossing her head and snorting. "Pat her neck, speak to her in a calm voice, maybe lean back a little if you feel able." His tones unruffled. While Lucy complied with his instructions, Rodney and Mr Garrick encircled her, hoping the presence of their horses stabled with Misty would calm the troubled mare. Nothing worked.

His suspicions aroused, the young viscount was possessed by a hankering to get Lucy home with all speed and leant forward to grab Misty's reins. At the same moment, Lucy shifted in the saddle, her knees pressing against the leather, the mare whinnied loudly and bolted. Lucy's wild shriek alerted other riders and those enjoying a morning constitutional that something was amiss, not to mention the thunder of hooves as Misty fled along the track. Lucy hung on for dear life, frantically deciding whether she dare hitch her skirts and straddle the horse, presuming, correctly as it happened, that if riding astride she would have less chance of falling off, memories of her childhood tumble rearing up in her mind.

The three men gave chase, torn between maintaining a judicious distance so as not to cause Misty further panic, but staying close enough to protect Lucy.

Risking a glance over her shoulder, Lucy saw her three guardians closing in. Dampening down her growing terror, she blocked out everything and concentrated on Misty, allowing the mare her head, somehow managing not to yank back the reins. She clawed at her gown, and with a sigh of relief, managed to slide it just high enough that she could swing her leg over the pommel. Lucy felt a little less vulnerable now, as they raced along the bridleway, dodging other riders who had no qualms at venting their opinion at her lack of equestrian etiquette, their outraged comments making Lucy's cheeks burn.

Imperceptibly, Misty began to slow down, Lucy leaned low over the mare's shoulder, relinquishing her death grip on the reins with one hand, so she could stroke the creature's neck.

"Whoa, Misty, come on girl, whoa," Lucy exhorted, her tones authoritative yet unperturbed in direct contrast to the fright coursing her. *Never, **ever**, would she get back on a horse.* She repeated the words, over and over again until, without warning, Misty came to an abrupt halt. So suddenly, that Lucy was flung forward and only held her seat because of how tightly she was clutching the reins and Misty's mane.

Frozen with shock, Lucy could not summon up the ability to move and remained prone over Misty's neck; her heart drumming, her breathing coming in painful bursts. The three men galloped up and quickly took charge. Mr Garrick carefully untangled her fingers from the rein; Rodney dismounted and held Misty's bridle, while William lifted Lucy down.

Chapter Eighteen

Lucy's legs were so wobbly she was unsure she could stay upright and, thus uncaring how it appeared, clung to the lapels on William's riding coat.

"Well, that certainly blew away the cobwebs." Her overly bright tones fooling no one. She was ashen and visibly trembling. William drew her close and cradled her head against his shoulder. Lucy fought for control, but feared it was slipping beyond her grasp.

Mr Garrick steadied Misty, and Rodney checked the mare over to make sure she had not injured herself in the headlong dash. While examining the saddle, he let out a long whistle.

"This might explain her behaviour." He held up a gnarly piece of wood. The others peered at it, and him.

"What on earth is it?' Garrick asked.

"An old rose stem, complete with thorns."

"Where was it?" This from Lucy.

"Wedged under the saddle. Probably planted there so it would slide down with the gait of the horse. Eventually one of the thorns stuck in her coat, and when you pressed your knee against the saddle it jabbed her. The more she fidgeted, the more you pressed trying to steady her until she had had enough." He snapped the twig and tossed it into the bushes. "You are fortunate she did not throw you."

"I did say horses and I were not compatible. It seems I was correct." Lucy offered a hint of a smile, her normal, healthy complexion beginning to replace the waxy pallor. "Moreover, I refuse to get back on Misty. I would rather walk through fire."

"Do not ever wish that, Lucy," William spoke quietly.

"Oh God, William. That was insensitive, please forgive my wayward tongue."

"Do not think on it." He dropped a light kiss on her forehead. "Only trust me when I say a bolting horse is far preferable to fire."

"I will take Misty home," Mr Garrick interrupted before Lucy could respond, but William's comment made her all the more determined he would confide in her soon. It was clear whatever he had suffered still haunted him and would continue to do so until he was able to face it, talk about it, and relegate it to the far reaches of his mind.

"Thank you, Mr Garrick, I appreciate it. Lord Westbrook…" Turning to the stern-faced viscount, as Mr Garrick trotted off, leading Misty who, now relieved of the barb, was her usual docile self, "… are you coming?"

"I… yes…" clearly lost in thought, Rodney gathered Dante's reins and the three strolled through Hyde Park.

When they reached the gate, Lucy said, "You two should ride home. I shall be perfectly safe." Both men turned matching frowns upon her and, had she been made of less sturdy stuff, would have quailed.

"Are you addled?" Rodney demanded. She shook her head mulishly.

"Of course not, but it seems unfair to deprive Dante and…" she waved her hand at the chestnut mare.

"Gypsy," William supplied.

"Oh, what a lovely name…" Beaming at William. "What was I saying? Oh yes, 'tis unfair to deprive Dante and Gypsy of their exercise, and 'tis the perfect day for a ride… if you enjoy that sort of thing."

"Lucy, someone just tried to have you thrown. We cannot assume you will make it to Rycote House unmolested. Do not be bothersome and indulge our alarm. Once you are home safe, I, or my groom, shall take Dante for a decent ride. Talk some sense into her, Blackthorne." Chuckling when Lucy muttered dire warnings against anyone asinine enough to *talk sense into her*.

On foot it took no little time to return to Rycote House, but it gave the three chance to discuss what happened.

"It must be someone who can access the stables without notice. That leaves family members, friends and staff." Rodney posited.

"Maybe, but what about delivery boys, tradesmen, staff from neighbouring houses?" queried William. "If Rycote is anything like my home, they come and go so often they seem part of the household, more especially if they regularly deliver fodder to the stables. The horses would not be spooked as their presence is not unusual."

"True, but to be so bold as to enter a loose box and affix something under a saddled horse takes guile and speed. What if Albert had caught them? The only way he would not confront someone is if they were known to him. Albert is very protective of his charges. That limits the suspects."

"We shall have to ask him with all haste. Also, check with the other staff. People often see things which do not register as being out of place at the time, but when recounting it later, in light of a specific event, something untoward might stand out." William suggested.

Lost in thought, Lucy walked between the two men, who continued to debate the possibilities. *Who on earth wanted to cause such harm? A throw from a horse could have killed her, easily, which perhaps was the intent.* In her heart of hearts, Lucy, although troubled by Elspeth's chapter of accidents believed — current evidence to the contrary — that someone was trying to frighten her half-sister, not kill her. Even the shooting incident, while terrifying, left her thinking death was not the perpetrator's ultimate goal. If he had wanted to kill her that day in the park, he could have done so. His skill with a rifle was not to be sneezed at. Unbidden, Edward Lindsay's expression that evening drifted into her mind.

"Excuse me for interrupting but might I ask something?" she

appealed when there was a break in conversation.

"Of course, what is it, Lucy?" Rodney smiled down at her, glad to see she was looking less distressed.

"How long has Edward Lindsay been part of the family?"

The young viscount stopped walking and faced Lucy properly. "Years. Since he was a child. He was only a babe when Rycote married Susannah. He's her nephew, her sister's... hmm... son."

"There is some doubt as to whether he is her son? Does he stand to inherit the title from his father?"

"Ahhh. Therein lies a sensitive subject." Rodney hesitated and Lucy waited, eyebrow raised.

"Well, you might as well tell us it could be pertinent," she said archly.

"Your father would be the better person to ask, but I'll tell you what I know. It gets a bit complicated, so stop me if you get confused." He paused until Lucy nodded. "Right, let me see whether I can get this straight.

"About a year after Susannah and Christopher wed, Serena, Susannah's younger sister, was married to Baron Winston Oakford, not a young man but they seemed to muddle along. I think their marriage was arranged to cement a business relationship involving horse racing, and because the two families' country estates adjoined. It was agreed, upon the death of Winston — regardless of whether there was an heir — that Oakford lands would pass to the Marquis of Segrave, Susannah's father, in their entirety. I have no idea why, or any other details of the agreement but apparently it was water-tight. There were whispers of debts owed, but whatever it was remained private.

"Winston died five years later, there were no children, but Edward Lindsay was a ward of the baron; the son of Winston's sister. She died in childbirth, followed to the grave soon after by her husband who apparently lost the will to live, even for his son. Winston took Edward in and brought him up as though he was his own child, but after his death, because of the deed, there was nothing to inherit. Edward's father was the youngest son, and there were three older brothers and their offspring in line before him. Serena remarried about two years after Winston's death, and now has two daughters, but she always treated Edward as though he was her son. He has never wanted for anything," Rodney paused, "except the chance of a title."

Silence fell while the other two absorbed this information. The sounds of a bustling city buffeted around them, but it was muted, as though they were cocooned in their own little world.

"I am at a loss here," William said. "How does hurting, or worse, killing Elspeth, or Lucy, gain Edward anything?"

"Edward is Susannah's nephew by marriage, maybe he assumes that if Elspeth does not marry and produce an heir, he might just, through the laws of primogeniture, inherit the Rycote seat as a collateral relative."

"It's a stretch, and does he not stand to inherit through Serena's new husband?" William posed.

Rodney shrugged, "If he is the one behind these attacks I would have to presume not."

"I confess I do feel rather sorry for him," William remarked, his voice tinged with sorrow. For there to be a legacy which would offer a lifetime of stability within your grasp, and to lose it, not once, but twice, would be difficult to swallow.

"And now we have Lucy, who although illegitimate, has been recognised by her father and will probably be included in a revised version of his will." Ignoring Lucy's startled expression. "Should it be Edward, and I find it hard to believe he could be so cruel, he knows of Lucy's existence, he knows she pretending to be Elspeth, he knows how Lord Rycote feels, and thus, it stands to reason he would also make an attempt on Lucy's life."

Lucy was so shocked, she could not keep walking and sat down on a nearby, and thankfully, convenient bench. "You think Papa would change his will? He does not need to do that. I never wanted anything from him."

"I know he has spoken to Garrick senior; the paperwork may already be signed," Rodney affirmed. "This is confidential information though, Lucy. I am only apprising you because of what happened this morning. We need to tell your father, but I think this has now escalated beyond our ability to control it. It requires someone more familiar with criminal activity."

"I know just the man," William said. "I served under him. He works in some covert capacity for the government but also undertakes business requiring the utmost discretion. He is of the highest integrity and I trust him with my life."

"Who?" Rodney demanded.

"Lucas Withers." William supplied. Lucy made a reflexive movement, prompting both men to glance down at her.

"I know him," she explained. "He married last year and his wife, Jemima, is a friend of sorts. We met when she came into the bookshop. She pops in every couple of weeks and, if I am able to take a break, we have hot chocolate together. Jemima is lovely." This last almost absently, pulling grins from William and Rodney, as though Jemima's character was the best recommendation for employing Lucas.

"Leave it with me. I shall send a note requesting he come to Harcourt House at his earliest convenience. Irrespective of whether it is Lindsay, we need an objective observer. I assume Elspeth's whereabouts remain undisclosed?" William addressed his last question to Lucy.

"As far as I know," she confirmed. "We implied she had gone to visit her maternal grandmother in Scotland but, in fact, she is far from there. Even if he intercepted her letters he would be none the wiser as she does not include a return address."

William took her hand and pulled her up from the bench. "Come along, Miss Lucy Truscott, let's get you home."

When they reached Rycote House. Lucy hurried upstairs to change, while Rodney and William sought out the earl. By the time Lucy joined them in the study, hot coffee had been served, and a plate laden with freshly cooked ginger biscuits, by the heavenly aroma, was offered round.

"Drink this, my girl." Christopher handed his daughter a glass half-filled with amber liquid. Lucy looked at him suspiciously. "'Tis only brandy. Good for shock so I'm told." He walked back around his desk to resume his seat and the room fell quiet while everyone sipped the hot coffee and nibbled on the biscuits.

"Right, let me get this straight. Misty bolted because someone deliberately interfered with her saddle? Scant weeks ago, you two were shot at," nodding at Lucy and William, "prior to that several inexplicable accidents befell Elspeth. *Now,* you feel it appropriate to bring in an outsider?" He raised his brows at the three who nodded in unison. At the earl's invitation, William supplied everything he knew about Lucas Withers and why he was suitable for the task.

Rodney added his opinion. "My Lord, if this is indeed someone we know, we need to let others handle it. We must be seen to be impartial. Too many times families cover up for wrongdoing out of a misguided sense of duty, and the victims are never free of their tormentor. Do you want your daughters to be in constant fear of their lives? Because if we cannot uncover who is behind this, or we try to sweep it under the rug, that is what will happen. Lucy might have been killed today. This is no game."

Christopher lifted his palms in resignation and blew a weary sigh. "I know, I know. I just find it difficult to envisage it could be someone I have welcomed into my home.

Chapter Nineteen

Their conversation went back and forth, suggestions made and rejected but, eventually, the earl had to agree William and Rodney were correct and a message was dispatched. Within two hours, Lucas Withers was being shown into the drawing room of Harcourt House.

"Blackthorne, well met." He strode towards his erstwhile captain.

"Major Withers, thank you for coming." The two shook hands and William offered Lucas a seat. Pouring both of them a drink, he took the chair opposite and stared at the whisky in his glass while he gathered his thoughts.

"Is this about the job I offered you?" Lucas grilled, reminding William his former commanding officer had invited him to join his shadowy organisation. It was a question Lucas posed every time they met, and one William always managed to avoid answering. For the first time in far too long, the prospect of working for his country in an undisclosed sphere sounded more than a little tempting.

"While your offer is something I should like to discuss further, 'tis not the right time." Grinning at Lucas' thunderstruck expression. "I have become involved in a tricky matter…" and proceeded to lay out the whole convoluted and somewhat bizarre tale. "You see why I think it requires your subtle touch?" William concluded, sitting back, and gulping the last of his drink, the aged malt searing his throat.

Leaning forward and resting his elbows on his knees, Lucas swirled the remnants of his drink while he pondered William's words. "It will take time and a little planning, but I have no doubt we can run whoever it is to ground. He, or she," he conceded, "I will go with he for now, took a great risk this morning. Had he been spotted questions would have been asked. Therefore, he acts with almost inhuman speed or is so well known to the family he can move around the house and grounds unremarked. You, or rather Miss Truscott, suspect this Mr Lindsay, is that correct? Why?"

William affirmed this was indeed the case and gave Lucas a condensed version of what Rodney had imparted.

"The man must be a fool." Lucas shook his head. By rights, he should not be surprised by the lunatic minds of the *ton*, yet he continued to be so. "Any petition would be controversial at best. I cannot think he could make a serious claim as a collateral relative even if he *was* successful in removing any who stand in his way. Never mind Lady Elspeth and Lucy, there is also the earl himself. No, no, this Lindsay character is addlepated. However, we must bear in mind, because of this, he could be more dangerous. He is not rational; thus, his actions will be irrational."

The two men soon became deeply engrossed in their discussion. Lucas took notes where necessary, adding his comments to the list Rodney had compiled of all the incidents and where they occurred. As Lucas and William were studying it, they noticed a pattern begin to emerge. Except for that day, most happened around the same time — late afternoon, and until the shooting, all in public places; Hyde Park, the street, a picnic and so on — suggestive of a person who has call on his time during normal working hours. The culprit might easily have been caught, although as William pointed out, the earlier mishaps were so minor they would be written off as mistakes, clumsiness, accidents or coincidence. Whoever was orchestrating them was either becoming desperate or reckless. To chance entering a busy stable without being seen was foolhardy, as was firing a gun in a quiet park.

Lucas accompanied William to Rycote House and

interviewed everyone in the household — from the scullery maid to the earl. It took some time, but he was able to rule them all out. Albert confirmed he was absent from the stables only a matter of minutes while preparing Misty for the morning ride and could not recall seeing anyone come or go. Lucy was not a suspect, she did not even know the Gillinghams existed until the day she met Elspeth. Moreover, Lucas knew Lucy; she was someone whose acquaintance he made when he was first courting Jemima and had always been impressed by her canny ability to grasp the significance of a situation without requiring all the finer points to be spelt out. He did, however, deem it necessary to remind her to take every care. He knew Lucy was as headstrong as his wife, and both had a tendency to be intransigent when they felt their hard-won, yet minimal, independence was threatened.

"I think it might be prudent to avoid working at The Wise Owl for a week or so," Lucas suggested, as he stood to take his leave. Lucy's grumpy expression made him chuckle.

"You must think me a pathetic milksop if you expect a runaway horse to prevent me from going about my daily business." She glared at Lucas.

"He has a point, Lucy," William interposed in conciliatory tones.

"What am I supposed to do all day?" she wailed. "I love my job, goodness, who will bake the cakes? What will Mr Abbot do without me?"

"I expect he will manage, arduous though he might find it, and I am sure the patrons can do without cakes," Lucas asserted, with dry humour. "I shall call on my way home and have a quiet word. Lucy, he will no more want you in harm's way than Lord Rycote, or Blackthorne here." Nodding towards William. A thought occurred to him and he continued, "Have you considered joining Elspeth?"

"No!" she snapped. Then in more moderate tones, "I beg

your pardon, but I prefer to remain in the city. I know what to look for here, I recognise what is out of place. I would be useless in the country, and Elspeth does not need me floundering around making things more worrisome. Added to that, if we are being watched they might take it upon themselves to come after me if I leave. That will place both of us in greater danger. No, I shall remain in the city."

"I have no mind to force you, Lucy, but I recommend you are extra vigilant whenever you go beyond these four walls."

"I am perfectly able to take care of myself," she responded a little imperiously.

"As this morning's jaunt proves," Lucas said wryly. Lucy blushed but did not retract her words, simply lifted her chin. "Fine." He raised his hands, placatingly. "All I ask is that you heed my advice. I do not want to have explain to Jemima that your unexpected demise was because you refused to listen." His droll smile softening the seriousness of his plea.

"I give you my word." Lucy nodded. "Hopefully, this will all be over soon, and I can have my old life back."

William frowned slightly, this was an odd statement. It sounded as though she wanted everything to revert to how it was before she met Elspeth. He assumed she did not want to go back to *exactly* the way it was.

Lucy, glancing his way, caught his perturbed expression and grinned. "With slight modification," she qualified her previous statement, watching the slow smile curve William's lips. Turning back to Lucas she added. "Please assure Jemima I will endeavour to arrange a meeting with her very soon. Mayhap she could visit with me here…" Lucy let that hang, looking at Lucas for confirmation.

"I am sure she would be very happy to. I shall be in contact as soon as I have anything to share." Lucas waved as he hurried down the steps and into the waiting, unmarked carriage.

Lucy and William watched until the coach rattled out of sight.

"I should be going too," William said, taking Lucy's hand, and bowing over it.

"Must you?"

"I cannot come up with a reason to stay."

"Am I not enough?" she chided, arching a brow.

"You are my all," he said, frankly. "How are your daffodils?" in neat diversion, grinning at Lucy's wide-eyed look of astonishment.

"Errr... they flourish. Each day a new flower. How long do they normally bloom?" Lucy was not fooled by his tactic but did not comment.

"Their season is brief, but you may be able to extend it by keeping them in a warm dry place and watering them regularly. I have not attempted to grow them indoors, so yours are an experiment of sorts." The mundanity of their conversation planted Lucy's feet back on the ground and they chatted a little longer, after which William bade Lucy farewell, assuring her he would call on the morrow.

*****

The next morning, William sent a note asking Lucy whether she would like to join him for luncheon at Harcourt House. She, of course, responded in the affirmative and in an effort to seem ladylike, changed into one of her new gowns. A simple dress in lilac silk, the pastel shade offset by a deep purple trim around the high waistline, hem, and sleeves.

Promptly at noon, she rapped on the imposing wooden door, greeting Mr Grantley when she was admitted.

"Good afternoon, Mr Grantley, is it not a glorious day?" Her bright smile tugging a responding grin from the butler.

"That it is, Miss Truscott, that it is," he agreed and ushered her into the library where she found William in deep discussion with two other people, both of whom she recognised immediately.

Without waiting to be introduced, she flew across the room. "Jemima! How glad I am to see you. It has been an age." She managed to gabble out a hello to William and Lucas, before she and Jemima fell into animated chatter, much to the amusement of the two men.

Luncheon was a cheerful meal; the four had known each other long enough that their conversation flowed freely and covered all manner of topics. As the dishes were being cleared away, William suggested they repair to the stone-flagged terrace which spanned the width of the back of the house. The others were easily persuaded; the day was warm, the view over the gardens and beyond to the park, spectacular.

They had been sitting sipping their drinks in companionable silence for several minutes when Jemima suddenly piped up.

"I wondered whether you might like me to help out at the book shop while you are unable to work there?"

"Do you not have enough to do with your work at St Bart's?" Lucy replied, shielding her face with her hand to stop from squinting in the dazzling sunlight.

"We should be wearing our hats," Jemima remarked absently, continuing with, "I have one or two free days. Mr Abbot might appreciate an extra hand."

"I am sure he would be delighted," Lucy assented. "I hope to be back soon, but William and Lucas seem to think I must maintain a low profile for a while longer.

"I should think so too," Jemima retorted. "This person sounds quite mad. I for one am happier knowing you are under watchful eyes, not wandering the streets on your own."

"I wander no more than you, my dear." Was Lucy's mildly indignant repost.

"Moreover, it gives me the chance to peruse the bookshelves to my heart's content. No Lucas breathing over my shoulder wanting to hurry me out, aware his coin will soon be diminished." Jemima ignored Lucy's comment and shot a sly glance at her husband who attempted to look affronted but failed dismally. There was little he would deny Jemima.

"If I give you a list, might you be so kind as to see whether Mr Abbot might be disposed to lending me one or two? He usually does on the understanding I return them quickly."

"I would be pleased to." Jemima and Lucy began discussing which books the latter was interested in reading.

William chuckled and interjected. "Only if you promise not to bring Lucy those contes de fées you insisted on reading to me."

Lucy swivelled in her chair to stare at William. "Jemima read to you?" She arched a quizzical brow, aware of a curious pinching in her chest. She knew Jemima was happily married, and there was nothing in William's demeanour to suggest he felt anything more for her than friendship, neither of which was enough to quash the stab of unreasonable and unwarranted jealousy.

Why and where had Jemima read to him?

Chapter Twenty

"It was when William was in St Bart's," Jemima clarified quickly, noting Lucy was striving to seem unaffected, "a year gone Christmas," sending Lucas a smile so full of love, Lucy felt her gaze drifting to William, surprising a similar expression as he stared back at her. She blushed and dipped her head, annoyed with herself for doubting his affection. "I had just met Lucas and had been rather impolite. Jack," referring to her brother, "informed me I needed to apologise, and when I finally tracked Lucas down, he was with William. Long story short, I added him to my visits, and he was subject to my penchant for fairy tales. To be fair," glaring at William, "it was not just fairy tales."

"No, you did read from Plutarch's *Love Letters* and Chaucer's *Troilus and Cressida*, not romantic mush at all." William grinned. "Then you added insult to injury by insisting my room be decorated to resemble a fairy grotto."

"I do not remember a word of complaint." Jemima replied, haughtily.

"*I* remember the scent of pine being quite uplifting," Lucas remarked, drawing an adoring smile from his wife.

"Thank you, Lucas, at least you appreciated my efforts."

William chuckled. "Forgive my teasing, Jemima, you know you were the one to bring much-needed cheer into my life. I still recall the snowflakes."

Lucy gaped in confusion. *Snowflakes? What on earth had gone on in this hospital?*

Spotting her bewilderment, William elaborated. "When I first met Jemima I was barely conscious and, in all honesty, wishing I had died in the fire that caused this." He flicked a hand towards his scarred face. "The pain was often unbearable, and I could see no end to the discomfort, or the pitying looks and hushed whispers. This particular morning, Lucas left Jemima to watch over me while he went to fetch something and, regardless of the fact this was our first meeting, she prattled on as though we had known each other a lifetime, about the snow and the frost fairs, all manner of wintery nonsense. Then she said… hmmm… what was it now…? Oh yes, something like, had I ever looked at a snowflake, and did I know they are like miniature pieces of the most fragile lace, made from cobwebs? That each one is different, and to be lucky enough to catch one, to see its perfect delicacy before it melts, was like a gift from God. Out of the blue, I realised I wanted to feel the cool snow on my skin, to hold a snowflake and observe its beauty. With those words, Jemima roused my will to live."

Listening to him, Lucy wanted to reach out and take his hand, to hold it and never let go. That he came so close to giving up before ever she knew him, made her heart ache.

"Of course, Lucas overheard me and thought I was developing a *tendre* for William," Jemima chuckled. "Tsk, men cannot see what is right in front of their noses." Her remark wresting instant denials from William and Lucas and a wry smile from Lucy. Jemima could see, however, her friend might need a little more, and stood, asking Lucy whether she fancied a turn around the garden.

Lucy was about to say no, when she caught Jemima's eye. "A short constitutional is always enjoyable after a meal." Standing also. The two, arms linked, strolled off watched by their men-folk.

"You need to tell her, Blackthorne." Lucy heard Lucas say — any reply William made lost as she walked out of earshot.

Jemima and she meandered through the garden and out into the park, gossiping like the friends they were. Lucy pointed out the daffodils and told Jemima about the gift William had given her, as well as the snippets of poetry. Jemima was flatteringly thrilled for her friend.

"You do know there is nothing between us, don't you?" Jemima queried while they made themselves comfortable under the shade of the same tree where Lucy sat the day of the shooting.

"Of course. 'Tis just I am still coming to terms with all these new emotions. Until I met William, I would not have imagined caring for someone so profoundly that I would experience jealousy, and until this afternoon, I never really thought about the women he might have courted or had an affection for prior to his meeting me. Why, I do not know; he is so handsome he must surely be quite the catch." She fell silent for a moment and Jemima did not respond, aware there was more.

"Lord Ryc… Papa tells me William has been more or less a recluse this past year or so, seemingly since he was released from St Bart's. I have no real idea what he suffered because he has yet to tell me despite my urging he do so. I know the horror will be never be completely vanquished, but I do believe if he talks about what happened with someone, not necessarily me, it will begin to dissipate to a level where he no longer suffers such a frequency of nightmares."

"If his reticence continues, maybe you should mention it to Lucas," Jemima suggested. "I know he and William had one or two deep and meaningful conversations during those first weeks after I met them both. He might be able to give you better insight."

"Wouldn't that seem as though I was going behind William's back?" Lucy countered, dubiously.

"Not at all. You are simply showing concern for his well-being." Jemima grinned.

Meanwhile, William was engaged in a similar conversation with Lucas.

"You have found her have you not?" Lucas quizzed while they watched Jemima and Lucy vanish into the garden.

"Found who," William replied, being deliberately obtuse.

"The one who challenges, confounds, intrigues and bewitches you. That extraordinary woman whom you never believed would see past your scars."

"You remember that conversation?"

"Of course, at the time, I thought you were in love with Jemima. Everything that was said, which might have in any way related to her over those few days, remains etched in my memory." Lucas grinned. "Nevertheless, you need to trust her with your story, my friend. If you cannot tell her, she will never truly understand you. Do not keep secrets. Poor Lucy has faced too many revelations this past month or two. If you love her..."

"It is not a tale I ought to burden her with," William interrupted, harshly, conveniently forgetting the promise he made to Lucy that he *would* share it with her.

"Maybe Lucy should be the judge of that," Lucas said quietly and without rancour. William started to shake his head only to change it to a slow nod.

"She implored me to tell her and I agreed. I admit I have been prevaricating, perhaps in fear it would prove too abhorrent."

"You do not give Lucy much credit, do you?" Lucas' dry question earned him a glare. "Come on, man, she is not some spineless debutante who has no desire to see what goes on in the world outside the endless round of soirees and balls. She mayn't have seen battle, but I have no doubt she has witnessed, nay, endured hardships all the same. Life in and around the rookeries can be as hazardous as any conflict, often more so because the danger comes from where you least expect."

William mulled over Lucas' words. His friend had a point. Dr Latham had encouraged him on many occasions to talk about the ambush, but he had not felt able to without the overwhelming concern he would start screaming and never stop. It was almost two years since that fateful day, and he acknowledged it was time. Time to confess that the nightmares were as bad today as they had been when he first regained consciousness. That the scars were more than skin deep. Lucy was one of only about half a dozen people who had never shown repugnance for the distorted mask that was once his face. Lucy was the *only* person to tell him he should not hide, to stroke the marred flesh with gentleness, to tell him she loved him *because* of it, not in spite of it.

"Much as it pains me to say so, you are correct. Lucy deserves to know, I should have told her long ago."

As Jemima and Lucy walked up the stone steps to the terrace, they heard Lucas crow in what sounded like triumph. They looked at each other and shrugged. Men!

Neither Lucas nor William saw fit to enlighten them as to the former's outburst, but Lucy noticed William appeared to be in a contemplative mood. A short while later, Lucas and Jemima took their leave. Jemima affirmed she would call in at The Wise Owl on the way home and discuss the possibility of covering for Lucy for the foreseeable future.

Lucy was about to follow, presuming William might appreciate some time alone after whatever it was, he and Lucas had been discussing, when William requested she stay.

"There is something I must tell you, Lucy. I have been putting it off and 'tis unfair of me to continue to do so."

Lucy felt a peculiar dropping sensation in her stomach and blanched a little.

William, seeing her pale face, hastened to reassure. "Do not fret, my love. 'Tis only that I want to talk about... errr... what happened in France. Please forgive my tardiness in this regard. I believed I was shielding you from the unpleasantness when, in actual fact, I was being cowardly."

"Cowardly? You? William Harcourt, you do talk rubbish. I

think you might well be the most courageous man I have ever met. Cowardly…" Words, quite surprisingly, failed her. Hands on hips, her brow creased, and her nose wrinkled, Lucy stared at William in astonishment. "While I believe that to discuss the trauma, frequently, until it no longer haunts your waking hours and torments your dreams, can only be beneficial, *not* talking about it is just as brave. To care enough to want to protect those who love you from hearing about the horror, holding it within yourself, is equivalent to falling on your sword, in a figurative sense."

William kissed her nose. "Thank you. Now, would you be more comfortable in the library?" Knowing how much Lucy loved the serenity of that particular room; it might make hearing what he had to say less… confronting.

Aware William was not wholly comfortable in the confines of the house, its vast proportions notwithstanding, Lucy pretended to muse over his question, before saying, "I would rather return to the terrace if you are agreeable. 'Tis so lovely in the sunshine, and the beauty of the garden may soothe the anguish I have no doubt you will suffer during the telling." Lucy slid her hand into his and squeezed lightly.

"I am more than amenable to your suggestion." Not releasing Lucy's hand, William tucked her arm through his and the couple sauntered through the house and out onto the sun-drenched terrace. A light breeze had begun to move the air; the gentle rustle of the leaves, the cheerful singing of the birds, and the light perfume of the blossoms, stark contrast to the images building in William's mind.

Once they were seated on the cushioned bench positioned just outside the doors leading into the library, and sheltered from direct sunlight, William tried to collect his thoughts. He was silent for so long Lucy began to consider whether recalling the ambush would be too difficult and was about to assure him he did not need to recount it when William started to speak.

"It was a day much like today. Bright and sunny, the birds were zipping about, trilling their cheerful melodies, which was unusual in itself. We rarely heard birdsong; almost as though the birds sensed approaching doom, and to sing was somehow disrespectful. Anyway, we had been moderately successful in our campaigns and there was a growing optimism that the war might be approaching its conclusion. We had not seen any major battles since April, and Napoleon had abdicated although none of us trusted this would be the last we would see of him. He was too determined to surrender. Nevertheless, we were tasked with making sure there were no pockets of resistance on our march back through France. Incidentally, it was just before this, Jemima's brother Jack, joined us. He was injured by shrapnel when a soldier fired on the contingent he was with. He was lucky not to be killed. Bloody *crapauds*." William ground out the curse — *toads*. "Beg pardon, Lucy, it was sheer idiocy on the part of the soldier who fired. By that stage we were disarming and sending any stragglers home, his impulsive action got him shot. Such a waste. War is such a waste." He paused, shaking his head. After a moment he continued.

"Most of the locals we met were similarly wearied of war and, although, in principle, remained loyal to Napoleon, many professed that all they wanted was peace. One day they were minding their own business going about their daily tasks unaffected by war, the next they could be in the middle of a skirmish between our forces and the retreating French. It transpired small bands of enemy soldiers had been instructed to lure any allied infantry pursuing them, into traps and then kill as many as they could. It was one of these pockets who fired on Jack's group. It was also one of these who ambushed my scouting party."

Chapter Twenty One

Lucy could see William was drifting back to the day he was injured, his expression hardened, and his gaze became shadowed. Unwilling to interrupt, she shuffled closer to him and took his hand, stroking her fingers over his knuckles, rewarded with a slight smile. He twisted around, his eyes refocusing.

"I do not wish to cause you undue distress, William. If you would rather not continue, I understand."

"'Tis not that, so much as I am not sure I can find the words to recount what happened in a mannerly fashion."

"I do not want you to skirt the edges of this in respect of my sensibilities, my love. All I want is to hear your words. If you feel moved to rant, to shout, to scream, do so. If it was me relating this incident, I would already be pacing up and down waving my arms about and growling balefully at my one-time tormentors living it up across the sea." She glanced at William who shook his head ever-so-slightly. "Dead? They are dead?" He nodded. "Oh, that *is* good news, saves me a trip to France." Grinning when William's mouth dropped open. "What? You think I would not hunt them down for what they did to you?" Her puckish expression assuring him she was *probably* jesting. "Although, had they been alive, maybe before I run them through I ought to thank them."

William started to stammer in disbelief.

"Well, if they had not ambushed you, you would not be injured." Lucy interrupted him. "You would not have spent the last however long seeking solace in your garden. Doubtless you would be courting some highly suitable young lady, maybe even already be wed. If they had not ambushed you, we would never have met..." Lucy's voice dropped as, with a slender hand, she traced the gnarly skin of his marred cheek, added a light kiss, then murmured in his ear "… and I cannot countenance my life without you."

Williams eyes closed when Lucy's cool lips brushed his maligned skin and her warm breath caressed his ear. His pulse quickened and, unable to stop himself, the instant she finished speaking, wrapped both arms around her, drew her against him, and kissed her with a reckless abandon, the inevitable heat flaring. Lucy fitted herself to him, meeting his passion with equal fervour, and they fell deeper into their ardour. Eventually, desire temporarily assuaged, their kiss became tender and languorous until William lifted his head.

"God, Lucy. I know I should apologise for my temerity, but heaven help me I needed to kiss you so badly." He rested his forehead against hers, both of them trembling a little from the raw intensity of their emotions.

"Never apologise for kissing me like that, William, that was one of the most exhilarating experiences of my life." Lucy's voice was husky, and she swallowed trying to regain her composure, totally wasted when William trailed a finger along her neck, stilling when he reached the hollow at the base of her throat. "However, this is not getting your tale told. I wager you will feel less troubled once 'tis out in the open, and we can always revisit this later?" she concluded, with an impish grin.

William gave a wry chuckle. "I shall hold you to that, tease." He inhaled on a sigh. "Are you sure."

"Positive certain, but I think I shall hold your hand to anchor you here while you revisit the past."

"I should like that, but please, if at any point you can no longer stomach it, you must tell me, and I will stop."

"That will not happen, but…" as William's expression indicated he would say nothing until she concurred, added, "… fair enough, I agree."

William stared into her spell-binding blue-grey eyes, which, as ever pierced his soul. Something had shifted between them during that kiss. He knew he loved Lucy, that was never in question but, as he prepared to divulge that which he had suppressed for so long, it struck him forcibly, that the rest of his life was sitting right next to him. Lucy was his heart, his whole, his beginning and his end.

She was his redemption.

The realisation rendered him speechless, and it took all his will-power to drag his mind back to the matter at hand. He would tell her, not today, but soon. Today was for the past, then he could embrace the future.

"Like I said, it was a bright sunny day and we were quite cheerful. We had been dispatched to check the route, along which were two villages, the inhabitants of whom we had become familiar during the previous months; our relationship bordering on the cordial. They knew we had no argument with them, and we treated them with respect. Although it was some time since we had stayed nearby, we trusted they would remember us with little rancour. Unfortunately, such villages are typical of where the French soldiers liked to lie in wait; small enough to put the fear of God into the inhabitants should they try to warn us, large enough to conceal a reasonable contingent of men.

"I really do not know what the French commanders expected to gain by these tactics for it certainly did not win them the support of the locals. Whether it was a last-ditch gambit to delay our advance, or whether they somehow believed they could turn the tide — we had been informed many in the French military refused to accept they had lost, and desperation engenders impetuosity. After all, we were the cause of their defeat, and I suppose I can understand.

"We arrived at the first village around noon. It was ruined. We presumed it was the retreating force who razed it to the ground, not the villagers. The destruction was recent… smoke still rose from the burned timbers. There was no one there, but neither were there any bodies, making us wary. Where had they gone? The countryside around was flat, grazing land, with only an odd thicket here and there, nowhere to hide a whole village. Thus, by the time we reached the second settlement we were on high alert. After witnessing what we had, the apparent tranquillity of this village sent the hairs up on the back of my neck. If those from the first village had fled here the place would be bustling, but it was too quiet, not even a dog skulked between the houses.

"Looking back on it now we should have retraced our steps a good five miles and sent a runner for reinforcements. Had I any inkling what was about to happen I would not have hesitated to do so, but in spite of everything, we never once assumed those we were tracking would kill for the sake of it. It is hard enough to kill someone in the heat of battle, but to do so in the cold light of day for no purpose other than revenge is not only heinous, it is also, under our laws, murder.

"At this juncture, I want to make it clear, the majority of French soldiers we came across were not so retaliatory. Like us they believed their cause was the righteous one, but that the fight should be restricted to the battlefield. To involve innocent bystanders was generally unacceptable to both sides."

Lucy observed. "It has been the same throughout history. There are always people whose anger and resentment is so deep-seated it can be extinguished only by eradicating those they presume to be the instigators, unable to comprehend they are merely pawns in a much larger and far more dangerous game. I would imagine most soldiers are like you, and Lucas, and Rodney. Good men sent to quell what those in positions of absolute power ought never to have incited."

"I am glad you understand. I would not have you hate the whole of the French nation for the actions of a few." William smiled at her.

Lucy returned his smile with one of her own, before nestling against his shoulder while he continued.

"We proceeded with extreme caution. I only had two sections with me — twenty men — and I separated them into four groups of five, with me tagging onto one of them. Each section took a side of the main street through the village and checked every house. One group of five went inside while the other scoured the outside. I thought it would be enough. Turns out it wasn't."

William hesitated, this was the hard part.

"My men were armed with a Brown Bess each — a musket with a bayonet," at Lucy's uncomprehending look. "I had a sabre and a flintlock. We held them at the ready, for even though all appeared peaceful we were not naive enough to presume it was. At the far side of the village there were several houses in tight formation, on either side of the road. Despite taking every precaution, as we reached the first in the line and without any warning, we were ambushed by maybe three dozen *chasseurs à pied*. How they managed to conceal themselves is a mystery and continues to haunt me. I must have missed something, some signal, a noise, a movement, but no matter how many times I go over it, it is the same. Everything was calm, then all hell broke loose." William stopped, his throat working as he recalled the horror of that moment. The rapidity of the attack by the French light infantry — the hunters of the French army — and the screams of his men, cut down before they had the chance to retaliate.

The silence lengthened.

"William," a soft voice broke through the tumult in his head. "You need to tell me, do not keep it inside. I need to hear it all."

"Sorry, sorry, 'tis…"

"Do not apologise, you have nothing to be sorry about, but you need to enunciate the terror, the torture, and the grief. The words need to be spoken; while they are trapped in your head, they have the power to destroy you. The ordeal holds you captive as surely as though you are still there. You need to liberate your mind. You need to talk about this every day until it is naught but a distant memory. I know you will never forget, do not try to forget, but you must reach a point whereby you can recall the attack without wanting to scream, without being engulfed in terror, without it seeming as though you are living it every day instead of it being part of your past."

"I do not think I can." There was an uncharacteristic catch in William's voice. Once again, Lucy pressed a gentle kiss to his injured cheek.

"Yes, you can. I am here, I will not leave; whatever you reveal cannot push me away. Come my rescuer, you have saved me from flying bullets and a runaway horse. This is child's play." She smiled, wickedly, "and I know of a most suitable recompense for he who bares his soul." She held his gaze, her eyes softening with tenderness, tinged with concern. "You need to let it go."

William nodded slowly. She was right, but the dark veil of guilt he had carried for so long was hard to shed. It kept him from slumber. Formless wraiths floating towards him, mouths open in a soundless shriek, their blackened bodies wrapped in torn shrouds — accusing.

"They were my men, my sections. I had known them all since they were assigned to me well over a year previously. Together, we had fought many battles, and survived. It was supposed to be a simple scouting party, not a bloodbath in idyllic countryside. They were my men…" his voice trailed off.

"Tsk, William, this was *not* your fault, this was the fault of those who ambushed you. I did not take you for a man to wallow in self-pity. Tell. Me. What. Happened." Lucy's bracing tones penetrated the fog in his head, and his brow furrowed. *Where was his sweet Lucy?* He met her narrowed eyes and registered her mutinous expression. Recognising her intent, he gave a rueful smile and finished his tale.

Chapter Twenty Two

"Where was I? Oh yes, so, there were twenty of us, well twenty-one if you count me, two groups with me and two bringing up the rear. When the French burst out of the houses, I knew myself and those closest to me were doomed, but the others had chance to flee. I bawled an order to retreat, but they refused to abandon us to our fate. They showed such courage, I think they managed to dispatch a goodly number of our attackers, but the French had the element of surprise and thus, the upper hand. The last thing I recall was seeing a rifle butt aimed at my head. To be honest I am stunned they did not kill me outright, but they had something far worse planned.

"I regained consciousness sometime later with no idea where I was. It was dark, save the odd sliver of light creeping through cracks in the wooden walls, and I hazarded it was some kind of barn or stable. I could hear lots of shuffling, relieved to discover it was caused by three of my men, not several rabid dogs or a mischief of giant rats in search of something to chew on. We had been positioned against the walls, arms above our heads, and wrists bound to rusted metal loops, which added to my belief we were in an outbuilding of some kind.

"I did not know whether any of our troops managed to evade capture, and even if they had, it would take them at least a day if not two to backtrack to our encampment, and the same to lead the regiment to the village. Lucas had no cause to presume any haste was necessary, and after months of fighting we were enjoying a relatively relaxed march north. Thus, I knew any rescue could be days away. My head told me this was our end, even while my heart clung to the hope our captors would simply walk away and leave us.

"We were not fed or offered any water, although several

times a day one of them would carry in a platter of hot food, waft it under our noses, and leave. We could hear them carousing, we could also hear screams from both men and women. It seemed the villagers were being abused, or worse. We never found out why, maybe because of their previous cordiality with their sworn enemy. I do not want to think about what they were doing to the women. Their own countrymen…" Unconsciously tightening his grip on Lucy's hand, William shook his head in disbelief, still unable to come to terms with such ignoble behaviour.

"Two of those imprisoned with me were badly injured; one died within hours of the ambush and the other, Morris, slipped away sometime during the next day. We — Fred, the other soldier, and I tried to encourage him to hang on, but Lucas informed us later, his wounds were grievous. He, Lucas, stressed, had we escaped or even managed to clean and bind Morris' injuries, we could not have saved him. I continue to be saddened that he died so close to us, and we were unable to offer anything other than our words as comfort. We could not even grasp his hand and tell him he was going to survive, to make him believe he would be going home. Such a waste of life.

"That left Fred and me. We could not understand why the French stayed. Surely, they knew if a regiment of soldiers came into view on the horizon, advancing to save us, any of their number loitering in the village would be slaughtered without pity after what they had done? Logic dictated they leave while they had the chance, but they did not. Their behaviour quickly deteriorated, becoming barbarous, and both of us were subject to maltreatment."

Words fell from William's lips almost too quickly for Lucy to comprehend, his tone eerily unemotional as he detailed the hours of suffering endured by the two soldiers. Under the outbuilding was a tiny cellar, its regular use unclear — possibly storage as there were a couple of chairs and a wooden manger, all of which looked to have seen better days. Currently, it was employed as a torture chamber. Dragged down into it and stripped naked, William was lashed to the floor, face up, and forced to lie for hours while water dripped onto him, out of a narrow pipe hanging from the ceiling above. Drainage was excruciatingly slow, meaning it did not take long until he was virtually submerged, straining against the ropes to keep his head above the water line. While he talked, memories of the darkness, the silence, the impotence, the feeling that the walls were closing in, the abject terror of facing your own death and being powerless to stop it, reared up. He could not prevent a shudder.

Once or twice he almost gave up, the effort was exhausting, and with no sustenance, his normal strength was sorely diminished. Only his dogged refusal not to die at the hands of the bloody French kept him going. Fred was similarly determined, and the two became each other's incentive to survive during those harrowing hours. Neither was ever subject to interrogation, so both remained at a loss as to the reasoning behind the prolonged torment.

William stopped, and took a gulp of the large whisky which materialised at his elbow, the fiery spirit bringing his focus back to Lucy. He had not felt her disentangle her hand from his, or seen her move, but assumed it was she who poured the much-needed drink. He smiled his appreciation.

"Weeks later, Lucas told me we were held captive for five days. Time meant nothing to Fred and me anymore, but one day, there was a lot of shouting and we were both pushed down into the cellar, unusual in itself, it had always been one at a time. We were not stripped — although by this stage, our uniforms were so ragged we might as well have been — but they secured us to the two chairs and tied cloths around our mouths. They were acting erratically, panicked almost, nothing like as methodical as they had been prior to that day. Shortly thereafter, about fifteen people, men and women, were dropped bodily into the cellar — all gagged, hands bound behind their backs. The hatch was bolted. There was not enough room for all of us. It was very dark and deathly quiet, too warm, and horribly confined, airless. No one knew what was going on and none of us could speak for the gags. I can still remember the dread I felt when I suspected their intent was to drown us. If they let the water run through the pipe at the normal rate, the cellar would flood long before the water had chance to drain away. We were at their mercy, and it was more terrifying than facing a whole army on the battlefield.

"It was soon abundantly clear, water was not going to be our death. Smoke began to filter through the cracks in the floor of the outbuilding above us. The smell of burning straw and wood was something I used to enjoy, it reminded me of November on our country estate when we had great bonfires to dispose of leaf litter and deadfall. Not anymore. Now, all it conjures up is the screams of the dying. Lucy..." his voice cracking with effort, "I..."

Uncaring how may so-called rules she was breaking, Lucy slid onto William's lap in a heartbeat. Her arms curved around his neck and, after stealing a chaste kiss, pillowed her head in the crook of his neck.

"You must do this. For Fred and for those who you couldn't save. You need to do this for you and also for me. While 'tis easy to soothe a nightmare, to know why they haunt you, gives me a better awareness of what might trigger them. You should know I am going to make you talk about this tragedy every day until it no longer holds sway over you, until it is relegated to your past."

"You would soothe my nightmares?"

"Do you not recall my pledge?"

William combed through his mind, relieved to be thinking about something less stomach churning for a moment. He stopped when he came to their conversation the day she promised to sing him to sleep if he trusted her enough to disclose what caused his scars.

Lucy sat up, her eyes searching his — winter's mist on summer blue. "Nothing since has given me cause to renege on my part of the bargain. I want to be the one who helps banish the horror that stalks your dreams, who holds you when you cannot sleep, who sits up with you, talking through the hours of darkness to ease the terror they bring. But I cannot do any of this until I have heard it all." She nestled her head back against him, slipped her hand into his and entwined their fingers. "When you're ready."

William capitulated. Lucy would not let him rest until he had done as she requested.

"To this day I do not know how he managed it, because they were sturdier than they seemed and we were weakened, but Fred broke the chair he was tied to. He kept ramming it against the wall until, eventually, it splintered. Once the chair was in pieces, he was able to loosen his bonds and remove the gag. After he released me, we untied those with us. The smoke was dense, and we could hear the crackle of flames. The only clear air was close to the ground and there was not enough room for us all to stay low. The villagers were hysterical, screaming for help, even though it was unlikely anyone would hear, let alone come. Then the fire reached the hatch. It ignited, and splinters of burning wood began to drop through.

"As luck would have it, except for the chairs and the manger... and us I suppose... there was little fodder for the fire in the cellar and the fragments burned out. Now, though we had a hole, a way out, a chance. It was dangerous, but we all decided it was better to die trying to escape than stand around and wait for death to find us. Fred volunteered to go up first, and the villagers shoved him through the gap. He helped two others out, and while they began hoisting up everyone else, he ran to see whether the water pipe the soldiers used to torture us, could help extinguish the blaze. Regrettably, it was made of clay and had fractured in several places, rendering it useless. Some of the villagers appeared with old buckets and, one by one, as the rest were pulled out of the cellar, they formed one chain from the fire to the horse trough, another to the well, doing what they could to douse the flames. Others who had fled into the fields returned in dribs and drabs and soon the whole village was working together to put out the fire before it destroyed any more houses. Apparently, the French soldiers had vanished."

He stopped talking, his vision turned inward.

"How did you get burned?" Lucy spoke quietly, aware this would be the hardest part to share.

"I was last through the hatch. I was determined no one would be left behind. These people had done nothing wrong, they did not deserve the treatment dished out by their compatriots. I could not have lived with myself had any of them been injured or worse because they helped me. They could see how debilitated I was and, to their everlasting credit, wanted to escort me out, but it didn't take a genius to know the building was about to cave in, so I shooed them off, saying I was right behind them. At the same moment, the roof began to collapse. The whole building was ablaze by this point, and I started to run, arms up to shield my face. I had taken maybe three strides when a huge beam, swung down and struck me with such force I fell back into the cellar, flames engulfing me. I heard screams of those who had been ahead of me and then nothing."

William drew a shaky breath. "I have no real memory of anything after that until I awoke in St Bart's, just snatches, nothing substantial. Lucas tells me I was in and out of consciousness for about a month. I am surprised they even bothered to check I was alive and am continually astounded *any* of us survived that fire. Ironically, the place where I thought I would die saved me. The beam which knocked me back into the cellar also stopped most of the burning debris from landing on me, and although I was caught by the flames, the lack of anything combustible meant the fire had nowhere to go. Sadly, three of the villagers who had not managed to escape the barn when the roof fell in, were not so fortunate and died from their injuries."

He heard a muffled sound, and out of the corner of his eye saw that Lucy was biting her bottom lip, hard. Twisting in his chair slightly, he ran a finger under Lucy's chin and tilted her head until she faced him. Tears were brimming in her eyes, their watery hue reminding him of a restless ocean. He could sense her determination not to let them spill over, and he did not think he would ever love her more than he did at this moment.

"Oh, my darling, do not weep. Yes, 'tis a harrowing tale, but 'tis done. The last eighteen months have been... challenging, but I found a peace of sorts in my garden, and now I have you. You have given me purpose. I want to throw open my windows, invite people to dinner, agree to the proposition Lucas made for me to join his organisation. Miss Lucy Truscott, Jemima may have been the one to give me hope, but you make me want to live."

Chapter Twenty Three

Two weeks had passed since William's revelations and, true to her word, Lucy asked him to repeat some part of his tale every day. It was still raw, and he had suffered a spate of recurrent nightmares since the initial telling, but he was prepared to confess they were not as disturbing as once they had been. He also explained his incarceration had initiated a mild claustrophobia, shedding light on why several of the rooms in Harcourt House were without doors.

Lucas visited several times to provide any pertinent information on his investigation, but thus far, had not uncovered anything of value. Everyone in Rycote House was on alert, and it was hoped somebody might surprise the perpetrator in the act. Until then all they could do was wait. Lucy apprised Elspeth of the news in a long letter, going on to suggest — just in case — that it might be sensible to send any replies to Jemima who had happily agreed to act as go-between.

Limited to where she was able to go, Lucy took the opportunity to get to know her father. They talked for hours about their lives. This was not necessarily always a comfortable topic because Lucy had not enjoyed an easy childhood, and Christopher carried a lot of guilt for allowing his family to dictate his future, one which did not feature Cecilia. Lucy was eager to learn everything relating to her mother, though, and plied Christopher with questions about what she was like during the time he knew her, returning the favour by regaling him with a variety of anecdotes about life in and around the rookeries.

Lucy was also flattered that William sought her out daily. He either came calling or would send a note asking whether she would meet him in the garden where it bordered the park. Lucy preferred the latter; to her it was akin to a secret tryst and she revelled in the privacy. During these stolen sojourns, they came to know each other; their likes and dislikes, fears, and dreams. William had not yet *officially* proposed marriage, but Lucy trusted it was implicit in his behaviour, his words and most especially his kisses which he bestowed with gratifying frequency… her own responses becoming harder to control.

*****

This particular morning, they were strolling towards The Wise Owl. Lucy was overjoyed William agreed to a constitutional with her, for she knew he found it difficult to pretend he did not see the horrified glances of passers-by, some of whom even crossed the road to avoid him. Lucy managed to keep his focus on her with artless gossip about nonsensical things, but it hurt her heart to see how many judged without pausing to consider their actions.

She squeezed the arm tucked through hers, and when he glanced down, gave him her brightest smile, eliciting a rueful grin in return.

"Pay them no mind, William. They do not know you," she murmured. "Instead of looking at them, admire this perfect day." She pointed upwards. "That sky, so blue, just like your eyes, those fluffy white clouds, which seem solid enough to walk on, I imagine they would make the most sublime pillows." She chattered on in this vein until they reached the bookshop, reminding William of the day Jemima spoke to him in a similar manner about snowflakes. He knew it was a technique to distract and loved that Lucy cared enough to do so.

"William, Lucy! What a lovely surprise." Jemima, who never stood on ceremony with her friends whatever their status, bustled up to the pair, smiling in delight, when they stepped into the airy shop. "Come in, come in, sit, sit..." she led them through to where they served a small selection of refreshments.

"Lucy, I..." William started to suggest they chose a table away from the large, bay window when he realised Jemima was ushering him to one, the seat of which meant his scar would not be obvious unless one looked closely.

"I am not so insensitive." She grinned. "Now, make yourselves comfortable and I shall be along with coffee and cakes."

"Thank you, Jemima." Lucy pressed her friend's arm in gratitude for her foresight.

"'Tis my pleasure." Jemima hurried away, calling a hello to another customer as she whisked passed the stacked bookshelves to the little kitchen at the rear of the shop.

Over steaming coffee and a plate of luscious cakes, Lucy and William were soon engrossed in conversation, paying little attention to the comings and goings in the busy bookshop. The morning slid by in a most congenial fashion. They were about to take their leave — William standing behind Lucy's chair — when a scream resounded throughout the shop. Twisting in her seat, Lucy saw a little girl of about six years old, mouth and eyes wide with shock.

"Mama," her childish treble rang out, "Will the monster eat me?"

"Hush, dear, do not stare at the poor man."

In that instant, Lucy knew she had to intervene, or this child would remain forever terrified of anything society regarded as 'unnatural'. Dropping to her knees in front of the little girl, she said.

"He is no monster, my dear. He is a soldier who was badly hurt in a battle. He was protecting people like you and your

Mama and was injured. How about you come and meet him and then you will see he is not scary at all." Glancing up for permission, it was clear the woman was uncertain. "Trust me," Lucy mouthed to the mother, glad when she saw her nod. "What is your name?" she asked the child.

"Hester," the little girl supplied with a shy smile.

"What a beautiful name. My name is Lucy and I am very pleased to make your acquaintance, Hester." She dipped a swift curtsy making Hester giggle, then put out a hand, pleased to feel Hester's tiny one slip into it. "Now, I would like you to meet William. William is the bravest man I have ever met, and he would be sad if people were afraid of him." Lucy motioned for William to sit in the chair she had just vacated. Crouching beside Hester, she spoke as though telling a story.

"Once upon a time there was a soldier called William. Along with hundreds of other men, William travelled across the sea to fight a battle to make sure we are always safe. He had been away for many, many months, and was finally on his way home when he and his friends stopped to help some villagers escape from a fire. Just as William freed the last person, the building fell down and one of the burning timbers knocked William over and into a cellar. The marks you see on his face are from that fire." Lucy took Hester's hand and lifted it to William's face. "Now, let your fingers touch the scar, that's it, nice and gently. You see? It might feel a little peculiar, but it is not scary at all, is it?"

"'Tis like tree bark, only softer," Hester said in wonderment and, feeling very brave, stroked her hand over the puckered skin again. "Oh, you poor, poor man." She stood on tiptoe and kissed William's disfigured cheek. "I am sorry I screamed." Hester rocked back on her heels, canted her head in the most adult fashion, and beamed at William who grinned back somewhat self-consciously. "Does it hurt?" Her concern clear.

William shook his head. "Not as much as it used to. Sometimes 'tis a bit sore, but I have a balm to use every day which makes it better."

By now a small crowd had gathered, listening with rapt attention. One or two people, aware there was far more to Lucy's tale, began to ask questions. Surprised by their unfeigned interest, William answered as honestly as possible while Lucy edged her way to the back of the group where Jemima hovered.

"Well done, Lucy. Mayhap this will lessen William's dread of being in public." The two women watched as William was quietly applauded for his courage, many clapping him on his shoulder or shaking his hand, and none any the wiser they were talking to a nobleman.

The day ticked by and it was well into the afternoon before William was able to extricate himself from the crowd of inquisitive customers — one even suggested he write a book about his ordeal — and even then, it was only by dint of promising to pop into The Wise Owl again soon. Earlier, Jemima, with an eye on the clock, nipped out and bought two slices of game pie, which Lucy and William munched with gratitude.

Arm in arm, the couple dawdled along busy pathways, content not to talk, just enjoying the balmy weather and cheerful sounds of a bustling city.

"Thank you, Lucy," William said after they had been walking for several minutes.

"What for?"

"For today. I confess, I never expected to enjoy being asked questions about my experiences, by so many strangers who genuinely wanted to know what happened, and it was oddly satisfying." He elaborated, catching a smug grin on Lucy's face. "I know, you don't need to say, 'I told you so'. Mind, 'tis taxing, my throat aches from all that talking." He remarked. The light pressure of Lucy's hand on his arm was enough for him to know she understood, and he moved their conversation to other things. The hour or so it took them to reach the relative serenity of Albany Square, passed almost without notice.

As he was wont to do, William invited Lucy to dine with him.

"Thank you, William, I would be delighted," Lucy accepted with alacrity, adding she would be there as soon as she had changed her gown. Her desire to wash off the dust of the day taking precedence over her need to be with William every waking moment.

"Come through the garden, I shall be waiting." William rapped on the door of Rycote House, ushering her inside when Harris opened it. Lucy smiled and disappeared into the cool hall, calling a hello to anyone who might be listening before dashing upstairs. Alice, no doubt primed by Harris, appeared moments later to help Lucy out of her gown. After a thorough wash, Lucy was sitting in front of the mirror suffering Alice's attempts to tame her wayward hair.

"How you have so many knots in your hair when all you did was walk to a bookshop is beyond me." Alice chuckled when she finally pronounced herself satisfied with her efforts.

Lucy shrugged. "You have more patience than I, Alice. Thank you," turning this way and that to admire the deceptively simple style Alice had created. "'Tis only dinner with William."

"'Tis never 'only' when a man is involved, miss," replied Alice sagely. Lucy grinned and stood, shaking out her skirts and slipping her feet into soft leather shoes. Popping her head into the study to see whether her father was there, which he was, Lucy apprised him of her plans for the evening.

"Have you heard from Elspeth recently?" Christopher enquired, smiling at his daughter's eager countenance.

"Not for several days, although she mentioned something about visiting some friends of Lady Rycote, so perhaps she has had no opportunity to write of late. Are you worried?" Lucy studied her father.

"Not especially, but with everything going on, I would like

to know where my other daughter is," Christopher replied. "I suppose I am concerned whoever wishes her harm has not only worked out our bluff, but also where Elspeth might be."

"Surely your mother has enough staff to protect her?" Lucy quizzed.

"She has, but Gillingham Park is quite isolated, it would only take a couple of careless decisions for Elspeth to be vulnerable."

"Send Rodney, wait, I have a better idea. Why not send Edward?" Lucy took the seat across the desk from Christopher, grinning when his face morphed from interested to confounded.

"Send Edward? Are you out of your mind? Send the one man we think culpable?"

"Papa," chidingly, "I had not finished. If you dispatch Edward with instructions to guard Elspeth it might prompt him to show his hand. He has his quarry, and he thinks she is alone and defenceless…" she paused, letting that sink in. "Of course, we, and by we, I mean you, James, possibly Lucas, and myself, would follow. I think we ought to send Rodney immediately; that way he is there before Edward arrives. I do not think he truly wishes Elspeth serious harm, but we have to force him into the open, however problematical that might prove. We have reached an impasse and are left waiting for the axe to fall. We should not be the ones cowering in our homes in fear of what might happen next, it ought to be him. If 'tis who we suspect, he knows we have brought Lucas into the investigation, he knows we will track him down sooner or later."

Lucy sucked in a breath, aware her voice was rising in her frustration. "Papa, I cannot live like this. I feel trapped. I am used to doing whatever I choose, and this is tantamount to being imprisoned, opulent though it is. Now, I can barely take a step outside, without words of caution or less than subtle hints I stay home being flung at me. 'Tis exhausting."

Christopher studied Lucy, noting her heightened colour and flashing eyes. *Lord, she was so like Cecilia*, the ever-present ache intensifying briefly. Ruminating over her impassioned plea, he had to acknowledge she was correct, although there was absolutely *no* chance of her accompanying him into what could be a dangerous situation.

"If," he raised his hand to stem her enthusiastic response, "if I agree to this fool-hardy proposal, you will remain here. I cannot be watching out for you *and* Elspeth. Neither am I prepared to agree to anything before further consultation with Westbrook and Withers. Give me some time."

"That is all I ask." Her immediate acquiescence causing a suspicious frown to appear on Christopher's brow. He knew she would revisit this again, but he would deal with that when it occurred. "I am dining with William, good evening." Bouncing up from her chair, she hurried around the desk to kiss her father and then was gone, her goodbye floating back to him in a soft echo.

Shaking his head in amusement at her blasé attitude, Christopher turned his attention to penning a detailed missive to Lucas Withers requesting his presence on the morrow if convenient. Rodney, who had been invited to stay at Rycote House for the duration of Elspeth's absence, would be home soon — they could talk at dinner.

Chapter Twenty Four

Lucy flew through the garden and into the park, conscious she had tarried longer than planned with her father. She found William deadheading some of the plants. He was aware of her approach before she spoke, and turned, his quirky smile sending a thrill rippling through her. She would never tire of seeing that smile.

"Forgive my tardiness. I was talking with Papa." She flung herself into his arms and lifted her face for his kiss, which he granted with fervour. "Oh my! Good evening, my lord," she murmured against his ear when, eventually, he relinquished her lips, but continued to embrace her.

"I admit I was beginning to ponder on what might have delayed you." Scattering featherlight kisses up her neck.

"I will tell you while we eat." She surveyed the garden beds. "Oh, William, the daffodils have died." Her tone sorrowful.

"They have but a short season, my love, and then go into a kind of hibernation for the remainder of the year. I have talked with other gardeners, and they assure me, if I heed their instructions on how to tend daffodils, they will flower again next year. We can only wait and see." He offered Lucy his arm and the couple sauntered slowly up to the terrace, chattering about plants and their flowering cycle, to find a tray with two tall glasses of cool lemonade awaiting them.

During the meal, Lucy told William about her conversation with Lord Rycote, a trifle irritated when William concurred that she ought to stay in London.

"You being at Gillingham Park will place undue stress on your father, Lucy, and 'tis unfair." He grinned at her disgruntled expression. "You know he is right in this. Let those more suited to tracking criminals do their job unhindered. Moreover, I would miss you." He rubbed his forehead, drawing Lucy's gaze to his face, which seemed a trifle pale, although his cheeks were ruddy.

"Do you feel unwell, William?" she asked, concerned, recalling, current discourse aside, he was unusually taciturn, and had little appetite.

"No, just a little tired. 'Tis years since I have conversed with so many people at once. I shall be much better after a good night's sleep."

Not convinced and, reminded of his earlier comment about his throat aching, Lucy said no more, but kept a close eye on him throughout the evening. Taking her leave much earlier than usual, she told William to stay put, and that she would ask Mr Grantley to see her home. Her anxiety increasing when William assented with nary an argument.

"Might I call on you tomorrow?" she asked dropping a light kiss on his cheek when he walked her to the door of the library, relieved to see an answering nod. His movements seemed slow as though requiring effort. While Mr Grantley escorted her to the adjacent house, Lucy voiced her disquiet, to be assured, Lord Blackthorne's health would be monitored closely.

Lucy placed her hand on the affable butler's arm. "Please, if William should ask for me, whatever the time, do not hesitate to send for me, even if 'tis the middle of the night. I…" she trailed off, unsure how to articulate what she wanted to say. "Forgive me, I am not questioning your care, 'tis only…" she paused again, and Mr Grantley patted the hand still resting on his sleeve.

"Fret not, Miss Truscott. If Lord Blackthorne requests your presence, I shall arrange for someone to rouse you."

"Thank you, Mr Grantley, he does look quite poorly." Lucy bit her lip torn between returning to minister to William and abiding by convention.

"Go and get some rest, miss. Hopefully, his lordship is simply fatigued."

Lucy nodded her agreement and, without thinking, brushed her lips to the elderly man's cheek. "I do not know what he would do with you, sir," she said, before dashing up the steps and into Rycote House.

Mr Grantley watched her go, a benign smile warming his face. "Aye, she's a rare one that," he muttered to himself. Retracing his steps, he checked on his master. William was dozing in the huge wing-backed chair by the unlit fire in the library. Mr Grantley ran an expert eye over the younger man's features, immediately spotting the unhealthy red flaring up his cheeks making the scarring appear angrier than usual.

Tutting under his breath, the butler suggested his master retire for the night. William agreed without demur, allowing Mr Grantley to assist him to his bedchamber where he fell asleep almost before the faithful retainer had left the room.

Aware William's injuries were susceptible to infection, the butler decided to send for the doctor. After dispatching Bill, the groom, Mr Grantley exhorted the redoubtable Mrs Hendry — William's cook and fixture in the Harcourt household for decades — to brew up some of the herb infused tea William swore by. While the staff attended to his instructions, Mr Grantley retrieved the pot of balm, Dr Latham at St Bart's had indicated was soothing for burns.

It was a long night. Dr Andrews, the family's physician, arrived and, after examining William, confirmed Lucy and the butler's suspicions. As promised, Mr Grantley had Megan fetch Lucy who, once she had spoken with the doctor and the household, did not leave William's side. She applied cool damp cloths to his face and hands, trying to reduce his temperature, and encouraged him to sip the sweet tea. Every so often, she massaged in the aromatic balm — the scent of which reminded her of the day she was shot at and, which she was pleased, finally, to identify. Towards the end of the night, William developed a harsh dry cough, something the doctor had predicted might happen, and for which he prescribed a peculiar smelling tincture. Lucy managed to coax William to drink the allotted dose, ignoring his disgusted grumblings.

"Surely, a momentary foul taste is naught if it settles the cough and allows you to rest comfortably?" her tones, gentle but adamant. She was rewarded by a brief smile and, within minutes, William succumbed to the mixture, falling into a deep sleep.

Exhausted, Lucy leaned back against the chair and shut her eyes. It felt like only seconds later she was jolted awake by rasping cries, prying open her eyes to see William thrashing on the bed, tossing off the covers and trying to rise. Although his words were garbled, it was obvious he was in the throes of a nightmare. Without thinking, and mindful of his scars, she scrambled onto the left side of the bed and, carefully, wrapped William in her arms. In a hushed voice, she talked about anything and everything, calling him back to the present, reminding him it was two years since his capture and subsequent torture, that he was safe in London in his own bed. Out of the blue, Lucy recollected her promise to sing him to sleep, and even though she needed him to do the opposite, or at least break free of the nightmare, it was worth a try.

One after another, Lucy crooned all the lullabies her mother sang to her when she was a child, then went back and started all over again. She sang until the room began to lighten as dawn pushed back the night. She sang until her voice was hoarse. Slowly, slowly, William calmed, and she was able to persuade him into another draft of the mixture.

This was a pattern she was to repeat several times throughout the ensuing days, only leaving William's bedchamber to perform necessary ablutions. She fought slumber, content to snatch the odd hour here and there while

William slept, to the consternation of the latter's household, who feared she might fall victim to the same infection. Lucy was more resilient than they gave her credit for, however, and although wearied beyond rational thought, made it clear she would stay with William until the crisis had passed.

Three days later, William began to regain consciousness, dimly aware someone was humming quietly. It was a melody he was familiar with although right then the title eluded him. He felt he should know the singer, her — for there was no doubt it was a woman — voice captivated him, the sweet notes ebbed and flowed around him, both soothing and tantalising. *Dear lord, who was it? He could love her for her voice.* As he swam up through layers of what felt like thick fog, images formed in his head. A tall woman, possessed of the most astonishing eyes, which could cool to silver or warm to the most entrancing blue-grey.

Lucy.

"I am here, William."

Had he spoken her name out loud? A hand cupped his face, cool on overly-warm skin. He mumbled something about needing to sleep and turned on his side. Voices talked above him, but he could make no sense of them and let the blessed darkness take him once more.

Lucy wanted to indulge in a temper tantrum. She was so tired she could barely see straight, and now the dratted man had half-woken, said her name and gone back to sleep. Dr Andrews, thankfully, had been there to witness the change and assured Lucy this was quite typical, affirming the crisis was passed, the fever had broken.

"I have no doubt he will be crotchety for a few days while he recovers his strength, but am confident, within a week, he will be back to full health. The hardest thing will be making sure he takes it easy until then."

"We shall ensure your instructions are carried out to the letter," Mr Grantley, who had just brought Lucy a cup of hot coffee and overheard the doctor's comment, interposed firmly. "Lord Blackthorne and I have an understanding." He winked at Lucy who smiled wearily, while she sipped her coffee, inhaling the rich aroma which had the added benefit of sharpening her senses.

"Thank you, Dr Andrews, you are a godsend and no mistake." Lucy's gratitude was heartfelt, and the doctor inclined his head.

"I do not think it will be required, but I shall leave some of this tincture with you, just in case. Any concerns, I am only two streets away." Nodding genially, the learned gentleman took his leave, hurrying out into the sunny morning.

Mr Grantley studied William for several minutes nodding to himself, then decided to take matters into his own hands. "Now, miss, are you going to come and have a spot of luncheon? I suspect his lordship will not stir for several hours and you need a break. Your papa is very worried." Secretly applauding himself when he cajoled Lucy into joining the rest of the staff in the kitchen for a proper meal, knowing she would find that preferable to sitting in isolated splendour in the dining room.

Acceding to gentle, but unyielding pressure, Lucy returned to Rycote House to update her father on William's condition, whereupon she was coaxed into a long soak in a hot bath. Hair washed, dried, and styled into a neat bun, and buttoned into a fresh gown, Lucy knocked on the study door. Invited to enter, she was surprised to see Rodney, James, and Edward, involved in what looked like a serious discussion with her father.

"Ah, Lucy, my dear, how delightful to see you. How is young Harcourt, sorry Blackthorne? I will forget he is marquis now." Christopher chuckled at his slip. Lucy informed them it seemed William had won yet another battle, but it would be a week or so before he was up and about. "Good, good, glad to hear it.

Might you spare us a moment before you rush back? You ought to hear of our plans." He held Lucy's gaze, a tacit message in his blue-grey eyes so similar to her own.

"I should be delighted." Lucy's immediate response indicated she had received and understood. Making herself comfortable, she listened while the earl outlined the, apparently new, plan to travel to Gillingham Park deep in the Herefordshire countryside. It would take about three days solid riding to reach the estate and, although not an easy journey, Christopher deemed it essential.

Unaware of their suspicions, Edward Lindsay fell right into the trap. "Might I be so bold as to propose I go ahead and warn them of your arrival? I imagine one man on horseback will cover the distance far more quickly than your carriage or the mail coach."

Christopher appeared to ponder this, tapping his chin in thought. "What say you, Westbrook?"

To all the world as though the idea was quite unexpected, Rodney pursed his lips, throwing out a question or two, before nodding his agreement.

"I do believe Edward's scheme has merit." He clapped the younger man on the back for good measure.

"As far as I can tell, you do not require my opinion, but for what it's worth, I think Mr Lindsay's idea is admirable. Thank you," Lucy interjected, beaming at the younger man, who flushed and glanced down, piquing Lucy's interest. "As I doubt, I am to accompany you, my presence will only complicate matters, thus I shall be next door if anyone needs me. It is lovely to see you all, and I am looking forward to having Elspeth safely home." Dipping a curtsy, she turned to leave, catching another one of those perplexing expressions flitting across Edward's face. Hatred, anger, disappointment, guilt? She could not decide which fitted and so just tucked it away with the everything else she struggled to explain.

Chapter Twenty Five

After popping her head into the kitchens of Harcourt House to tell the staff she would be upstairs, Lucy made her way to William's bedchamber, pleased to note he was still sleeping peacefully. Now he had overcome the fever, he was no longer tormented by laboured breathing and that harsh cough, his chest rising and falling in a steady rhythm.

Resuming her seat, Lucy studied his beloved face. Two sides so drastically different, yet to Lucy, scarcely noticeable… he was just… well… William, and as ever she had to quench the almost irresistible urge to stroke her hand along his jaw, to press her lips to the damaged flesh. He needed sleep far more than he needed kissing. While she sat, thoughts meandered in and out of her head, her worry over William mixing with concern for Elspeth, and she brooded over the knotty problem of how to induce her father to allow her to travel with them to Gillingham Park.

She still struggled to accept Edward meant any real harm to befall Elspeth. She was just a young woman, who, as far as Lucy could work out, had never done anything to cause affront. Was it really to do with inheritance or was there something else going on, something no one had considered? As the day wore on, Lucy came up with and discounted a multitude of possibilities, none of which were credible, and several utterly nonsensical. Not for the first time, she wished she had known the family longer, for perhaps that would have provided deeper insight into what might cause Edward's smile to be so easily extinguished.

It was dusk before William came back to full wakefulness, the sky outside the open window morphing through shades of deep pink and purple to quieter greys as the sun disappeared behind the horizon. The evening was pleasant, and Lucy was standing on the stone balcony, off William's bedroom, taking the time to breathe in the clean fresh air, while trying to distinguish the fragrances drifting up from the blossoms below. The garden and the park were in shadow, dark shapes stirred in the breeze, their movements following a coordinated rhythm, almost like a dance. Lucy leaned on the parapet, and rested her chin in her hands, letting the peace wash over her.

"Lucy?" The quiet question banished all thoughts of admiring the view. Lucy spun on her heel, retreating into the bedchamber with alacrity.

Sinking onto the chair beside the bed, she lifted the candle from the table standing alongside, offering just enough light that she could examine his pale features. "William?" She remembered to speak in undertones. "When did you wake?"

He shrugged. "A moment ago. Why are you in my bedchamber? Not that I am complaining by the way, just curious." The hint of a frown creasing his forehead.

"You developed a fever. I have been helping care for you," she replied lightly, deliberately understating her involvement. "I must inform Mr Grantley you have woken, he has been so worried." She replaced the candle on the side table and was about to seek the butler when a hand grasped hers.

"Not yet. I feel unutterably tired, and doubtless will fall asleep again before you reach the staircase." He studied Lucy in the soft glow thrown by the candle, registering the lines of fatigue etched on her face, and that her hair, which rarely remained confined in its style, seemed more unruly than usual. Her sleeves were rolled up and she was wearing a pinafore. "Lucy?" He raised a brow and squeezed her hand. "How long have I been unwell?"

"Not long," she evaded. "Dr Andrews assures us you are on the mend but will be expected not to throw yourself at life for at least a week." She rested her free hand against his face, gauging his temperature, relieved to feel cool skin under her fingertips.

Disengaging their hands, she stretched over to plump the pillows up behind him. "That should be more comfortable. Here, please try to drink some of this." She reached for a tall glass of water, to which had been added a drop or two of peppermint; steadying it while he sipped.

"That is refreshing." William drank most of it, then leaned back against the pillows, panting a little. "Goodness, I feel weak as a new-born lamb."

"It will pass, my love. You will be back to normal before you know it." Once again, Lucy made to stand, but he caught her fingers and tugged until she had no option but to sit on the edge of the bed. "I really ought to apprise Mr Grantley," she murmured, making no effort to move.

"I have the oddest recollection of you singing to me. Did I dream it?"

Lucy blushed. "I promised I would, and it seemed the only way to settle your night terrors. Now, let me go and speak with your staff. I am sure you would appreciate a clean nightshirt and while I can sing the night through, I daresay I do not have the strength to assist you in and out of your sleeping attire." An image of William naked flickered into her mind and she felt her heart rate increase. *Tsk, really? Not the moment for **that**, Lucy,* she chided silently. Shaking her head to rid it of the picture, she bent to kiss William's cheek. He moved his head at the last second and their lips touched. She tasted the mint, while the aroma from the balm on his scars swirled around her and it was all she could do to stand upright, fighting the temptation to slide into the bed next to him.

"I will return before you notice I've gone." She kissed the back of his knuckles and, sending him a tender smile over her shoulder, hurried from the room.

William watched her leave, his eyelids already drooping. He registered, vaguely, that Lucy looked thinner than of late and her eyes were shadowed but he was so tired, his brain could not deduce why that should be. Even though he was absolutely determined to stay awake until she returned in order to ask her, slumber re-claimed him before she reached the bottom of the stairs.

A week slid by during which William continued to sleep for much of the day, although, with assistance, he managed to get out of bed for short periods. A residual haziness and lapses of memory lingered, causing those caring for him some concern but, eventually, William's naturally robust constitution took over, and he was soon chafing at the limitations imposed by Dr Andrews, upheld by Lucy and Mr Grantley. The doctor suggested William ought to contemplate a sojourn at the Blackthorne country estate to recuperate in more conducive surroundings, a proposal William had thus far resisted.

"You might find the country air more beneficial than London, William," Lucy said one afternoon two weeks after he had fallen ill, while they were enjoying a cup of coffee in the library. William still found being out of bed for the whole day gruelling; rising much later than was typical and retiring immediately after dinner.

"I cannot conceive of travelling at present. The mere idea of a coach journey is enough to dispatch me back to bed, but…" when Lucy started to interrupt, "… I promise to give serious thought to the possibility once I have beaten this maddening lassitude." And with that Lucy had to be satisfied.

Meanwhile, at Rycote House plans were unfolding apace. Rodney informed Christopher, in Edward's hearing, that he required leave to attend family business. The Westbrook estates were on the southeast coast of England, far from Gillingham Park, which to all intents and purposes took Rodney in completely the opposite direction from Elspeth. Christopher behaved as though this irked him, but as Rodney was viscount — with all the responsibilities attached to the title — there were frequently matters only he could deal with, and thus with an admirable show of reluctance, agreed.

James and Christopher began to organise their visit to Gillingham Park, urging Edward to travel with all haste, assuring him they would follow within the week. Lucy, despite haranguing her father to be allowed to join them, was denied permission in tones that brooked no argument. She accepted her father's directive with little grace, stomping up to her bedchamber in a fine old temper. Once there, she plonked herself down at the escritoire and ruminated over the situation. After dipping her quill into the inkwell, she hesitated while her thoughts coalesced, her hand poised over a clean sheet of paper. Then she began to make a list of what she knew.

Edward Lindsay...

Ward of Lady Serena Mayhew from her marriage to Baron Oakford.

Does he still live with her? Ask Papa.

No chance of inheriting a title or estate - need to confirm this.

Does he love Elspeth?

Does he hate her?

Is his intent to kill or frighten? Why?

Might he resort to kidnap?

What of me? Again, is his intent to kill or just to scare me away?

How does Papa fit into this?

Lucy studied what she had written, doodling a little before replacing the quill in its holder when the ink ran out. As she had been from the moment she saw Elspeth fall into the path of the carriage all those weeks ago, Lucy was still baffled by Edward's actions, *if* indeed he was behind them. They made no sense. He knew they were investigating the incidents, and he had to be aware Lucas Withers was now involved. Why continue? If he stopped now, no one would question it. They would be relieved, eager to forget the whole thing. None wanted to accuse a fellow nobleman, however lowly, of murderous intent. He could not be beetle-headed enough to believe himself above suspicion. Those closest to the family would be the first to be accused.

"Nothing for it, Lucy my girl," she murmured, "you are going to have to get to the bottom of this." Obstinately ignoring the voice of reason which insisted she take her suppositions to Lucas, who — if he had not already — possessed the means and expertise to deal with it unobtrusively. Denied the opportunity to travel outside London to see her sister, and the woman she resembled so closely, Lucy's disgruntlement became another link in a chain of events, which would have dire consequences.

Folding the paper, she tucked it into one of the slots in the writing desk and then made her way back downstairs. Poking her head around the door to her father's study, she informed him she was taking a walk and would probably be gone some time.

"No!" Remembering her manners just in time, she softened her sharp retort, with a 'thank you,' when Christopher mentioned a chaperone. "I do not require a chaperone or a guardian. I am perfectly capable of going next door by myself, even if I choose to take the long way around through the park."

"Lucy, please do not be angry with me. In any other circumstances you would be more than welcome to join us, but your safety is paramount, and I will not risk it even if that means suffering your ire. I will introduce you to Mama at the earliest opportunity, you have my word."

Lucy bobbed a curtsy, and although she did not smile at her father, he detected a softening of her expression. "I might not like your reasoning, but I suppose I understand," she conceded grudgingly. "When do you leave?"

"Two days hence. Edward leaves on the morrow and I have told him we depart on Monday."

Lucy could see the sense in this, it was only Wednesday. Unaware Rodney was probably already halfway to Gillingham Park, Edward would believe himself inviolable — at liberty to follow through with whatever scheme he was concocting.

"I shall miss you," she muttered gruffly, a pink blush staining her cheeks, while she studied the pattern on the rug with fierce concentration. Lucy found overt demonstrations of affection in word or deed, awkward. It was not because it had been lacking, but after her mother died there was only her, familial affection no longer part of everyday life, and its revival was taking some adjusting to.

"I will miss you more." Christopher grinned at Lucy, seeing Cecilia in their daughter's exasperated demeanour. "Oh, how I wish your mother was here to see you. Doubtless, she would berate me for being over-protective, while at the same time, telling you not to be so headstrong and listen to reason."

"I wish she was too." Lucy blinked back unexpected tears, silently cursing everyone from William to Edward for such feminine weakness. "I have to go." And hurried out, brushing the dampness from her eyes.

Chapter Twenty Six

Two days passed in the blink of an eye and, suddenly, Rycote House was almost empty, save Lucy and the staff. Now all she could do was wait. It was already interminable, and they had barely left. Tired of traipsing along silent corridors and sitting in empty rooms, Lucy decided to expend some of her nervous energy with brisk promenade. Making her way through the garden, and out into the little park, she began marching around its perimeter — something she repeated twice. It did not help; her mind was a whirl of confused thoughts and emotions. She slowed her pace and scuffed through the undergrowth with little care for her shoes until, without conscious thought, came to the daffodil garden. Unfamiliar plants — all manner of colourful blooms — filled the place where the bright yellow flowers once grew, and the change, despite knowing it to be inevitable, caused the melancholy which had descended on her father's departure, to swamp Lucy once more

She sank onto the grass and buried her hands into the fine soil, lifting a fistful then letting it flow through her fingers. Again, and again, inhaling the loamy scent of the tilled earth, shutting her mind off to everything else around her. William was now in good health and did not require further monitoring. She ought to be able to sleep, but slumber proved elusive, leaving her lethargic. The monumental changes wrought on her life over the past three months suddenly weighed heavily; saving Elspeth, discovering who she was, finding the father she thought long dead, and meeting William — the bright star in her convoluted world. The strange incidents plaguing the Rycote family of which she was now part, William's fever, and the underlying fear that the madman hounding them would never give up.

Unbidden, her mother's face swam over her vision. "Oh,

Mama, why did you leave me?" Her desolate cry was caught by the breeze as Lucy finally succumbed to long-suppressed grief and burst into uncharacteristic tears.

William, after waking at his normal early hour and partaking of a substantial breakfast — glad his appetite had returned — was heading to his study to read the broadsheets, when an urge to visit the daffodil garden possessed him. Glancing through the windows he saw it was a beautiful morning. The sun was shining, and a light breeze rustled the trees, a perfect late-spring day. Unclear what prompted the impulse, William saw no reason *not* to take a brief constitutional; it was over three weeks since he walked with Lucy to The Wise Owl, and the exercise would do him good.

Reaching the boundary of his property, William was startled when he recognised a voice keening in sorrow. Hurrying now, he broke clear of the trees, astonished to see Lucy in a huddle on the grass, weeping as though her heart was breaking. His own heart stuttered at her misery and he was by her side in seconds.

"Lucy my darling what on earth has happened?" William lowered himself onto the ground next to her and gently enfolded her in his arms.

"They've all gone... everyone has gone... you nearly went... I can't lose anyone else." Her less than coherent explanation offered little clarification, so William just held her close, his cheek pillowed on her head, one hand stroking up and down her back in what he hoped was a comforting gesture, talking in soft tones about nothing of any import. It took some time but, eventually, Lucy's sobs began to lessen, and several deep, shuddering breaths later, she had, more or less, collected herself.

"I do beg your pardon, William. I am not usually such a watering pot." She sniffed disconsolately; hiccupping a little. William handed her his handkerchief and she scrubbed at her eyes.

"What brought it on?" William enquired quietly, feeling her shrug.

"Naught but childish nonsense," she parried, but William was having none of it.

"Come, Lucy, I know 'tis not like you to give in to tears, so please do not prevaricate. Tell me what bothers you."

Lucy huffed a sigh and after a moment or so during which she tried to gather recalcitrant thoughts, elaborated. "My life feels like a runaway carriage which is silly really because things have not changed precipitously. Maybe 'tis more that I feel as though I have no control anymore. When Mama was sick, I had no time to think about what might happen, I was focused on tending to her. Then she died. I was sure she would recover, she always seemed so vital, so enduring. One minute she was holding my hand telling me not to waste my life, the next she was gone. I had no time to grieve, although to be honest, I refused to. Mr Abbot and Jemima suggested I take a spell away from work, but what was the point? Mama was dead, no amount of moping about would bring her back and if I was at the bookshop, I could not be tempted to wallow in self-pity." Her voice, a sad little wail.

"Then I meet Elspeth, and the man who is revealed to be my Papa; the man Mama categorically refused to discuss. The only time I ever knew her to be angry was when I pressed her to talk about him." Unconsciously, she nestled against William, taking comfort from his solid presence, while she chattered on in this vein for several minutes.

"Forgive me, I digress. I have never spoken thus of Mama, perhaps in dread that I would become irrationally discomposed, or worse deranged. She was all I had and even though I appreciate my independence, I miss her sorely," she trailed off.

"I am happy to listen to you talk of your mother whenever you feel so moved," William assured, feeling her relax against him, "and the rest?" he coaxed.

"You will think me bird-witted," she mumbled, blushing.

"I sincerely doubt that, my love." Tightening his embrace, briefly.

"William, 'tis just... I know 'tis ridiculous, but I cannot bear the thought of losing anyone else?"

"That is not a ridiculous concern, but who do you think you might lose?" Curiously.

"Papa, Elspeth..." she hesitated, then almost inaudibly, her head bowed, "... you."

"Lucy, I have no intention of going anywhere. Your papa will ensure your sister's safety and, with luck, Lucas will catch the miscreant."

"You do not know that. The person is clearly taken by some kind of mania, and as for you..." she hesitated again, unwilling to voice her fear.

William pulled back and studied her features. Her normally lightly tanned and healthy complexion was a trifle sallow, her eyes looked bruised and lacked their usual brilliance, and her features appeared strained as though she was carrying a burden.

"Lucy..." he slid a cool finger under her chin, tilting her face so she had to look at him, "... are you not sleeping?" She nodded but did not meet his gaze. "Lucy?" William ran his mind back over what he could recall of the last couple of weeks which, to be fair, was very little; the woman singing to him; it happened with frequency, and he knew it had been Lucy. Cool cloths being applied sporadically, gentle fingers massaging in the ointment that never failed to soothe his burns. *How long had she been doing that?* "Lucy, sweetheart, what am I missing here?" He skimmed a thumb over her bottom lip, seeing the vestiges of tears shimmering in her remarkable eyes, and willed her to trust him.

Then, it was though a dam had broken. Words spilt over Lucy's lips so quickly, William wasn't entirely sure what she was saying but he guessed the gist. Long nights keeping vigil, terrified the fever would snatch William away like it had her mother. The daunting prospect of being on her own in a huge house, regardless of the fact that until three months ago she had been on her own for several years. All on top of the niggling suspicion, everyone and everything she was only just beginning to know, to love, and to cherish was about to be ripped from her grasp.

"… and all the daffodils in my pot have died…" this last was so mournful a lament, William had to bite his lip to keep from smiling, she sounded more devastated about the loss of the flowers than anything else. He hugged her close and dropped a kiss on her head as she groused. "I hate change."

"While I wish I was able to tell you otherwise, 'tis an undeniable fact that things change. Time cannot stand still for where would that leave us? Seasons come and go, the world turns, the moon rises as the sun sets, and in among all this, flowers, and yes people, die. 'Tis sad, and we must grieve for them, but we are not granted the gift of foresight, and I cannot predict when or how I will leave this life. We do, however, have the here and now, and we should celebrate it with every fibre of our beings. You have faith that the sun will rise, that the stars will glow, that a new day will follow the last, do you not?"

He waited until he felt her nod. "Then, have faith our coming together was decreed before ever we met, for it required a host of seemingly unrelated things to align at just the right moment. My life would still be as a hermit and you never would have known your heritage. I have long believed that you are my fate, my destiny — why else would you have tripped me up after falling asleep under a shady tree on a quiet spring afternoon?"

"I did not trip you up." Affronted, Lucy twisted to glare at him.

"That's better, I was beginning to wonder whether you'd lost your spirit." Smiling his rare smile.

Lucy offered a lopsided and rather watery grin, but it was a grin all the same, and William responded in kind. Uncoiling his tall frame, he stood, holding out his hand to help Lucy. She followed suit but did not release her grip. The moment she was upright, she stretched on tiptoe to kiss him.

"Thank you, William. You always come to my rescue."

"And I always will," he replied, returning her gesture of thanks with passionate interest. Time slowed, and all sound faded as he wrapped her close and let their kiss deepen. Hands roved, lips teased, and breathing quickened. It was only when he heard Lucy's soft moan that he remembered where they were. "Dash it all, Lucy, you undo me," he husked, his need for her barely restrained.

"The feeling is mutual, my lord," she murmured, adding another, "thank you." She did not have to say for what. "Before we get carried away, if you have a spare moment, there are some things I should like to discuss with you."

Her abrupt switch to the practical took William by surprise, but a quick glance at her glazed eyes and flushed cheeks told him she was as moved as he, her control hanging by a thread. For Lucy, changing the subject was the only way she prevented herself from begging William to make love to her right there in the middle of the park.

"Then let us adjourn to Harcourt House where I expect Mr Grantley can be prevailed upon to brew us a cup of coffee." He paused. "I hope I have been able to assuage your worries somewhat."

Tucking her arm through his, Lucy affirmed this was the case, and the two chatted about nothing at all until they were comfortably ensconced in the library, sipping steaming hot coffee.

"I made a list," Lucy stated, scrabbling about in the pocket of her skirts to withdraw a crumpled sheet of paper. She handed it to William who smoothed it out and read it carefully.

"Do you not think Lucas has already investigated these angles?" William queried.

"I daresay he has, but if so, he has not seen fit to tell me and

I'm the one being targeted of late. I have found out, Lady Mayhew is in town for the Season, so I am going to pay a call. I understand that is what ladies do." She looked at William for confirmation. At his nod, she continued. "If she agrees to see me, yes I realise a visit from the illegitimate daughter of her dead sister's husband might be rather confronting, I would like to ask her the questions pertaining to Edward." Indicating the sheet.

"Then, while you do that, what say I consult my man of business about whether he is in line to inherit anything?" William petitioned, and with which Lucy concurred.

By the time luncheon was served, they had made a plan.

Chapter Twenty Seven

Two days later, Lucy was being ushered into an elegant drawing room. With no cards of her own, she had appropriated one of her father's and written her name in neat script on the back. She rather expected Lady Mayhew to pretend she was not at home which, according to William, meant she preferred not to meet. Trembling at her audacity, and relieved to see she was the only caller, Lucy executed a flawless curtsy when she entered the room. Modulating her tones, Lucy greeted her hostess and after making one or two trivial remarks about the weather, decided to come straight to the point.

"Thank you for being kind enough to receive me, Lady Mayhew. I realise my visit might seem impertinent, but I am involved in an urgent matter and, if you would be patient with me while I explain, I believe your help would be invaluable."

Her hostess was not incognisant of Miss Lucy Truscott. She had made it her business to learn all she could after the sudden appearance of the bastard daughter of her brother-in-law — once the secret was revealed — and admitted to being intrigued. A woman, slight of figure, with piercing blue eyes, and perfectly coiffured hair which still retained its youthful blonde, Lady Serena Mayhew was no fool, her refined features in stark contrast to her sharp wit and acerbic temper. She studied Lucy for several moments, the silence in the room only broken by a ticking of the clock on the mantel, although Lucy was certain her heart was thudding loudly enough for the whole house to hear.

"So, you are the child of the woman, Rycote bedded prior to marrying my sister?" Serena's refined voice held no judgement, she was merely posing the question.

Lucy, slightly pink in the cheek, dipped her head. "I am she, my lady."

"Pray, what is this information you seek?"

Lucy took a deep breath and, as succinctly as possible, gave Serena an abridged version of the events of the last several months. Concluding with their concerns Edward might be behind it in a misguided attempt to claim an inheritance.

Serena stood and paced the room while she pondered Lucy's words. The Edward she knew would never resort to such cruelty and she said as much.

"Whatever his feelings towards the Rycote family, I cannot imagine him stooping so low as to hurt Elspeth over the very slim possibility he might come into an endowment."

Lucy mentioned those odd instances when he appeared to be fighting some deep-seated emotion, possibly hatred or even love of Elspeth, but these too Serena refuted.

"Edward does not care for Elspeth, and in this, you must trust me, Miss Truscott. His…" she hesitated, then continued diplomatically, "… preference is not for those of the female persuasion." Lucy stared at her in bewilderment, the viscountess' words, meaningless. Serena raised a finely arched brow and held Lucy's gaze until comprehension dawned.

"Oh my," she managed. Her kind heart ached for the young man who due to the rule of law, never mind Society's constraints, would be required to keep his predilections secret. Lucy knew of brothels and 'private' clubs who catered to those of a certain taste, the discretion of its patrons of utmost importance. The slightest inkling the authorities were closing in, and they moved. Regardless of her own opinion, she acknowledged the clandestine nature of the clubs would challenge the most tenacious adherent. "Poor Edward," she said her tones gentle.

Observing Lucy, Serena nodded to herself, her brow clearing as though she had reached a decision. "Come, Miss Truscott, there is something you ought to see." Leading Lucy upstairs, along a carpeted hall to what appeared to be a whole different part of the house, confirmed when Serena said. "After I remarried, my husband offered Edward this wing as his own, it gives him some privacy from the rest of us."

Lucy did not reply, assuming it was unnecessary. They came to a room at the end of an airy corridor where Serena paused, her hand on the doorknob.

"This is Edward's study. The day before he left for Gillingham Park, he asked my husband's advice on something that must have been bothering him for a while. Mayhew told me about it later. He wanted to know what to do if he felt his life was being threatened. As Edward is such a retiring young man I laughed, for who on earth would want to hurt him? Now you are here with your questions and revelations. He has been a good son, solicitous of me, loving to my other children, and even though not related by blood, I consider him as much mine as they. Please do not let anyone harm him."

Lucy was astonished to hear the plea in Serena's words. She truly believed Edward incapable of what he was suspected although, as yet, Lucy was not prepared to take her word for it. Growing up in a questionable neighbourhood, she learned never to accept anyone at face value, for that could be your downfall. Proof was as important as instinct and, currently, Edward looked to be the most likely culprit.

"If he is innocent, I will do everything in my power, which to be honest is very little, to ensure he is not wrongly accused." Was the best Lucy could offer.

Acknowledging her guest's assurance, Serena offered a grim smile and opened the door, standing to one side to let Lucy go in ahead of her. "I shall let you look for yourself. Please do not disturb anything. I will return shortly." Closing the door quietly, Serena left.

Amazed she was being trusted in this manner, Lucy remained where she was for several seconds, letting the silence of the room surround her. It was immaculate. Two walls were filled with bookshelves, she could read the spines of those closest to her and they were the tomes of someone who read for pleasure, adding to her burgeoning disquiet. Three chairs were grouped at regular intervals around the fire, a huge globe stood alongside an ornately carved cabinet. The furniture was very masculine — rich walnut and heavy oak inlaid or cushioned, where appropriate, with plush leather of the deepest claret. The sun poured through the large windows to her right, its rays falling on a large desk, which in contrast to the rest of the room was a mess. Papers were scattered across the polished surface, their haphazard arrangement suggesting Edward had been rummaging through them right up until his departure. Might they hold the key?

Lucy took a step forward, then hesitated. This was a gross breach of privacy. Did she really want to go through Edward's papers? While she vacillated, the sound of the gunshots, the terror of clinging to the reins of a runaway horse, and Elspeth's anxious face reared in her mind. She swallowed her scruples. Marching over to the desk, she sat herself down and twitched the closest pile of papers towards her.

With no small amount of trepidation, Lucy lifted the first sheet and began to read. Time passed. At some point a cup of coffee and a plate of biscuits appeared at her elbow, she *did* remember to thank the bearer, even though somewhat abstractedly. Absorbed by the information contained within the papers, Lucy forgot where she was. Realising there was an order to the pages, Lucy surmised Edward had produced a journal of sorts, documenting all the incidents, but in greater detail than she had yet heard or seen. He had done the same as Lucas and William, created a timeline, complete with dates, places, people, adding his own comments — connecting then disconnecting should an avenue of enquiry fail to provide what he was looking for, and any similarities between events were compiled on yet another page. Not wanting to forget anything pertinent, Lucy opened the top drawer and found a little stack of blank sheets. Withdrawing one, and hoping Edward didn't mind, she began making her own notes.

By the time she read the last page, Lucy was confident Edward had nothing to do with the accidents. Leaning back in the chair, she let her thoughts roam, revisiting the occasions she was in Edward's company, whether it be at dinner, a carriage ride, a walk; whatever the instance, she wanted to recall every single facet. Placing the last sheet on top of the rest, she began pulling open drawers just in case Edward had left anything else of note. Then she wandered the room, scanning the bookcases, staring out of the window onto the street below, her eyes seeing a whole other scene. Those two moments when she had caught Edward glowering at Elspeth continued to perplex her. If he was not the one behind it, what had prompted such depths of emotion. More importantly, why had he offered to go to Gillingham Park ahead of the others?

Something pulled at the back of her mind, but just when she thought she had pinned it down, it skittered away. Maybe something in the papers prompted it; she would be going through the notes she had made, with William — hopefully it would come back to her then. Nothing she could do for now. Making sure the desk was tidy and the room exactly she found it, Lucy was about to pick up the tray, when she spied something in the fireplace. Owing to the warmer weather, and the study's usual occupant being away, the fire was laid but not lit. There, stuffed between the logs, was a scrunched-up ball of paper. Plucking it out carefully, Lucy flattened the sheet on the desk and peered at the text. It bore nothing save a name. She stared, her brain refusing to accept what her eyes were reading. It was not possible. She was so shocked, she did not hear the door open, nor the whisper of silks as Lady Mayhew came into the room, nor the mention of her name.

"Miss Truscott." No response. Serena was presented with a fine view of Lucy's bent head, the latter seemingly transfixed by the paper in front of her.

"Miss Truscott!"

Lucy's gaze lifted to that of the speaker, and she shot upright, her cheeks flaring with hectic colour. "Oh, my lady, forgive me, I did not hear you." Embarrassed by her discourteous behaviour.

"As I can see," Serena replied wryly. "Did you find what you were seeking?"

"I did, and I am astounded. I must inform Major Withers," she waved her hand towards the pile of papers, "the information therein is irrefutable but mystifying, and while I hope we might eventually be privy to the reasoning, I cannot say the knowledge gives me any satisfaction at all."

"Please take those." Serena pointed to the same sheaf Lucy had just indicated. "They might be of help to those investigating."

"Are you sure? What of Edward?"

"After what you have told me, 'tis imperative to do what is necessary to prevent Edward from being implicated. If these papers support that end, I daresay he will forgive me for handing them to you."

"Thank you, you have my word I will keep them safe." Lucy bundled the papers together and tied them neatly with a piece of string she located in the top drawer of the desk. One final glance around, and she followed Serena from the room, closing the door behind her.

Back in the drawing room, over a cup of hot chocolate, Lucy updated her hostess on what she had discovered. "Please I beg of you, keep this to yourself for the moment. Of course, you may tell your husband, but only him," she hastened to clarify. "As it stands, 'tis only Edward's supposition and, although my instinct tells me he is correct, we must have more than someone's thoughts."

The two ladies conversed in an amiable fashion while they sipped their drinks, then Lucy ventured. "Your welcome today was more than I dared expect. My presence in your home must raise painful memories."

Serena studied Lucy for a long moment, taking in her guest's tidy appearance, her polite manners, and ingenuous smile. "What your parents did is not your fault, my dear. Susannah had a good marriage. Christopher was never anything other than attentive, but she knew about Cecilia. Yes…" when Lucy's jaw dropped, "… there is always someone who takes gleeful delight in gossiping. She knew Christopher loved your mother, such things are quite common in Society. Your mother showed great strength of character in removing herself, in not becoming his mistress. Had she agreed, your life would have been much easier."

Lucy bowed her head, more tears threatening; she really was a veritable spring shower at the moment. Regaining her self-possession, she lifted her blue-grey eyes back to Serena's intuitive gaze. "Thank you, my lady, not many in your position would be as… open-minded."

"Sometimes, I surprise myself." Serena grinned, and suddenly, the atmosphere relaxed, any residual tension between the two women vanishing like the morning mist. They chatted a little longer, then Lucy, eager to show William what she had uncovered, took her leave.

"If you are moved to call upon me again, I should be glad," Serena said, unexpectedly, when the butler came to show Lucy out. Lucy dipped a curtsy and affirmed she was already looking forward to it.

Chapter Twenty Eight

Albany Square was not far, and Lucy used the time it took to walk to Harcourt House, to collect her thoughts. Arriving, she went around to the domestic entrance, as was her habit, calling a hello to those in the kitchen.

"Is William home?" she asked brightly. Lucy never used his title, William having told her long ago he preferred his given name in his own home.

"He is, Miss Lucy, but…" Mr Grantley stood, as though to escort her through.

"Stay where you are, Mr Grantley, I can find him." Lucy waved the roll of papers. "You would not credit what I have found today. I promise to share it with you once I have told William." She beamed at the friendly staff.

"Miss, wait…" the butler tried again, but Lucy was gone, whisking through the doors, her footsteps fading along the flagged passage. The soft thud of the baize door galvanised Mr Grantley. "Oh dear, I should have warned her."

"Don't you worry about Miss Lucy, she'll sort them out," Mrs Hendry replied cosily. Not convinced, Mr Grantley hurried after Lucy, hoping to catch her before she reached drawing room.

Lucy, excited to tell William about her afternoon, had peeped into the study, the parlour, and the library and was currently standing in the middle of the hall, her nose crinkled in confusion. Had William decided to take a nap? It seemed unlikely so late in the day. Then she heard voices, several of them. Visitors? Thinking it might be Lucas and Jemima, Lucy was heading towards the drawing room when she was halted by a hand on her arm.

"Miss Lucy, please…"

She turned to see the butler, his expression mildly distressed. About to ask what bothered him, her question died in her throat when one of the voices drowned out the others.

"Lord Blackthorne," the voice was that of a woman and, although cultured, was also grating, "surely you can see how troublesome this will become? She is naught but a gold digger, after your coin. What proof have you, has anyone, she is who she claims to be? Lord Rycote is gullible indeed accepting her into his home without proper investigation."

Another voice chimed in, "Why saddle yourself with the chit anyway? Bed her by all means, but *court* her or, heaven forbid, *marry her*?" The speaker was clearly aghast at the mere possibility. "Come now, I did not take you for a fool. There are plenty of eligible young ladies who could be prevailed upon, given suitable incentive, to marry you. You risk being snubbed if you choose to wed a bastard."

An angry rumble. William. Lucy strained her ears but could not make out his reply. She stared at the butler who held her gaze, his eyes sympathetic. For a split second, she wanted to run; run back to her miserable little room in the pokey house in Seven Dials. The memory of the rude countess came back, and it still nettled her. Lucy glanced down at her attire and saw the tanned skin of her hands — no amount of finery could disguise the fact she was a child of the rookeries. That curious notion she was adrift between worlds descended upon her, and she felt her shoulders sag.

Shrewd and worldly wise, Mr Grantley guessed her thoughts and, aware of the change she had wrought in William, the vitality she had brought to the household, took a gamble.

"Miss Lucy, these are the very same people who shunned him when he returned from the war. Until you came along, there has only been the major and us. Everyone else avoided him because of his burns. You have never judged him or recoiled from him. You have made him happier than I have ever known him to be, yes, even prior to his departure for France. He was never one for parties and the like, always preferred the solitude of books and his garden, something his parents could not understand. In you, he has found someone who sees him for who he is and loves him because of it. Do not undervalue yourself or presume you will be doing him a favour by leaving." He paused and studied her speculatively. This was the latest in a steady stream of visitors trying to sweet-talk their way into Harcourt House. Lucy's presence, and her somewhat controversial heritage had caused some ruffled feathers among the *ton*, especially as she appeared to have snared herself a marquis.

"Gossip travels fast, it is known he has begun to spend time beyond this house. I have been fending off *well-intentioned…*" the butler almost sneered the term, "callers for weeks now. This is the first time they have managed to get beyond the doorstep, and that was only because they assured me and his lordship they were here regarding a ball in aid of some charity or other. That they have resorted to subterfuge in an attempt to induce him to marry some empty-headed debutante shows their desperation. These women are vultures, Lucy, only after his wealth, and he knows that. Lord Blackthorne is nobody's fool."

Lucy listened to the genial retainer and knew his words to be the truth. She loved William and he loved her. Most people were never fortunate enough to find their soulmate and, despite their difference in status, she knew this was no frivolous dalliance. Moreover, although they had never specifically discussed marriage, William *had* declared his intentions to her father, and they often talked of their future together. Was she going to allow a deputation of meddling old battle-axes to interfere with her life in so spiteful a fashion? No, she most definitely was not!

"You are correct, Mr Grantley. For a moment I allowed my insecurities to overwhelm me. I know who I am, and I know I am not the most suitable woman for William, but dammit it all to hell, I am not about to let him go without a fight," she hissed the words in angry undertones and saw a wicked grin curve the butler's lips.

"Go get him, my lady." Grinning, when Lucy gaped at him. "Practising," he said and, whistling a merry tune, strolled back to the kitchen.

Head held high, Lucy walked into the drawing room. Three ladies — and she attributed that moniker with reluctance — were standing shoulder to shoulder, creating a barrier, reminiscent of protestors she'd seen marching against the latest government reform with which they disagreed. William was leaning on the mantelpiece, his face dark as thunder. His eyes flicked to hers when she entered the room, his expression morphed from furious to pained, aware she must have heard something of the discussion.

Any last-minute reservations vanished when, as she passed the trio, Lucy heard one of the women remark that if his lordship left it to them, they *knew* they could persuade a suitable young lady to look beyond his scars, her companions murmuring their agreement. Ignoring them, Lucy went straight to William, and slid gentle fingers over the blemish on his face, before standing on tiptoe to brush her lips to his.

"Leave this to me," she murmured in his ear, rewarded when he grasped her other hand and squeezed her fingers.

"'Tis not your fight," he replied, turning his head so their eyes met.

"It most certainly is." Lucy held his gaze, and the immeasurable devotion they bore for each other flowed between them.

"I love you, my William." It was the first time she had uttered the words. Neither felt it necessary, it was clear in the way they behaved but, upon her admission, Lucy felt a wave of unadulterated happiness course through her. They were bound.

William smiled his slow, tender smile, lifted her hand and kissed her knuckles. "I love you more."

There was absolute silence. Then one of the visitors coughed, bringing the couple back to reality

Another quick kiss and Lucy spun on her heel, prepared to do battle.

She took her time to scrutinise the three. Fashionably dressed, of course, but their gowns although of the finest material, were fussy — she could hear her mother's voice 'too much frippery' — fingers heavily be-ringed and cosmetics a tad garish, reminding her of the chickens all trussed up, at the market. An image that made her want to giggle, effectively banishing her anxiety. They were just people, no better or worse than she who, by luck of birth, presumed themselves entitled to dictate to others. Quite pathetic when you knew how constrained they actually were, prompting her to speculate whether this was the reason they deemed it acceptable to manipulate the lives of those who dared flout the rules. It gave them a sense of power, when in reality, it was just an illusion but was all they could cling to.

In turn, the women, not prepared to give an inch, glared at this upstart who had inveigled her way into Lord Blackthorne's affections.

"Good afternoon," Lucy dipped a low curtsy, "my name is Lucy Truscott, how do you do?"

Years of discipline came to the fore and all three responded in kind — without the curtsies.

"I understand your... concern for Lord Blackthorne. After all, I am sure you have heard I am not of your class. I grew up in one of the disreputable areas of the city and learned from an early age, nothing would be handed to me on a silver platter, unlike yourselves," the devil inside made her add. Her tones were so reasonable, however, none in front of her registered the jibe. She *did* hear a quickly smothered sound from William but did not dare look at him, for fear she would lose her concentration.

"His lordship has suffered greatly over the last year or so, first the war, then his injuries and their aftermath. At a time when he might have benefitted from the succour of his peers, he was neglected, treated like a pariah, and left to overcome his wounds all alone save his staff and his commanding officer. While the neighbourhood of my childhood was rough and harsh, no one in need was abandoned, especially those brave enough to fight for our freedom. We might not have great wealth, or fine clothes or grand houses, but we have riches beyond compare.

"I knew a mother's devotion; a woman so in love with my father she kept his identity a secret so as not to embarrass him and his new wife. She gave me everything she was able to and I am forever grateful. She taught me to be respectful, regardless of people's attitudes; to show compassion, to be empathetic. It was hard. I thought you Society folk abominably rude, your inconsiderate treatment of those who work their fingers to the bone to keep you in the lap of luxury, appals me. Nevertheless, I heeded my mother's advice and, for the most part, I can curb my indignation at your slights and am able to feel sorry for you, a caged bird has more freedom." She paused, knowing that when annoyed, the urgency to voice her ire, often came at the detriment of coherence.

"Now, after all this time, during which you have ignored his existence, offered him no support, no consolation, no companionship, no encouragement, no welcome; no invitations to your homes, to balls, to any kind of gathering at all, you feel it appropriate, nay, essential, to pay a call, to warn him of the folly of associating with the gold-digging, social-climbing, bastard daughter of an earl." Horrified gasps penetrated her fury, and Lucy sucked in another breath. Striving for control, she felt a hand on her back, as William moved from the mantel to stand alongside her. He started to speak but she shook her head.

William, who prior to Lucy's arrival, had given the three busybodies short shrift was fascinated by the skill with which Lucy insulted his guests while making it sound as though she was disparaging herself. Knowing he could stop this right now, he was inclined to let it play out and only intercede if necessary, amused that Lucy had no qualms about ticking off anyone she felt had overstepped the mark. He dragged his attention back to what she was saying.

"This man has more integrity in his little finger than the rest of you put together. You assume because he is outwardly scarred that he is inwardly addled, unable to make sensible decisions, and in dire need of your wisdom. To suggest you might, oh so generously, be able to find a lady who is prepared to *look beyond his scars*, makes you not only insensitive but the most patronising women I have had the misfortune to meet. William's scars are a badge of honour, not something to excuse or conceal, and to me are inconsequential." Her tone had cooled to just above frigid and the icy steel of her eyes bore into them, noting two of the three had the decency to blush. "I am the first to admit, a woman with my heritage should preclude me from being anything other than mistress to a man of his lordship's pedigree, but that is not for you to decide. You forfeited any right, if indeed you *ever* had the right... goodness me you people beggar belief... to meddle in Lord Blackthorne's life when you neglected to provide one iota of comfort, or one ounce of sensitivity upon his return from the war.

"Whether, and whom, he chooses to wed is none of your

concern, never has been. Now, if there is nothing more, I have important business to discuss with his lordship, so I suggest you scurry off and impart your newly acquired gossip among your clique. I daresay they'll be avid to hear what a shrew Lord Blackthorne may or may not be bedding. William…" she let that dangle, indicating the papers she was clutching, deliberately addressing him by his given name, a liberty granted to very few in his world.

William rang for Mr Grantley who arrived with an immediacy that indicated he had been loitering close by. The innocent expression on his face, compounding the supposition.

"Ah, Mr Grantley, please show these ladies out, they do not have time to enjoy refreshments." William smiled at the butler who responded with barely-concealed exultation.

Lucy sank onto the chaise by the French doors, trembling from her audacity. It was not her place to dispatch William's visitors, but once she started to speak, she could not stop nor had she any desire to do so. Their brazen assumption anyone, never mind William, could be swayed from a chosen path by their very presence infuriated her and, if she was honest, scared her.

Having escorted the visitors out of the drawing room, leaving them in Mr Grantley's capable hands, William came over and stood in front of Lucy, noting the way her hands were twisting on her lap and the quiver of her shoulders.

"William forgive me, my mouth…"

"Lucy, you never cease to…"

Spoken in unison, each stopped aware the other was speaking.

"Ladies first," William invited. Lucy cocked her head to look him in the eye.

"Forgive me, William. I should not have behaved thus to guests in your home, but they… and I… because you see… and

I *am* totally unsuitable…" she halted and shivered, reaction was setting it. There was really no justification, so she shut up and began pleating the soft material of her gown over and over until it started to resemble a scruffy rag.

William crouched, and took both of her hands in his. "Lucy do not ever apologise for having an opinion, nor standing up for what you believe. I was about to say you never cease to amaze me. And, of course, you are unsuitable…" he put a finger to her lips when she started to voice an indignant repost. "Whoever said I want *suitable*? I want gloriously, ridiculously, blissfully *un*suitable and on that, I remain resolute. You have more class and courage than any woman I know, and any man would be privileged to have you by his side." Straightening up, he raised Lucy to her feet, and leaned close to touch his lips to hers. "But I do hope mine will be the side by which you stand… forever."

Lucy searched his eyes, her own beginning to sparkle, and arched a quizzical brow. She was not going to say it.

"Lucy Truscott, my love, my life, my redemption, please will you bestow upon me the greatest honour and agree to become my wife?"

Lucy's smile could have lit the whole of London.

"Yes, oh, William, my love, my heart, my rescuer, and whose side I promise to stand by, forever — YES!" she squealed the last in unmitigated joy, as William swung her into his arms and kissed her most emphatically.

Chapter Twenty Nine

Following a lengthy interlude during which William demonstrated, most satisfactorily, how happy he was Lucy agreed to marry him, they shared their news with the household. The latter declared themselves ecstatic, proceeding to pat each other on the back for having predicted it. After a celebratory dinner complete with champagne, Lucy and William remained in the dining room poring over the documents Lucy brought from Lady Mayhew.

"It seems unequivocal," William said, shuffling the sheets into some semblance of order.

"I know, and while I found it difficult enough to accept it was Edward, this is even harder. He was with us when Misty bolted. How could he…" she trailed off staring into space. Shaking her head at the sheer gall of the man. "What do we do?"

William grinned. "*I* shall inform Lucas, whom I expect will have a chat with his father. You, my dear need to enjoy a relaxing week, you have been running yourself ragged. Moreover, we have a wedding to plan, so I expect several hours a day to be given over to discussion surrounding said nuptials.

"Pfft! Relax? I do not know how to do that, I would be bored witless in five minutes. Anyway, I am rather hoping you will allow me to help with this," waving her hand at the papers. "There was something…"

William tried to look severe but, fortified by two glasses of champagne, Lucy simply smiled winsomely, placed her hands together as though she was praying, and batted her eyelids.

William chuckled. "You bamboozle me, my betrothed." Shaking his head in mock resignation.

The endearment sending a prickle of delight through Lucy. "I know," she replied and, pushing back her chair, walked around the end of the table to where he was sitting, "and I intend to bamboozle you for the rest of our lives. 'Tis so much fun." She took his hand, drew him out of the chair, and led him through to the library. "We have the rest of the evening, naught we can do until the morrow, and I can think of a far more interesting way to spend the next hour or so." She lit a handful of candles, then perched on the desk to stare up at him through innocent eyes.

"You can?" William's lips quirked in a slow smile.

"Oh yes," she almost purred. "I should like to continue where we left off this afternoon."

"Would you now? Am I not supposed to be the one to seduce you?" He came to the desk and, nudging her legs apart until her gown prevented further movement, stood between them, enfolding her in his arms.

"I am of the belief, seduction should work both ways." she murmured. "Now kiss me."

"As you command, my love." He captured her lips gently; savouring the sensation, as he became aware Lucy was unfastening the buttons of his waistcoat. She slid her hands underneath it and around his back, pulling at his shirt until she freed it from his buckskins. Slender hands stroked over flesh, which prickled in anticipation, and he swallowed a groan when her fingers stroked across his abdomen, languidly describing the outline of his muscles upwards to his chest.

Shoving papers and ledgers out of the way with little care, William gently reclined Lucy until she lay flush against the gleaming surface of the desk. Bending from the waist, he scattered kisses from her décolletage to the hollow at the base of her throat. With his right hand, he caressed her neck, and around the sensitive spot behind her ear, to entangle his fingers through her lustrous hair, completely destroying the neat bun Alice had twisted it into that morning. His left hand trailed down her dress, seeking under the layers, fingers tracing her shapely calf, while his thumb massaged her skin in a hypnotically circular motion.

"William…?" at Lucy's breathy moan, he lifted his head.

"Do you want me to stop?"

"Don't you dare," she husked. "I never want you to stop. I was just wondering whether we ought to lock the door?" Endlessly glad the library was one of the rooms whose door had not been removed.

William chuckled, and in three strides was turning the key, the click of the lock sending fiery colour over Lucy's cheeks. From her recumbent position, she watched him through half-lidded eyes, admiring his lithe body when he stalked back to where she lay. She wanted to see him naked, to watch the flex of his physique while he adored her body, uncaring how wanton it sounded, attributing her lowered inhibitions to the champagne. A thought occurred to her. Was this it? Was he going to make love to her tonight? That they were not yet wed, did not particularly worry Lucy, and despite her innocence, knew she desired him as much as he desired her, evidenced whenever they kissed. Moreover, she had faith if all he wanted was to bed her, he would have done so long ago. The notion that history was about to repeat itself drifted through her mind, banished when William's lips were once again on hers.

Unaware of the thoughts cartwheeling through Lucy's head, William gathered her into his arms, and carried her over to the fireplace, in front of which was a sizeable, deep-pile rug. Kneeling, he was about to lower her onto the rug, when she squirmed in his embrace until she faced him, straddling his legs, her skirts bunching up around her calves.

Scattering kisses, featherlight, over his scars, and along his jawline, she pushed the waistcoat off his shoulders. "I want to see you," she murmured, "I need to touch you." Tugging at his shirt, she dragged it over his head with little resistance from William, it must be said. "Oh my…" any other opinion died in her throat as her pupils dilated at the sight of him. "William, I… oh my…" they were the only words she could dredge up. Tentatively, Lucy stretched out her hands, placing them palms flat against his chest, fanning her fingers over his taut frame, hearing William inhale sharply. Emboldened, she inched closer, the gap between their bodies reduced to a hair's breadth.

The air around them fairly sizzled.

"Lucy?" His voice held a plea and a question.

"You may take this as far as you wish," she whispered in his ear, gently biting the lobe, before kissing her way down his neck. "I know this is brazen, and I am doubtless breaking even more of your rules, but if you do not ravish me, I might just expire." She pulled away slightly, and held his gaze, molten gunmetal on smouldering indigo.

"Which would be a travesty," William concurred, his fingers swarming up the back of her gown, to make short work of the multitude of buttons.

"Hmmm… you managed that very easily. How much practise have you had unfastening lady's buttons?" she quizzed, lazily.

"Apparently just enough," the wicked grin pulling at the corners of his mouth was extinguished the instant her bodice fell forward to expose the delicate cotton of her chemise. He paused and looked her in the eye. "Lucy, I may have been witness to things which, tempted me to find ways to blank out the horror." His lips grazed the rise of her breast, wrenching a thready whimper from her throat. "I may have lived among those who availed themselves of whatever was offered," cool fingers slid the chemise off her shoulders, "but I have never been intimate with a woman. You will be my first, my last, my only." Swathes of gauzy material pooled at her waist and as his fingers began a detailed exploration, he felt a tremor run through her. "Oh God, my darling Lucy, you are perfection."

Wrapped in William's arms, Lucy became aware of an ache,

or was it a throb? in her core. Her head fell back as William kissed his way from the base of her throat to her stomach, his tongue swirling around her navel. It was the most exquisite torture. In swift succession, her gown and underthings were gone, tossed to one side, then William lowered her to the rug, his fingers tracking up the inside of her leg. The throb, *yes it was definitely a throb*, intensified and involuntarily she arched towards him.

"William…"

"Mmmm," he was concentrating on not losing control.

"Are you going to make love to me?"

"In a manner of speaking," he ground out, the tips of his fingers skimming against her heat. Lucy gasped at the unexpected touch, then wriggled needing more.

"William! Don't stop, please don't stop."

"I have no intention of stopping, my love." His thumb inciting ripples of sensation, while his fingers moved inexorably towards their objective. William knew the moment she reached the edge. He flicked her over, his lips stifling the scream ripped from her as she fell off the cliff.

Lucy felt as though she was flying, soaring on a wave of an emotion hitherto unknown and wholly indescribable. The throb remained but was dull now as she floated back to earth, to the quiet of a dimly lit library. Nestled in William's arms, she became aware of his fingers stroking up and down her arm; occasionally his thumb caught the side of her breast sending infinitesimal quivers coursing through her.

"That was incredible," she murmured shyly, her breath still coming in gasps, and her heart pounding. "Your talents know no bounds."

William kissed her hot cheek. "You bring out the virtuoso in me," he growled, "now let us see what other skills we can master."

"Good sir." She raised herself on one elbow — causing her

hair, now totally dishevelled, to spill over her naked shoulders —
and tapped him on his chest. "I do believe I intimated that
seduction works both ways, for which you are wearing far too
many clothes." Tilting her head pensively, she studied him.
"These must go." She fiddled with the fall of his trousers, her
ministrations threatening to undermine William's rapidly
evaporating restraint.

"Allow me," he croaked, divesting himself of the remainder
of his clothes. Lucy gawked. There was no polite way of
describing her expression; her eyes widened, and her jaw
dropped.

"William…" she pulled him back down onto the rug. "… if
I was a person of faith, I would thank all that is holy for whatever
deity placed you in my path. Being ambivalent in that regard I
shall assume it was Fate, to whom I am eternally thankful. My
turn." And giving him no chance to respond, she proceeded to
discover her betrothed until he was the one writhing. Eventually,
determined not to take her innocence until they were wed,
William grabbed her inquisitive hands and kissed her into
delicious delirium.

"While I can think of nothing I want more than to make love
to you tonight and every night, I want to wait 'til we are husband
and wife, even though I might die in the interim." His mock
doleful expression making Lucy giggle. "You mean more, are
worth more to me than a quick tumble. You are the woman I
never expected to meet, the one who loves me for who I am, who
sees the man *beneath* the scars, and even though I crave you like
a man starved, I will not dishonour you by taking you out of
wedlock."

They were facing each other, and Lucy shuffled closer until
their bodies aligned, her curves fitting into his hollows. "While I
am eager to know you as intimately as is possible, your desire to
delay until we are married pleases me more than I anticipated."
She yawned, "I should probably take my leave. We have much

to do on the morrow."

"Permit me another moment or two…" William kissed her objections, few though they were, into silence.

It was a very sleepy Lucy whom Lord Blackthorne delivered to Rycote House as the clock on the tower of the nearby church struck midnight. Having made sure she was properly dressed — although Lucy barely recalled being helped into her underclothes and buttoned into her gown — William draped her wrap around her shoulders and walked her home.

"I apologise for the lateness of the hour, Harris," William murmured when the butler answered his soft knock. "We had much to discuss and time got away from us." William had not been able to do anything with Lucy's hair, her slightly rumpled appearance not lost on Harris. His lips twitched but he made no comment other than to thank the marquis for escorting Lucy home.

Alice took over. She led Lucy up to her bedchamber, assisting her into her nightgown and tucking her under the covers. Lucy was lost in dreamland long before William, who decided to treat himself to a nightcap while perusing the notes they had made earlier, sought his bed.

Chapter Thirty

Lucy shared her news with the staff of Rycote House when she finally awoke the next morning. Appalled she had slept until nearly luncheon, her apologies were waved away by those behind the baize door, especially after adding, rather more diffidently than was her wont, she was betrothed to Lord Blackthorne. Most guessed his lordship would ask for her hand and were gratifyingly pleased for the couple. Her unusual status aside, Lucy was well-loved among the domestic staff, her determination not to make their lives any more arduous than they already were, endearing her to them long ago.

"We cannot confirm a date until Papa knows. But you have been so kind and welcoming to me, I could not wait until his return to share my joy." She beamed at them while sitting on the well-scrubbed kitchen table, swinging her legs, in complete disregard for etiquette.

In light of her betrothal, Lucy finally gave up her squalid attic room. She had no more need of somewhere she could run to — her future secure.

*****

The ensuing days were spent gathering as much information as possible. Lucas arrived as dusk fell the following afternoon and, after William provided an abridged version of their content, took the papers Lucy brought from Lady Mayhew's into his safekeeping, before confirming he would visit Lord Rycote's solicitor.

"I am astonished at Garrick's duplicity," Lucas said, sounding almost impressed. "That he managed to maintain the ruse of a concerned friend while simultaneously devising these attacks indicates a man of steely resolve. Probably the more dangerous because of it." He steepled his fingers together, resting his chin on their tips as he ruminated on this unexpected twist. Then, he reached for and gulped the last of his hot chocolate, before propelling himself out of the comfortable seat with renewed vigour. "I am glad we have something more tangible to work with. Although Edward seemed the likely candidate, something did not sit quite right with me, there were too many inconsistencies. Now I know why. I shall endeavour to convince Garrick's father to tell me anything pertinent, but he is a solicitor, so doubtless my powers of persuasion will be sorely tested."

He grinned, the thrill of the hunt coiling through him. This was what he and his men loved to do, peel away the layers until all that remained was the truth. "Harcourt, when you're ready..." leaving that dangling. Lucas wanted William on his team; he knew the man to be methodical, diligent, and conscientious, he was also meticulous to a fault and would leave no stone unturned when involved in a case. Such a man would be an asset to his organisation. He had been soliciting William since before the latter was discharged from St Bart's. The recent awareness his friend and one-time captain, was beginning to conquer his aversion to appearing in public, in the main because of Lucy, encouraged Lucas to strike while the iron was hot.

William chuckled at Lucas' persistence and decided to put him out of his misery. Wanting a relatively objective perspective, he had discussed the major's offer with Lucy, in depth. Lucy was of the opinion that it would bring variety and interest, not to mention excitement to his days and he would also be able to work from home as well as in the city office where Lucas and his team were based.

"Once this fiasco is done we shall revisit this conversation but, as it stands, I am inclined to accept your offer." His chuckle blossoming into outright laughter at Lucas' whoop of delight.

"I knew I would wear you down sooner or later," was his friend's gleeful response. "Now, I'm going. Lucy," he pinned that young woman with an unwavering stare, "please do not do anything rash. Jemima would never forgive me if anything happened to you." Knowing Lucy's penchant for stepping in where angels feared to tread. Her impulsive nature would have her dashing around the countryside chasing maniacs with murderous intentions without a second's thought. He waited until he saw Lucy's reluctant nod, and with that, he had to be satisfied.

Ducking his head in nonchalant acknowledgement of William's title, Lucas strode out, calling a goodbye as he left, the front door slamming on his heels.

"May I add to Lucas' request by begging you to be careful?" William adjured when they were alone again. "I know you have been vigilant and, that with everyone travelling to Gillingham Park, you think yourself safe, but there are wheels within wheels here. We do not know whether he works alone, whether he has people watching you and what will happen when he is confronted. Once cornered, people lose their ability to behave rationally…"

"You think any of this is rational?" Lucy interrupted.

"No, I do not, but we need to have him think we do not suspect him, for as long as possible. We cannot get a message to Gillingham Park, without showing our hand. Maybe we ought to travel there. We could use the excuse of our betrothal. It would be natural for you to want to share it with your father and sister, and my doctor does keep insisting I visit the country."

Lucy pondered his suggestion. It might just work. "What if we make plans to travel but wait until Lucas has spoken with James' father, before we set off. I should like to hear whether there is any other pertinent information we ought to be aware of." She paused. *Travel, why did that ring a bell?* "Was there anything among all those papers about travelling?" she asked. Scouring her brain, her mind's eye scanning each sheet. That same niggle, the one she had felt when she had finished going through the papers yesterday, and again last evening when she and William were discussing their import, continued to frustrate her. *What the devil was it?*

William shook his head. "I cannot recall any mention of travel. Ask Lucas when next we meet. He will have one of his men reading every page at least three times."

Nodding distractedly, Lucy's mind was careening off on several tangents. "How long will you require to prepare for this journey? I have little to pack, and I do not think we should delay once we have spoken with Lucas." Tapping her chin in thought while she mentally assessed her relatively meagre wardrobe. "Do we take a carriage? It will be quicker to ride." Her tones were casual, but her stomach tightened at the prospect of getting back on a horse, something she would have flatly refused to do had not Elspeth's safety been under threat.

William chuckled at her attempt to sound indifferent. "Before we go rushing off into the wilds, let us wait for Lucas. There may be no need to leave the city. How would you fancy a turn around the garden? 'Tis too beautiful a day to remain inside." A welcome distraction and one which kept them occupied until dinner was announced.

*****

Twenty-four hours passed with no word from Lucas, then on Friday morning, two things happened which precipitated their next move.

Lucy received a letter from Elspeth. One which was delivered direct to Rycote House instead of coming via Jemima. It was a bit garbled as though Elspeth had written it in hurry, and it took Lucy several attempts to unravel what she surmised her sister was saying. She confirmed all four men, across the space of a week, had arrived safely and nothing seemed out of the ordinary. Then, the morning Elspeth wrote her letter, Edward and James disappeared. According to the groom, they had gone riding, but it was now long past their expected return and neither had been seen. In itself not particularly unusual, one of their horses might have slipped a shoe, and it *had* rained heavily, so they may have taken shelter in one of the disused cottages scattered around the estate, but with everything else going on Elspeth believed their absence had a more sinister overtone.

Lucy hurried around to Harcourt House, waving the letter excitedly under William's nose, when she found him breakfasting in the dining room.

"Please forgive my intrusion, but you must read this." She hopped from foot to foot while William, chewing on a slice of crispy bacon, perused the missive. As Elspeth noted, and Lucy pointed out, under normal circumstances, two adult males missing on an estate was no cause for alarm, but these circumstances had progressed way beyond what could be classed as normal. Had James lured Edward away? Was he contriving some kind of incident to point the finger more firmly at Edward? They were embroiled in a conversation about this when Mr Grantley announced Lucas.

"Fill a plate, Lucas. I'm sure you can manage another breakfast," William invited. Lucas piled his plate with food, sat down opposite the couple and, while munching his way through half of what was on his plate, divulged what he had learned from Mr Garrick senior.

"It transpires the Garrick family have relatives who are of the *ton*. Vernon's sister married a baron. In turn, their oldest daughter married an earl. Thus, James' cousins hold considerably loftier positions within Society, than do Vernon's children. Until recently he, Vernon, did not think James was particularly perturbed by the difference in status, but of late and this was after I pressed him, he admits his son seemed out of sorts, his petulant attitude out of proportion to perceived grievances. He also mentioned he would be marrying soon but has yet to apprise his father anything about his supposed bride."

Lucas paused, took another mouthful of bacon, chewed thoughtfully, and swallowed before continuing. "That was all he had to say, other than James has always been a model son."

'So, we have two men who seem above reproach, yet one of whom has malicious intent?" Lucy interjected.

William nodded. "It seems to be the case. Lucas, read this." He thrust Elspeth's letter at the major, who read it quickly, while gulping his way down a cup of aromatic coffee.

"My, my, the plot thickens," he muttered "Good coffee this." He waved the cup absently, making Lucy and William grin. "I think we must travel to Gillingham Park."

"Just as I said after last you were here," Lucy crowed, clapping her hands.

Lucas glanced across the table at William who shrugged helplessly.

"You know she will find a way to come whether we permit her to accompany us or not," he said. "At least this way, we know where she is."

His plate empty, Lucas leaned back in his chair, studying Lucy, speculatively. "I do not know why I waste my breath," he growled, but Lucy spied the smile beginning to twitch at his lips.

"Thank you." She bounced out of her seat, went around the table to where he was sitting, and planted a kiss on his cheek. "I will do exactly as you instruct. I must pack." She accorded the two men a bright beam and then shot off through the house yelling a goodbye to anyone who might hear.

"I hope we do not have cause to regret this decision," Lucas remarked.

"As do I," William concurred, a kernel of apprehension

beginning to form.

*****

Bearing in mind Elspeth's letter had taken three days to arrive, with the best will, and the fastest horses in the world it would be at least another four before Lucy, William, and Lucas could reach Gillingham Park and that assumed nothing delayed their journey. As far as anyone else knew, Edward was their chief suspect. Therefore, if James accused Edward of wrong-doing, everyone would assume it was part of the pattern. That James might have orchestrated it would never have entered the heads of those residing on the estate, which at least had the benefit of keeping them relatively safe. None of the three about to set out could fathom why James was taking his vexation out on the Gillingham family, but they hoped to get to the bottom of it in the not too distant future.

*****

Lucy, aware she would have to ride a horse if she wanted to travel with William and Lucas, confessed her fears to Alice while they packed a valise with the absolute essentials. Lucy would wear her riding habit, take one gown, and several underthings. Hopefully, should she require any other clothes, there was something suitable at Gillingham Park she would be permitted to borrow. It was essential they travel with as little luggage as possible. The staff of Rycote House knew why his lordship had hastened to the family's Herefordshire estate, so Lucy's sudden decision to follow was not unexpected.

"Do not fret, Miss Lucy, there's none here to stick a thistle under a saddle, and Albert says you have a fine seat when it comes to Misty."

"I might have to risk Pepper," she grumbled gloomily. Alice

chuckled and patted Lucy's shoulder in a motherly fashion.

"I daresay you will be fine if needs must. Albert would not let you ride a horse he did not think you could control."

"I did not do too good a job when Misty bolted," Lucy countered. A displeasing thought struck her. How *could* James have been so solicitous the day she was nearly thrown, when he was the cause. The man was without compunction. "Is there anything else I should include?" she asked, as Alice tucked the last item in the small valise.

"I think you should be able to manage with what we have packed, miss," the maid assured her.

"Good. If anyone needs me, I shall be with Albert." Whirling out of her bedchamber and down the stairs — with little regard for decorum — to the mews at the rear of Rycote House, finding Albert and Tip, one of the stable boys, mucking out the horses.

The aroma of fresh straw and warm animals assailed Lucy's nostrils when she opened the door. "Albert, might I beg a moment of your time?" she called from where she stood, unwilling to chance stepping in something unsavoury, should she walk through the stables. The affable groom rested his vicious-looking pitchfork against the wall and scuffed through the straw towards her.

"'Ow can I 'elp yer, miss?" he asked.

"Do you think me capable of riding Pepper, or should I stay with Misty?" she appealed, twisting her fingers together anxiously. "I do not want to be the one to impede Lord Blackthorne and Major Lucas if I was to ride Misty, neither do I want to ride a horse for three days that I could not master if anything... errr... were to spook her."

"As long as you act confident, like, Pepper will follow your lead, not the other way around."

"But she's so big."

"She is huge, I'll grant you, and she takes careful 'andlin', but I reckon as you can manage 'er, miss. 'Ow about you take a turn on her now. I can have her saddled in a trice."

Lucy agreed, and fifteen minutes later was trotting around the park quite competently. An hour after that, Albert declared himself satisfied she was able to manage Pepper.

"You were able to rein in Misty when she were in agony, me dear. After that, most mounts would seem calm."

Reassured, Lucy left Pepper in Albert's capable hands and confirmed they would be leaving first thing on the morrow.

Chapter Thirty One

The following morning, just as London was suffused in the pale pink glow of dawn — the soft pearlescence turning even the most downtrodden neighbourhood into something unexpectedly arresting to the eye — three riders set out, bags strapped to their saddles.

Riding along roads recently swept, they chatted about this and that — the journey mostly, occasionally calling a hello to a passing merchant, or one of the lamplighters on his rounds, dousing the lights on those streets lucky enough to sport them. Lucy was fascinated. Although an early riser, she had yet to witness the bustle in the more fashionable areas of London as they awoke to a new day. Maids scrubbing front steps, traders ready to ply their wares to the more discerning households, chimney sweeps balancing all manner of brushes and poles on bikes of questionable stability; so many people.

Without knowing them personally, they were familiar to Lucy. These were the people she grew up among, goodness — she had probably rubbed shoulders with some of them, but she was no longer *one* of them and that strange impression of being disconnected nudged at her subconscious. Then William caught her eye, and smiled with such devotion, the sentiment vanished with the last of the night, and she turned her concentration to staying on her horse.

It took a little while to reach the outskirts of the city, they had to manoeuvre around a surprising amount of traffic to say it was barely six o'clock. Soon, however, they were in open countryside, and Lucas asked whether Lucy felt able to increase her pace. Nodding, and swallowing her apprehension, Lucy pressed her knees to Pepper's flank and the horse rose from a sedate trot to a steady canter. With the blessing of Albert, Lucy had eschewed the typical side-saddle for women, which after the incident with Misty, she thought ridiculous in the extreme, and was sitting astride, her skirts artfully arranged to conceal the fact. It gave her much better control of the creature and she felt quite at home with the rhythmic cadence of the mare. Alice had been heard to mutter, 'Lawks, but the master will have something to say,' when she saw the unorthodox style her new mistress had adopted, but as Lucy was anything but conventional, the young maid had to admit she was not unduly surprised.

It flummoxed Lucy how any woman managed to keep her seat, riding side-saddle, especially at speed, although perhaps the women of the *ton* were not prone to such a fast pace, preferring a more genteel gait. She was pleased that she was able to keep up with the two men, never for one second thinking they were the ones matching her pace.

*****

They broke their journey every couple of hours. This served a triple purpose, the first being that Lucy was able to stretch muscles she did not know she had; the second, allowed them to take refreshments and avail themselves of the privy at the coaching house, and the third, gave the horses a well-earned rest, a chance to quench their thirst and dip their heads into a tasty nosebag. By nightfall they were well on their way, repeating the pattern over the next two days, arriving at the enormous wrought iron gates marking the boundary of Gillingham Park in the late afternoon, three days after leaving London.

Lucy, unused to riding, wondered whether she would ever walk properly again. Her poor muscles rebelled every time she tried to ease the knots in them, and her skin was chafed from long hours in the saddle. Assuring her it was an essential addition to her luggage, Albert had given her a small pot of ointment the evening prior to their departure, which she applied lavishly every time they stopped, silently praising the groom to the heavens and back. Despite her discomfort, she had not complained once, and although both William and Lucas guessed, they made no mention, allowing her the dignity of silence, impressed with her stoic determination not to slow them down.

"This is it?" she asked as they reined in their horses.

"This is it," William affirmed, dismounting to open the gates. In the centre of each gate two gilt letters were intertwined — a G and P — evoking for Lucy, heroic tales of gallant knights and their castles in the books she borrowed from The Wise Owl. The intricate lettering would be splendid on a shield, or a standard. Once they were through the gates, William closed them, and swung back up on his mare, the horses' hooves crunched on the gravel, now the only sound, even conversation had dwindled. The drive curved slightly and, as they rounded the bend, the estate unfolded before them. Lucy could not contain her gasp. It was magnificent.

To her right, an extensive, yet graceful, building nestled in a dip, which — along with the dark green forest on the hill behind — offered a modicum of shelter from inclement weather. Built from the warm, yellowish-grey, local stone, Gillingham Park's elegant facade was punctuated by dozens of mullioned windows each reflecting the sky. Spread out in front of her, as though drawn by an artist's hand, neatly manicured gardens, not a blossom or a leaf out of place. The abundance of flowers filled the air with a faintly exotic scent. So many colours and varieties, Lucy longed to wander through them, to admire the dainty petals and bury her nose in the fragrant blooms. Surrounding the formal gardens and away to her left, swathes of less tamed land. *This must be the great park of which people speak* she thought, *one could get lost in the wilds… what an exhilarating idea.* She turned to say something to William, then stopped, feeling warmth flush up her cheeks, remembering they were not alone.

William glanced across at her. The waning heat of the day

had created a haze, softening the late afternoon sun, wreathing Lucy in an almost otherworldly aura. One or two strands of hair had escaped the confines of her detested hat, to be caught by the breeze. Her eyes were shining, and her eager smile was full of anticipation. William sucked in a breath… *dear lord, but she was exquisite.* Before he made a fool of himself and hauled her from the saddle to make love to her in the lush grass, he said,

"Quite impressive, isn't it?" His mundane understatement proving an adequate diversion. Having taken their fill of the view, they trotted towards the main house where it became obvious their arrival had been noted. As they approached, uniformed figures appeared from every direction. Grooms to tend to the horses, maids to assist Lucy, and footmen for William and Lucas. The front door opened, and three people came out, one of whom could not curb her excitement and, hitching her skirts, flew down the steps and across the crescent-shaped frontage to the new arrivals.

"Lucy, Lucy oh how wonderful. I cannot believe you are here, I have missed you so much." Elspeth was virtually jumping up and down in her enthusiasm.

Lucy grinned and responded in kind. Unsure quite how she was going to dismount without it being obvious she was in pain she fidgeted in her seat. "I cannot get off Pepper here, Elspeth. I need a set of steps."

"A moment and I shall assist you," William called, as he slid off Gipsy with all the skill of a seasoned rider. Coming to where Pepper was stamping impatiently, he patted the horse's neck then reached up and said, "Trust me, I will not allow you to fall."

Lucy stared at him dubiously but did as instructed. Placing her hands on his broad shoulders, she felt herself being lifted down as though she weighed nothing more than a child.

"Thank you," she whispered as he stood her on her feet and held her for a moment until she regained her balance.

"My pleasure." He leaned down and brushed his lips to hers,

even so slight a contact sending a quiver down her spine and reminding her of *that* night in his library. She blushed again and dipped her head.

"Come on." Elspeth took her hand, effectively breaking the moment. She was about to drag her sister to the house when Lucy implored in frantic undertones.

"Elspeth, slowly, please."

Turning, Elspeth noticed Lucy was walking with an almost comical bearing, a kind of unsteady teeter. It took her seconds to work out what was wrong with her sister, and when it dawned on her, burst out laughing, her merriment echoing off the walls. "I expect you are rather stiff from all that riding?" she posited. "A hot bath and a proper sleep will help alleviate the soreness, but you might wish to consider returning to London by coach." Amusement still playing around her mouth.

"Shush," Lucy hissed. "The whole world doesn't need to know. Just take it steady and I will be fine." Pulling on all her reserves, Lucy straightened her back and made a credible attempt to look composed while they walked to the front door. Her effort totally ruined when Christopher gathered his older daughter in his arms to crush her in a bear hug. Unable to prevent an agonised squawk, she had to admit how difficult it was to put one foot in front of the other and was immediately dispatched up to her bedchamber where a bath was already being drawn.

"I must say hello to our hosts, your mother and..." she started, then stopped. His father must have died otherwise he wouldn't be the earl and she had no mind to remind him of his loss, even if it be long ago.

"They can wait, I expect you will feel more sociable after a warm soak." Christopher waved her off with Elspeth. Lucy gave in, submitting to assistance provided by the Gillingham Park staff.

Meanwhile, Lucas and William after being introduced to Lady Rycote, and thanking her for their welcome, unexpected though it might be, greeted the others whom they already knew, then asked whether they might have a private moment with his lordship.

Lady Rycote had no objections and informed them light refreshments would be served as soon as Miss Truscott joined them.

Following Christopher into the cavernous study, William was quiet, stunned by the likeness between Lucy and her paternal grandmother despite the age difference. It was uncanny and a tad unnerving.

"What happened?" Christopher wasted no time with pleasantries. Lucas provided a concise account of what they had discovered, adding that Lucy had received a letter from Elspeth, which mentioned the inexplicable disappearance of James and Edward.

Christopher, perching on the edge of the desk, rubbed his chin thoughtfully, trying to make sense of this new information. "They returned the next afternoon, a bit bruised and battered, but otherwise unharmed. Any mail to send would have been collected that morning." He paused. "So, 'tis not Edward but James who is behind this?"

The two younger men nodded. "'Tis all but incontrovertible," Lucas added. "When Lucy gave me Elspeth's letter, my first thought was that James was setting Edward up, that he would come back here alone and point the finger at Edward for what happened, increasing our suspicion that Edward is the perpetrator for everything."

"That is not far from the truth," Christopher said, "Edward has not spoken since their return. I have spent several hours with him over the last few days, but to date, he has neither refuted nor conceded James' accusation that while they were exploring the estate they fell into a discussion, which deteriorated into an argument. Edward goaded James until they came to blows. Edward is currently under guard in one of the rooms in the east wing. We deemed it sensible to separate him for his own good. Rodney wants him strung up. Good job I didn't let him." With a rather macabre attempt at humour. "Dammit all to hell, how do we let this play out?"

"I think we must leave things as they are. We do not want James to know, so keep this between ourselves. If we tell the others it may affect the way they behave in front of James and that would tip our hand. I shall make it clear I am to conduct an interview with Edward. As an investigator for the crown it would be expected." Another thought dropped into Lucas' head. "Has James said anything about travelling?"

Christopher shook his head. "Not that I am aware. He has been his usually affable self. Oh, I did so hope it was a random stranger, even a disgruntled ex-employee or someone I had inadvertently thwarted. That it is a man whom I have treated as one of my family galls me." His expression darkening as his fury mounted.

"You must conquer your anger, my lord, at least for a little while. We are so close."

Christopher knew Lucas was correct and he strode about the room thumping his fist into his palm, for a minute or so. "This needs to be over. See to it, man," he barked at Lucas who nodded in acknowledgement. Christopher rang for a footman, whom he instructed to escort the major to Mr Lindsay's rooms.

Chapter Thirty Two

Lucas did not reveal the details of his interview with Edward but took pains to applaud James for his quick action, saying that he hoped he hadn't suffered unduly as a result of the violent exchange. James assured the major he was fine, just sore.

The early part of the evening saw the first meeting between Lady Rycote and Lucy Truscott.

Dressed in her only other gown, her riding habit removed for cleaning, Lucy was nervous about meeting the woman whom she so closely resembled. Her dress was of soft grey and shimmered blue when she moved, the mercurial colour almost matching her eyes. She came into the library, clutching Elspeth's hand, striving for equanimity, and failing dismally, her reticence, palpable.

Lady Rycote was sitting in a high-backed chair. More than seventy years old, she still held herself ramrod straight, and although her hair was snowy white and her face not as smooth as once it was, her eyes still twinkled, and they were the exact same shade as Lucy's.

"Come closer, my dear, let me see you, my eyes are not what they used to be."

Lucy inched forward, as slowly as she dared.

"She does not bite, Lucy." Christopher chuckled, watching his daughter, oddly proud he was able to introduce her to his mother.

"She might," mumbled Lucy when she passed him. Reaching the dowager countess, Lucy sank a perfect curtsy and then stood like a criminal awaiting the order for execution.

"Why, my dear, you are quite beautiful." Lady Rycote stretched out a hand. Lucy, unclear as to what to do now, grasped it and was drawn to the countess' side. "You are

Cecilia's daughter?" Lucy nodded. "That poor woman, left to bring up a child on her own because my husband refused to overturn a gentleman's agreement."

Lucy's head shot up. "You knew of Mama's... errr... entanglement?"

"Of course, everyone knew, but such things were never discussed, it is not done."

"They should be," Lucy muttered.

"Maybe so, but whether they should or not is moot. We cannot turn back the clock, and I would not be without Elspeth." Smiling at her other granddaughter who beamed back happily. "I would like to hear about your mama and your childhood. Mayhap tomorrow you could sit with me and we can talk?"

"I suppose," Lucy replied, a little confused as to why this elderly woman wanted to dredge up a past of which, until recently, she had been blessedly ignorant.

Lady Rycote, reading her thoughts, patted Lucy's hand. "You are my granddaughter, Lucy, and the image of me at your age. I have missed out on nearly three and twenty years of your life and have no mind to miss out on any more." She paused. "That is for tomorrow, tonight we enjoy a meal and some light-hearted conversation. No business talk, Christopher." She pinned her firstborn with a gimlet gaze. Lucy's father raised his palms in acquiescence, "we have three weary travellers, who are no doubt more interested in a good night's sleep than a large meal and weighty conversation. Lucy, you shall sit beside me at dinner, I want to hear all about your William."

Lucy gurgled with laughter at William's shocked expression. "How did you know he is my William, my lady?" she asked grinning at her betrothed.

"Why your father told me. Moreover, I see how he watches you, he knows where you are at all times, and his gaze rarely leaves you."

Lucy blushed, then lifted her eyes to William who, although

perhaps slightly red in cheek, smiled slightly and inclined his head.

"You see." Her grandmother nudged her. Lucy took a chance and twisting her head, whispered in the old lady's ear.

"We are betrothed but have not told Papa. William asked for my hand just before we left London."

"Duly noted. Your secret is safe with me," the dowager countess replied *sotto voce.*

Any further comments were cut off because, just then, a footman announced dinner was served in the dining room.

The meal was sumptuous, as befitted so grand an estate, and comfortable conversation flowed around the table. Later, while the men were smoking cigars and sipping fine whisky, William informed Christopher he had asked Lucy to marry him and she had said yes.

"I apologise for not approaching you first, but I think you knew my intentions. Moreover, I get the feeling Lucy would not have been best pleased had I petitioned you prior to asking her." Grinning at the earl's wry nod. "Neither of us wants a big wedding, Rycote, just family and one or two close friends will suffice. I have a plan and would appreciate your help implementing it." He explained what he wanted to do, delighted when the earl clapped him on the back, then shook his hand.

"You will make Lucy a fine husband. Very glad, very glad. I must congratulate Lucy."

The rest of the evening passed in good cheer. Lucy — who was heard to murmur to Lady Rycote, 'so much for keeping it secret' — and William were congratulated on their betrothal and everyone declared themselves delighted for the couple. As glasses were being topped up to salute the couple, Lucy, her spine prickling, caught a strange expression on James' face and in that moment knew, what they had hoped to be a mistake — was not.

The next day Lucy and Elspeth spent time with their grandmother, sharing anecdotes of their lives, and in the afternoon the sisters enjoyed a long walk around the gardens, Elspeth acting as tour guide. The men closeted themselves away in the study apparently in discussion regarding Edward. By evening the atmosphere was tense. Lady Rycote, aware of what had been happening, but preferring not to become involved, retired to her rooms immediately after dinner, while the others chose to have a drink in the library. James excused himself shortly thereafter, and although Lucas itched to go after him, managed to keep his seat.

Lucy, still tired after their journey and a little sad after talking about her mother, was tempted to follow her grandmother's example, but hoped to contrive a few moments alone with William. She needed to feel his arms around her and the touch of his lips — even if that was a simple kiss on her cheek. Glancing across to where he was sitting, she relished observing him in the flickering light shed by the numerous candelabras, while he chatted with Rodney. She was seated to his right, his injured side, and as she studied him, she was reminded of the fact it was this scar, from the first moment they met, that had drawn her to him. While so many had been repelled by, were even afraid of, his deformity, to Lucy it gave him a mysterious quality, like a story not yet read. The thrill of opening the cover, of smoothing your fingers over the flyleaf, of reading the title, to that magical moment just before you turn the first page and let the words consume you. Yes, William was like a book, one she could not wait to get lost in.

A smile tugged at her mouth and she was about to reach out to run her fingers up his sleeve when the door opened and James returned, carrying a tray.

"I met Bennet at the bottom of the stairs, he was bringing these and I said I would save him the bother." Placing the tray on the desk and handing out cups of steaming hot chocolate.

"Thank you, James, very thoughtful," Christopher remarked, blowing over the top of the cup to cool the drink before taking a sip. "Mmmm, nothing nicer at the end of a busy day." He raised his cup in a toast and took another swallow. The others followed suit, resuming their various conversations, but when Lucy tasted hers, she thought it might benefit from a little extra sugar.

"Is there a sugar bowl on the tray?" she enquired, the peculiar taste making her crinkle her nose.

"What's wrong, Lucy?" William asked, his cup hovering near his lips.

"The chocolate needs sweetening," she replied, watching William gulp another mouthful. She walked over to the desk spying the sugar bowl on the tray. Helping herself to a generous measure, she stirred it in, then took another sip. It was still bitter. Disinclined to drink anymore, Lucy leaned against the desk, and enjoyed the warmth of the cup between her fingers, while watching the others chat.

The ambience of the room, the glow from the fire, and the rumble of men's voices as they talked was soporific and Lucy felt quite sleepy. Time for bed. She turned to replace her cup on the tray, only to notice the desk seemed to be melting. *That couldn't be right.* "William…" she tried to move but her feet felt as though they were stuck to the floor, a floor which was, incomprehensibly, undulating. Something was awry. She wanted to giggle at so gross an understatement, but it was too much effort. By sheer force of will, she dragged her gaze to James who was perched on a window ledge, arms folded, watching, expressionless. *Oh God, what has he done?* "Jam…" she planted a hand flat on the surface of the desk to steady herself, as the room began to spin. "Oh God," she repeated, this time out loud, her words slurring, as she pitched forward — she tried to break her fall, but her arms refused to do her bidding.

She heard a snort of laughter.

Then nothing.

*****

Her head was pounding, her face hurt, and her mouth felt like it was stuffed full of straw. Peeling her eyes open, Lucy registered that it was dark and cold. *Was she in bed?* It did not feel particularly comfortable and she could not feel the warmth of blankets. She was in a half-reclining position, and aware of an unaccustomed heaviness across her legs but when she tried to rid herself if it, the sudden movement made her stomach roil. She sucked in a steadying breath to combat threatening nausea, to no avail. She was violently sick. The bout passed and, mortified she was probably now covered in her own vomit, again tried to sit up, but it was too hard. Panting a little, Lucy closed her eyes, it was easier to go back to sleep.

The next time she awoke the room was a little less black. Maybe it was dawn. She ached all over, and her recollection of the previous night was hazy. Frowning, she tried to determine why this should be. Surely, she had not overindulged? Not in someone else's home. Lucy thought she had only drunk two glasses of wine, one with dinner, and another when everyone was toasting her betrothal. So why was she so befuddled? Running her tongue around her mouth which was dry as dust, she had a sudden memory of unsweetened hot chocolate which prompted a recurrence of her earlier sickness. This time she managed to quell it, breathing slowly until the sensation dissipated.

Cautiously shifting until she was in a more upright position, Lucy narrowed her eyes and peered into the gloom. She could not see much beyond her feet but that was more than she had been able to do when she awoke the first time, however long ago that was. The room was frigid, and she was shivering, belatedly registering that her clothes were wet and clinging to her. An ice-cold finger trailed down her spine, nothing to do with her current surroundings or sodden gown. This was bad, this was very, very bad.

Swallowing the urge to scream, Lucy decided it would be a good idea *not* to be here, wherever here was, a moment longer and made to get up off the floor. The weight which prevented her from moving earlier, rolled off, the action adding to her disquiet. Twisting around, she stretched out a hand until she came into contact with something solid. Smothering a yelp, she shuffled until she could use both hands and felt along what became clear was a body and they were wearing a jacket. It was a man, but who, and was he alive or dead?

Unable to stop an anguished moan spilling over her lips, Lucy continued, coming to a shoulder and then a face. As her fingers traced the skin, she heaved a sigh of relief, it wasn't William. *Thank God. So, who was it?* Finding the pulse in his neck, she pressed her fingertips against it. It was rapid and a bit thready, but it was there. He was alive, but for how long? Shaking the shoulder firmly for several seconds, she was gratified, when she finally heard a grumble.

"Wake up, please wake up. We cannot stay here, we shall catch our deaths." Lucy begged. He did not respond, so she shook him harder and then began to beat him with her fists, battering his arm and his chest. "Wake up. You *must* wake up. I am not going to die here. I have a wedding to plan."

"Hell's teeth, Miss Truscott, are you always so demanding?"

She knew that voice, weak though it was. "*Edward?*"

"I believe so, although the way I feel right now, there is a distinct possibility I am mistaken." A tinge of humour in his tone.

"Are you injured?"

"My ankle hurts like the dickens."

She sensed movement, then heard a long groan when he sat up.

"Where the devil are we?"

"I do not have the slightest idea. It is dark, cold and wet. There is some light that way." Lucy pointed then giggled realising Edward could not see her hand. "Sorry, it comes from behind you." She elaborated. More shuffling, then.

"I see it. Are we in a tunnel?"

"I do not think so." Lucy replied. "The light source is too high, and I expect if it was a tunnel, we could see light at both ends?"

"True enough. Please help me up. I am taller than you, mayhap I can see what you cannot."

Lucy ignored her aching muscles and stood. After fumbling in the dark for several seconds, she caught Edward's hand. Clasping his arm, she braced herself.

"Ready?"

"Yes."

She heaved and heard Edward's grunt of pain, as he steadied himself by resting his free hand on her shoulder. "Damnation, that tickles." He bit out. Frustrated at not being able to see much of anything, all Lucy could do was wait.

"Do you see anything?" she quizzed. The deathly silence bothered her more than she cared to admit so, accepting it was undoubtedly a wasted effort, tried to distract herself by scooping palmfuls of water to rinse the front of her dress. It did the trick.

"My best guess is that we are in the disused ice-house."

"We are where?" Lucy squeaked.

Edward repeated it, adding, "We just have to hope someone finds us, before this water gets too high.

"What do you mean?" Her sense of foreboding increased.

"I mean, if this was the working icehouse we would be balancing on blocks of ice and could probably climb out without assistance, as it would be almost full so early in the summer. I have to assume this is a disused one. Firstly, it is empty of ice and secondly, the water is not draining away. Ice houses are built near water courses, like a lake or a stream, so any meltwater can flow out through a channel. I daresay this one was abandoned because it was built too close or too far from either. Given that we are standing in water, my guess is that the stream which the meltwater drained into is too close. Maybe at some point the course of the stream shifted, and the water started to run into the icehouse instead of around it."

Lucy didn't fully comprehend the technical details, but she *did* understand their prospects of survival decreased the longer they were trapped. "Surely, even if unused, the water will eventually drain away?"

"Only if it has somewhere to go. We had torrential rain last week; the lake is full, as are the streams which feed it. If the base of this icehouse is lower than the bottom of the lake, the water will back up into it."

"Bloody hell," she ground out. "We are in a pickle."

Chapter Thirty Three

In the library, three peers of the realm and a major, were awoken just after dawn when Tess, one of the maids, came into the library to lay the fire and tidy the room. Having flung back the curtains, she turned to attend to her tasks and spied the four sprawled in their respective chairs. Her shocked yelp disturbed William, who opened his eyes, squinting against the light from the windows.

"What the he—?" he bit off the expletive in deference to the young girl and tried to stand. His body protesting after being in so awkward a position for hours. "Rycote," he barked.

His soon-to-be father-in-law groaned. "Keep your voice down, I have the devil of a headache." There was silence then. "Wait… why are you in my bedchamber?"

"I am not, we are in the library. Rodney, Lucas," William raised his voice as much as he was able, the hammering in his skull reaching epic proportions. "How much did we drink last night?"

"Not enough to cause this hangover." Christopher groused. "You'd think my daughters would have called someone to escort us to bed. Thoughtless girls."

Seeing Lucas was waking, William ignored him and staggered to where Rodney was spread-eagled on the chaise and shook him. "Come on, Westbrook go find your bed for the rest of the night. Ugh, my mouth tastes like a Turkish brothel."

"How in the hell do you know what a Turkish brothel *tastes* like?" Christopher quizzed blearily. "And if you have ever frequented one, you are not marrying my daughter."

"I don't. It was a figure of speech. Suffice it to say I feel as though I have been flattened by a carriage and eaten dung. A Turkish brothel sounded less disgusting."

Christopher could not quash his mirth. "No, don't make me laugh, it hurts." He glanced blearily around the room his gaze settling on the maid. "Tess, were we the only four in here?"

Tess nodded. "Yes, my lord."

"Where is Mr Garrick?"

Tess shook her head. "I expect he went to bed, my lord."

"Hmmm, maybe." The earl pondered that for a moment. "Ask Bennet to check for me would you? Oh, and please look in on Lady Elspeth and Miss Truscott. Do not disturb them if they are asleep. I just need to know they are safely in their beds."

"Rycote?" William spoke in uneasy tones.

"Something is not right, Blackthorne. Something is not right at all." By this time both Lucas and Rodney had finally roused, the latter was running his fingers through his hair, making it look as though he had been dragged through a hedge backwards.

"What's going on? Why did we sleep in the library?" his voice, scratchy.

"Not sure, however, I do not think it was out of choice." Christopher walked over to the desk and picked up one of the tall glasses, seeing the dregs of chocolate coating the bottom. Tilting it, and sniffing suspiciously, he jerked his head away. "Ugh, laudanum." Closing his eyes until the room stopped spinning

"No wonder Lucy wanted more sugar. How did we not recognise it tasted peculiar?" William interjected.

"Probably, because we drank more alcohol than she. I think Lucy only had two small glasses of wine, we had rather more as well as a couple of shots of whisky. Maybe our sense of taste was dulled."

"Surely James would not stoop to poisoning us?" Rodney asked, only mildly perturbed.

"I imagine he is desperate and, at this point, I would put nothing past him." Lucas countered. "I need to speak to Edward." He reeled away in the manner reminiscent of a sailor just on dry land after months at sea. "Damn, but I cannot walk in straight line," he complained, using the furniture to balance. The door opened as he reached it, and Tess dashed in, Bennet on her heels.

"They're not there, my lord, either of them." Clearly panicked.

"Mr Garrick is not in his chamber, my lord," Bennet intoned, "and, after what happened last week, I took the liberty of checking on Mr Lindsay. He is not in his suite. The door is ajar."

"Thank you, Bennet. While breakfast is prepared, please arrange for all who can be spared to search the house. Every room, every cupboard, every alcove, even the domestic quarters. Malice is afoot and we need to stop this before it is too late.

*****

Miles from Gillingham Park, Elspeth regained consciousness to the sensation of being jostled violently.

"Stop it. Just stop it," she moaned, as the rattling of wheels penetrated the wooziness clogging her mind. She was in a speeding carriage. *How on earth…?*

"We must get to the docks, my darling. The ship leaves on the tide four days hence. We must not tarry.

My darling? Who was calling her my darling? It did not sound like Rodney. Elspeth groaned again, trying to banish the sluggishness engulfing her. Her limbs felt too heavy to move, but her brain told her she needed them to. "Where am I?" she mumbled.

"On the London road," the voice answered, brightly, as though that explained everything.

"But I was at Grandmama's," she said, confused.

"Yes, your ploy fooled me for a while, Scotland indeed, but I soon caught on to your ruse? Why did you not tell me you were coming here?" In faint rebuke.

Elspeth struggled to manoeuvre herself into a sitting position, feeling an arm come around her and lift her upright. Blinking in the dim light of the interior, her eyes began to focus on the person speaking to her. She got such a shock she nearly fell off the bench, only the hand gripping her arm prevented it.

"*James?*" Her horrified tones rang around the carriage.

"Why so surprised, my love? You surely did not expect me to dally once I knew you were here? I was just waiting for the opportune moment, to whisk you away. So many people determined to keep us apart, first Westbrook, then that busybody, Lucy, *tsk*. Why you did not listen to her that day, and let her walk out of your life, I shall never know. Thankfully, she is no longer a bother. I tried to warn them off, but either I was too subtle, or they were too stupid to get the message. Witless idiots the lot of them. No matter, the only effect their interference had was to delay the inevitable."

Elspeth, her poor head whirling, tried to make sense of what James was telling her.

"It was *you?*" she gasped. "*You* pushed me in front of the carriage? *You* shot at Lucy? *You* stuffed the thistle under Misty's saddle? You were behind *all* those bizarre incidents?" He nodded. "I thought I was going mad, that I was imagining things, at least I did until you made the mistake of firing a gun at my sister." She glared at him, her anger eradicating the last of her disorientation. "What about Edward? We thought it was him. Wait... what do you mean Lucy is no longer a bother? James, what have you done?" Her voice dropped to a whisper. "If you have harmed one hair on her head, I will never forgive you."

"Do not fret, my dearest Elspeth. I daresay someone will find her. As for Edward, he is an abomination. We have a ship to meet." He reached out to stroke her cheek, and it was all Elspeth could do not to bite his hand. A shudder ran through her as another question popped into her head.

"Ship? What ship? Where are you taking me?"

"The East Indies, my darling. I have secured passage on a merchant vessel departing the Pool of London at week's end. We cannot dawdle."

Even in the gloom of the carriage, Elspeth detected the faraway look in his eyes. Notwithstanding whatever else was going on, there was *no* way she was spending months on board a ship. Knowing she had little time to act, she thought quickly.

"James, I cannot go to the Indies. What about my clothes? I understand the voyage takes months. How do you expect me to travel without suitable luggage? You cannot expect me to wear this dress for months on end? No, no, no, this is not good at all. We must call at Rycote House on the way to the docks. Alice will pack my belongings in the blink of an eye. No!" She raised an imperious palm when James tried to speak. "Let me think. Are we to be wed on board?" She held his gaze and although he looked bemused at her abrupt change of heart, accepted it, nodding sheepishly, "and you were not going to tell me that? *Tsk*! I cannot be married in any old gown. I need something special, now…" she began muttering about gowns and shoes and for all the world looked to be mentally perusing her wardrobe. In reality, she was trying to think of how she could jump out of a moving carriage without breaking every bone in her body only to have James jump out after her, lift her back in, and continue on regardless.

Out of the blue, she recalled Lucy's lessons before she left London and her sister's plea that she practice, even at Gillingham Park. Did she dare? In the pretence of stretching her tired body, she flexed her arms and legs, then yawned and leaned against James' shoulder. As she anticipated, his arm came around her hugging her to him. She swallowed her abhorrence and relaxed.

"I'm so sleepy, James, wake me when we reach the coaching inn."

"Shut your eyes, my darling. You are safe with me."

Elspeth's mind was as busy as her body was frozen. Coming up with and discarding escape scenarios, in the end, she realised she would just have to chance it. In the guise of getting more comfortable, she turned into James until her head was nestled under his chin, one arm tucked between the seat and his back, the other loosely draped across the top of his thighs.

She could feel how her touch affected him and a wicked imp within encouraged her to sigh heavily and slide her arm a little higher as though simply moving in her sleep. Her gesture was rewarded, when she heard him suck in his breath and shift slightly. Counting to ten, she paused, drew a long slow breath, then using the back of the seat as a brace propelled herself across the small gap between the seats, spinning on her heel and bunching her fist threw a creditable punch to his jaw. Stunned and roaring his fury, James bolted to his feet, reaching for her, and that was all Elspeth needed.

Recalling her lessons, she seemed to crouch, then before he had time to comprehend her next move, straightened, and with considerable force, rammed one of her knees into James' groin. She heard a wheezing sound as he toppled forward, utterly incapacitated.

Leaning her head out of the window, Elspeth recognised Robbie, one of the grooms, and shrieked at him to stop the coach. Robbie glanced down, his mouth falling open in surprise when he saw Lady Elspeth, looking decidedly harried, shouting up at him. *How had* she *got in the carriage?* He reined in the horses with alacrity, and the coach slowed.

"Robbie, help me," she pleaded when the groom opened the door to help her down. "Mr Garrick was kidnapping me. He wanted to take me to the East Indies. I have never heard such nonsense. Do you have any rope?" At the groom's nod, she instructed him to secure Mr Garrick in a manner that offered no possible chance of escape. Once satisfied James could not untie his bonds, she stuffed his kerchief in his mouth for good measure. James himself was still dazed, prompting Robbie to ask what had happened.

Fright loosened Elspeth's tongue, and she gabbled somewhat incomprehensibly about what she knew. "And we must get back to Gillingham Park, I fear for what he might have done to Lucy."

Robbie turned the carriage and they were on their way home in a flash. Elspeth elected to sit up with the groom; the fresh air and the gentle hues of the early morning, allaying her panic somewhat. Here and there, pockets of mist — scattered with miniature iridescent rainbows — hung like gossamer blankets, fading as the sun rose. The countryside near Gillingham Park was breathtaking. That Mr James Garrick expected her to leave this for some hot dusty foreign country, astounded Elspeth.

It was mid-morning by the time they reached the gates, whereupon Elspeth heaved a sigh of relief. They trundled up the driveway, coming upon a scene of organised chaos. People milled about everywhere and when the carriage was spotted, a shout went up.

A veritable stream of people ran towards them, led by Rodney whose white face was etched with worry lines she had not seen before. He was up on the driver's seat before the carriage had even come to a complete halt. Uncaring how inappropriate it was his hands searched her, checking for injuries, while he kissed her forehead, her cheeks, her lips, making Elspeth giggle in spite of the gravity of the situation.

"Rodney, I am unharmed, although I am quite desperate for a glass of water," she assured him, delighting in his attentiveness.

"I thought you..." he stopped unable to articulate what he thought.

"James is trussed up inside." She flicked her hand at the door through which muffled roars could be heard. Rodney gaped at her, as two more men skidded to a halt in front of the carriage.

"Is Lucy with you?" William spoke with a calm he was far from feeling.

The faces of all three fell at Elspeth's decisive,

"No!"

Chapter Thirty Four

Not so very far from all the commotion, Lucy and Edward were trying to come up with a way to climb out of the icehouse. The ladder, typically propped up against the wall under the arch through which the ice was deposited, was nowhere to be seen, probably in use at the new icehouse. As the day dawned, the darkness in the cavernous space lightened to a grey gloom. It was still difficult to see, but better than the pitch-black of night. Lucy proposed she crawl along the drainage channel then go and get help — a plan immediately rejected by Edward.

"Firstly, while I admire your enthusiasm, these conduits are very narrow, you would probably get stuck fast. Secondly, if the water is already filling up in here, there must be blockages along the channel; leaves and twigs forming a sort of barrier. Even if perchance it was wide enough for a human to crawl through, you do not know how far it is to the other end, or whether, if the water filled the cavity, you can hold your breath until you find an air pocket. I will not have you drown under my watch, Lucy Truscott."

She grinned, "I am so sorry, Edward."

"What for?"

"For ever suspecting you. Although you did seem the most likely. There were several instances when I caught you glaring at Elspeth as though you wanted to harm her. What did she do to warrant such hatred?"

"Elspeth? I do not hate Elspeth, or wish her harm, what gave you that idea?"

Lucy told him about the times she caught him studying her sister. Edward frowned, obviously perplexed. Lucy could see him ruminating over what she said, then it came to him.

"It was not Lucy I was glaring at, but Garrick."

"Huh?" Lucy cocked her head and peered at him through the obscurity.

"I already had my own theory about who was behind the campaign of curious incidents, but I could not for the life of me work out why. Elspeth has been like a sister to me, I would never hurt her. I knew you were beginning to have misgivings about me, and it was easier to let them develop, that way I could garner my own evidence against James. I confess I did not think he would stoop so low as to shoot at you or accompany you on a horse ride he had already sabotaged. He is brazen, that is for sure."

"Is *that* why you offered to come here before the others?" she asked, light dawning.

"It seemed the only way to get one step ahead of him. To be here, to be prepared before he arrived, and look how well that turned out." Edward said ruefully.

"I still believe he was only trying to scare me off, to get me to run back to my attic room away from the Gillinghams. The day he shot at us, he could easily have killed either William or me, but he didn't. We just need to know why."

"I think I might have figured it out." Edward offered, going on to explain about James' unhealthy obsession with Elspeth as well as his preoccupation with acquiring status. "I believe his ultimate goal is being recognised, being acknowledged as somebody, by the *ton*, and regrettably, I think he will use any means at his disposal to gain the latter," he concluded.

"The man is deranged if he thinks Elspeth will fall out of love with Rodney and into love with him, just because he wants her to, or to help him achieve his aim."

"I never said he was of sound mind, as you and I being here attests."

Lucy could hear amusement in Edward's voice. "We are not dissimilar you and I," she mused.

"How's that?"

"I am trying to find my place in a world where I do not belong, among people who judge me without ever knowing me. I imagine 'tis the same for you." There was a long silence, then she heard a resigned sigh.

"What did Serena tell you?"

"Not much. 'Tis clear how deeply she cares for you. I am sorry Edward. I wish it could be different."

"Me too, but it is what is it."

"And that still doesn't help us get out of here." Her practical tones alleviating an atmosphere becoming pensive. "Would you be strong enough for me to stand on your shoulders? I do not want to cause further damage to your ankle, but it might be our only option. Maybe I could reach the access shelf?"

"Hmmm… it is certainly worth a try." Edward hobbled until he was under the narrow shaft of light which illuminated the bricks at the lip of the pit. "Oh, for a candle," he grumbled. "Lucy, if you put one foot on my clasped hands, I will hoist you up. Then, using the wall to balance, climb onto my shoulders."

Lucy did as she was bid. Edward bent forward, allowing her to place one foot on his interlinked fingers. With no small amount of apprehension, Lucy let him lift her. She scrabbled at the bricks in the wall, finding and holding onto any that jutted out. Once confident she was not going to fall, she lifted first one foot then the other onto Edward's shoulders. Her gown, now dripping wet, stuck to her legs making movement difficult. Slowly she levered herself up, pleased when she realised she was head and shoulders above the lip of the pit and could see the access passage. She looked around for anything that might offer her a purchase to pull herself up.

"Are you all right, Edward?" she called back. Her voice boomed around the cavern, making her head spin. Swallowing rising nausea, she focused on the floor in front of her beyond the opening. "I might be able to drag myself up, but not with this wet gown hampering me. I am coming back down." Gingerly, she lowered one leg until she felt her foot settle into Edward's hands, and seconds later she was on solid ground. "There is a slim chance I can wriggle up. If I can grab some of the bricks lining the floor of that passage, and if you can push my feet at the same time, I think I could manage it. I need to get out of this dress though."

Edward's ankle was throbbing, every movement, agony, and he too felt dizzy from the after-effects of the drug they unwittingly consumed, but he was not about to tell Lucy. If there was a chance she could get out to alert the others, allowing them to rescue him, it was worth the pain. "Let's do this."

"Please unbutton my gown. I cannot reach around; the material has stiffened being so wet." She turned her back to him and, even though he was wholly unaccustomed to divesting ladies of their clothes, either in or out of the dark, Edward eventually managed to unfasten enough that she could slip it off. Dropping the sodden article on the floor, she also removed her petticoat, stays, and slippers, until she was only wearing her chemise. "Right, that should make climbing out of here a whole lot easier." She said, brightly and with a confidence she did not feel. Edward interlocked his fingers, and taking a breath, Lucy readied herself.

*****

Above them, the hunt continued.

James refused to speak, resolutely ignoring Elspeth's pleas.

The throng of people searching the grounds were stumped.

William, desperately worried for Lucy's safety, not to mention Edward's, suggested they saddle their horses and ride across the estate. They could cover a far greater area more quickly. The others agreed, and soon several men set off in different directions, each taking a sector of the grounds.

William had been riding for about ten minutes when he

came to a sizeable lake, sheltered by the surrounding wood. A heron stood in the reeds at the bank, poised to catch an unwary fish. Sunlight flickered through the trees casting intricate patterns over the water and for a moment he was transfixed. Gypsy was restive and he was about to let her gallop off her fidgets when something caught his eye. An odd mound at the far side of the lake — camouflaged by the dense woodland, making it difficult to see — too small and too solidly built to be a folly. *Was it a boathouse?* It was worth checking. Nudging Gipsy into a trot, he skirted the lake, scattering flocks of waterfowl as he went.

Upon reaching the building he realised its purpose. An icehouse. It looked rather dilapidated. The domed roof was in need of repair, and what should have been a solid wooden doorway to the entrance was crumbling. Ivy tendrils clung to the walls and clumps of grass had taken root in the gaps between the bricks. Clearly abandoned, now nature was reclaiming its own.

He noticed the door was ajar, and his senses went on high alert. Was this where James had brought Lucy and Edward? How the devil had he managed to transport them this far from the house? Scanning the perimeter of the structure, he spied a sturdy cart, probably normally used to carry animal fodder or even ice. Had James used that? William shrugged, he had no clue, and it was more important to check the building. Dismounting, he slung Gipsy's rein over a convenient tree branch and descended the steps to the door. Seizing the edges, he pulled. It creaked ominously on its hinges and a few splinters came away under his fingers as the wood dragged over the bricks, the noise harsh in the quiet.

An indistinct sound. Unsure whether it was a shout from one of the other searchers or from within the icehouse, William paused, waiting, straining his ears. It came again. It sounded as though someone was swearing, and despite the seriousness of the situation, he felt a grin tug at his lips. The voice was dearly familiar.

It was Lucy.

"***Lucy***!" he bawled.

Silence. Then, "William?" A shocked question.

"Yes! I'm here."

"You came for me," wonder in her voice.

"Of course, I came for you. There are promises to be kept and I am not prepared to lose you before they are fulfilled." He heard a 'tsk' and grinned.

"Edward, it's William. I can't believe it, oh thank goodness! William, please hurry, I think I might be stuck."

Her placid tones, completely at odds with her predicament, made William chuckle. "Hang on," he shouted. "I just need to force this door all the way open."

*****

In the icehouse, Lucy had managed to clutch at a piece of brick which was not quite flush with the others. Unfortunately, as she was pulling herself up, she felt it lift. In a quandary now, did she trust it would hold long enough for her to climb out, or did she try for a better purchase? Even though there was a glimmer of light through the gaps in the door, it was not bright enough to give her a clear view of the floor. She was also conscious Edward was fading. She was not naive, aware his ankle pained him far more than he claimed, and the longer he steadied her, the more agonising the injury.

Chilled to the bone and debating whether or not to give up and try again later, Lucy had just suggested the same to Edward when she was temporarily dazzled by sunlight, making her jolt backwards, very nearly losing her balance and her grip.

"Dammit all to hell!" she cursed, adding various other choice expletives. She could hear the rumble of Edward's laughter. "All very well for you to laugh," she groused. "I..." Her next remark cut off when she heard her own name.

"**Lucy!**"

Was that William? She asked, and hearing the affirmative was like music to her ears, he had come for her. He mentioned something about promises which made her tut at the same time as the most delectable warmth infused her whole body. *Goodness, but he knew how to woo a girl*, covering an uncharacteristic shyness by yelling over her shoulder to Edward that they were rescued.

William finally opened the door wide enough to get through and stepped into the passageway. His body blocked the light, and all he could see was the gloom, all he could smell was damp. Images slammed into his mind. A cellar, in an outbuilding, in a village, in France; lying on his back, no strength to keep his head above the rising water, fearing he would drown.

The walls closed in and he stumbled backwards, his chest tightening. He had to get out.

He sucked in a breath.

No, he had to save Lucy.

He *could* do this.

"William?" A plaintive wail echoed along the brick tunnel. He could go and summon help, one of the others would be close enough. *No*, he chided himself, *this is not France, it is not a cellar, and you are not a prisoner. Lucy is depending on you to save her. Get a hold of yourself, man.*

"Coming, sweetheart." In an attempt to flood the passageway with light, William yanked the door back as far as it would go, then edged along sideways. Narrow by necessity to keep the cool air in, the brickwork — he was glad to see — while aged and coated here and there with green moss was of sound construction. Underfoot, the surface was slippery and, unwilling to hurry in case he fell into the pit, William proceeded with caution, forcing back the horror circling his mind. It was harder to see the further in he ventured, but as he came to what seemed to be a slight curve in the passage, he heard another yell.

"William, stop."

Peering down, he saw a grubby hand, hanging on to a brick, which was standing proud of those around it. *Lucy*! Kneeling, he placed a hand over hers. "I'm here." He heard a quiet sob.

"The brick is coming away, I dare not move."

"I've got you." Without removing his hand, William glanced around, noticing that there was a ridge around the arch which marked the opening to the pit. If he sat on the ground and placed his feet in the gap between the ridge and the wall of the passage, he should be able to pull Lucy out. He, or someone else, would need to find a ladder to get Edward out, but first things first. He explained his plan to Lucy, who in turn explained it to Edward.

Closing his eyes and taking a deep breath, William repeated the three phrases his doctor at St Bart's had suggested he use when memories threatened to overwhelm him; *you are not locked in, you will not drown, this is not France*. Composure more or less restored, he shuffled around in the limited space, getting himself in position, knees bent to give him impetus. Sliding his hand under Lucy's wrist, he curled his fingers around her forearm and gripped it tightly, gratified when he felt her reciprocate the gesture. Now she was at the mercy of his strength, and Edward's ability to hold her.

"I am going to count to three. Edward, on three I want you to push Lucy up. Lucy, I want you to hold onto my wrist and let me take your weight. If you are able to propel yourself forward with your other hand, try to do that. There will be a second when my hand is the only thing stopping you from falling back into the pit. Do not, I repeat, do not panic and let go."

"Panic, as if I would panic," Lucy huffed in indignation. William grinned, glad she sounded her usual insouciant self.

"Ready?" he asked her

"Ready."

"Ready, Edward?" he bawled and heard an exhausted 'ready' float up through the opening.

"William?" Lucy could not prevent the tremor in her voice.

"Yes, my love."

"Don't let go."

"Never," William replied, with firm conviction. His nightmares prowled, but he held them at bay. They were his past, he refused to let them interfere with his present. Taking a breath, he began to count. "One, *Two*, **Three**!" On three, he shoved his body away from the opening, bracing his feet on the wall, praying the arch was as solidly built as it appeared. Hauling Lucy with him, he landed on his back, with her on his chest, knocking the wind out of both them.

"Urrgghhh," they groaned in unison.

"Sorry," he heard her muffled apology, her face still buried in his chest. Relinquishing his grasp on her wrist, his arms went around her, as he pressed his lips against her hair, the relief at having her safe, indescribable.

"Why, Miss Truscott, seems 'tis your lot in life to end up lying in the dirt with me." He felt her giggle, at the same moment as he registered she was sodden, cold as ice, looked as though she'd been in a fight with a compost heap and lost, and was wearing naught but her chemise, which had ripped on the brickwork, when he dragged her out of the pit.

"Lucy, you are frozen. Where is your gown? Did he…" his voice roughened as another thought struck him.

"No, William. No, he did not. I had to remove my dress because it was soaked through and made it difficult for me to climb. James must possess the strength of ten men to drag both Edward and me in here and drop us into the pit. I am amazed we are not both dead or badly injured, although I fear Edward has broken his ankle." A hint of awe in her tones at James' feat.

"We must get you warm. Can you stand?" He felt her nod and unable to do much in the confines of the passageway, William got to his feet and helped Lucy up, leading her out of the gloom. As the rays from the sun touched her face, Lucy released a sigh.

"Oh, thank goodness. I was beginning to suspect I might never see daylight again."

William shrugged out of his jacket and wrapped it snugly around her shoulders. He studied her face which was bruised and scratched. "What happened to your face?" He kissed her nose, gentle as a butterfly's wing.

Lucy's forehead crinkled as she tried to remember. "I vaguely recall landing face first on the rug in the library, and I expect I gained several extra bumps on my way here." She flung her hand towards the icehouse. "What about Edward? We cannot leave Edward."

"I have no intention of leaving Edward, my sweet, but I do not have the ability to pull him out too. We need a ladder." Scouring the undergrowth around the edge of the icehouse, William found the ladder James must have removed from the pit, to prevent his victims' escape. It was clean and relatively dry, not a piece of equipment left to the mercy of the elements for more than a couple of hours. Carrying it into the icehouse, William shouted for Edward to move aside, then he slid the ladder over the lip of the pit and let it drop until it bounced on the ground. Angling it so it would not slip, he told Edward to check the stability at his end. He felt the ladder wobble as Edward steadied it.

"Can you climb up?" William queried.

"I can certainly try." Edward's weary reply rose from the dank depths. William wanted nothing more than to be out of this chamber of darkness, but he would not leave Edward.

The ladder moved, then settled, as Edward placed his good foot on the lower rung, but when he tried to bear weight on his injured ankle, pain lanced through him. Lights flashed in his vision and he bit down on a crude oath.

"It's no good Blackthorne, I cannot put my weight on this blasted ankle."

William swore, then told Edward to hang on. Going back to the door of the icehouse, he asked Lucy to take Gipsy and find the other men. Edward would have to be carried out. He could do it, but someone needed to hold the ladder. White with fatigue, Lucy nodded and went to take off William's jacket. "Keep it on, you need it more than I. Drawing her against him, he kissed her forehead and her cheek and her lips. "God, Lucy, I have never been so…"

Her finger came to rest on his mouth. "Hush my love. I am here, you saved me. Although I apologise that while you think 'tis my lot in life to wallow in mud with you, seems 'tis yours to rescue me." She offered the ghost of a grin. "Thank you." She stretched up and kissed him, relishing their connection. "Now, I must get help." Ignoring the persistent grogginess and the shivers she could not control, she followed William to where Gipsy was nibbling some tasty looking leaves.

"William…?" The ground beneath her bare feet was falling away quite steeply. *Not possible, surely it was flat a moment ago.* Her headache, which had worsened gradually, over the past hour or so, had become blinding, and she needed to squint to focus. "William…" she repeated. He said something, but it seemed to come from a vast distance, there was a roaring in her ears and for the second time in twelve hours she pitched forward, only this time William caught her.

Chapter Thirty Five

William, Lucy in his arms, called along the passageway to Edward. "Lucy's fainted. I need to get her back to the house. Someone will be with you shortly." Hoping he sounded reassuring.

"Not to worry, I'm not going anywhere," Edward's wry response, drawing a chuckle from William, who, using the cart as a step, lifted Lucy into Gipsy's saddle, before settling himself behind her. Half-way back to the house, they met Lucas and Rodney who dashed off to rescue Edward.

Lucy, floating in and out of consciousness, was fairly sure she heard her father and Elspeth chattering around her, but acknowledged it could have been her imagination. There was definitely a warm bath somewhere in there, but the rest was never any more than a hazy memory, like a dream, which skitters away upon waking, leaving naught but tantalising wisps.

Climbing up through layers of sleep, Lucy opened her eyes to find she was in her chamber at Gillingham Park, she was blessedly warm, and her headache had lessened to a dull throb — *thank goodness*. Fleetingly, she contemplated whether the whole thing had been a nightmare, quickly dismissed when she shuffled onto her side, to see William, fast asleep in the chair next to her bed. He was holding her hand — *oh, how romantic*. No, that would definitely *not* be allowed if the only thing disturbed was her slumber. The room was dim, the curtains drawn almost closed, but she could still make out the fatigue etched on his face. His scar looked a little angrier than usual, a typical reaction to over-exertion. She wanted to stroke her fingers over the reddened flesh but did not want to wake him.

Lying back against the pillows, questions flooded her mind.

Had William been drugged too? Had everyone been drugged? What happened to the others? Was Elspeth safe? While she was meditating on the consequences of James' actions, William roused. She felt him squeeze her hand and turned her head. He smiled, that beguiling quirk of his lips making her heart flutter.

"Lie with me?" she beseeched, "you cannot be comfortable in that chair." He shook his head, but she tightened her grip on his hand and tugged. "I presume I made an idiot of myself and fainted?" She raised a brow. He nodded, amusement still playing around his mouth. "In that case, you must pander to my every whim. Please…" wishing, for once, she could weep to order, and guilt him into obeying her. She tugged again. This time he moved and lay alongside her, on top of the coverlet, enfolding her in his arms. She snuggled against him, one arm creeping over his stomach, coming to rest on the waistband of his pants. Pressing her lips to his chin, currently all she could reach, she murmured,

"You didn't let me go."

"Of course not, my love. Go back to sleep."

"I love you." Drowsily.

"I love you more." She felt his lips on her hair.

"Not possible." She heard her words slurring.

"Not going to argue with you."

She started to sit up. "Edward?"

"Is in his own bed. Everyone is safe."

Lucy heard him begin to hum a lullaby. "I'm supposed to be the one singing *you* to sleep."

He chuckled. "Hush, love." The humming resumed, she could feel it resonating through his chest, where her head lay. The sound was soporific and, within seconds, slumber had reclaimed her.

William stared down at Lucy. Her dark lashes formed a sooty curve over bruised cheeks — livid against her pallor — and

261

her hair tumbled over his arm in honeyed rivulets. The fear he experienced when she was missing, lingered, and only served to increase his conviction, they were meant to be, that somehow fate had conspired against immeasurable odds to place her in his path, that she was the answer to a prayer he had never dared utter. Holding her close and whispering his love for her, William pillowed his cheek on Lucy's head and closed his eyes.

The next time Lucy awoke, William had gone. Instead, Elspeth and her grandmother, were sitting either side of her bed. Sunlight flooded the room, and she could smell the balmy air through the open windows.

"Finally, you are awake." Her sister's clarion tones banished any hope of going back to sleep. Lucy stretched, groaning when her muscles protested.

"What happened, Lucy?"

"Which part?" she mumbled, still half-asleep.

"How you ended up in the icehouse."

"I have no idea, and did James hurt you?"

"Ha! Hurt me? I did not give him the chance. Those lessons you gave me came in very handy." Elspeth bunched her right hand into a fist and blew across the knuckles. Lucy raised a quizzical brow. "You first," her sister entreated.

Too tired to argue, Lucy yielded and went on to describe what she could recall. "How is Edward?" she enquired when her story was told. Her grandmother patted her hand and assured Lucy he was resting comfortably. Then Elspeth took up the tale and provided a graphic description of her wild carriage ride, making Lucy laugh when she related the moment she punched James Garrick and then brought him to his knees. "I told you that knowledge would come in handy." She caught her grandmother's horrified expression. "I grew up near the rookeries, Lady Ry— Grandmama," she amended quickly at her grandmother's frown. "To be able to look after yourself is essential."

She paused and fiddled with the coverlet. "What of James?"

"He is on his way back to London, guarded by Major Withers.

"Where was he taking you, Elspeth?"

"Apparently he thought I might appreciate living out my days in the East Indies."

Lucy's mouth fell open, but upon hearing James' destination, several small and seemingly insignificant details coalesced. She slapped her hand on the top of the covers.

"That's it! That's what was bothering me." The other two stared at her in astonishment. "Forgive me, but I have been trying to fathom why the word travel has been pestering me." She elaborated, telling them what she had overheard in the Rycote's library one evening not long after Elspeth and she had met. She shook her head. "How did he think he was going to get you on board ship?"

Elspeth shrugged. "He was of the opinion, I would fall in with his plans without complaint. The man is insane. It was very satisfying to land one on him." She smiled beatifically, her use of the vernacular drawing an exasperated 'tut' from her grandmother.

"I apologise, Grandmama, I am a bad influence." Lucy did not appear particularly repentant, and the dowager countess swallowed unexpected mirth at her irrepressible granddaughters. To her relief, neither was any the worse for their adventures.

"All that just because he wanted to *be* someone," Lucy remarked. "I used to think Seven Dials was bad, Society is far more dangerous." She flung back the covers. "I am getting up. I cannot lie abed all afternoon. I need to see William."

Smiling knowingly, the other two left the room, and without Lucy lifting a finger, a maid, Liza, appeared to help her dress. "Oh dear, my clothes are in the icehouse." She started to explain, then the incongruity of her statement hit her, and she burst out laughing. Sobering, she submitted to the maid's ministrations and was assisted into a gown which Liza informed her was one of Lady Rycote's. As she stood in front of the mirror, Lucy realised it was very similar to the one worn by her grandmother in the painting at Rycote House; the dove grey silk, the perfect complement to her eyes and hair. She smiled at her reflection. Hopefully William would be impressed.

He was!

*****

By the end of that day, all the tales were told — the enormity of James' duplicity only now beginning to sink in. That he had perpetrated the incidents in the first place was bad enough, that he deceived everyone into suspecting Edward, was heinous. Edward confessed that when James and he were delayed while out riding, their fight was because James threatened to reveal what he, Edward, had managed to keep hidden. Edward, undaunted by the prospect of being blackmailed, rejected James' proposition, preferring to risk being shunned.

Hence the fisticuffs.

Blackmail, kidnap, and bodily harm, not to mention the drugging of several members of the nobility and one high-ranking government operative, could not be brushed aside and James would be in front of a judge immediately upon his return to London. The local magistrate willing, nay, relieved to defer his jurisdiction in this case.

After dinner, William asked Lucy whether she would like to take a stroll.

"If you promise not to take me anywhere near that smelly old icehouse, I should be delighted." She smiled and took his proffered arm. When they stepped out into the evening air, however, it was clear their constitutional would be curtailed. Across the horizon, lightning flickered, and black clouds were massing, signalling the onset of a storm.

"What a shame." Lucy sighed when she heard a distant rumble.

"Well, dash it all, that rather spoils my plans for the rest of the evening.

"You had plans?" Lucy arched a brow. "Pray, enlighten me."

William bent his head and whispered in her ear. His breath caressed sensitive skin, sending frissons down her spine.

"Oh my." She blushed and pretended to fan her face. "I shall hold you to that, but as the weather seems to have thwarted your designs, might we at least take a short walk? The tempest is a way off."

"I can think of nothing I should like more." William chuckled at her slightly dazed expression. The two stepped out across the gravel of the driveway, seeking the path leading to the formal gardens. They had barely reached the neatly trimmed flower beds, however, before the breeze strengthened, whipping Lucy's skirts around her legs, and tearing at her hair. The oppressive air seemed to crackle, as forks of lightning rent the sky, and the thunder grew louder with every passing moment. Even in the grey gloom, the strange haze heralding torrential rain, or possibly hail, driven ahead of the encroaching storm was unmistakable.

"This is madness we need to get indoors." William hurried Lucy back to the house. "I should check on Gipsy," he added, "she is liable to panic during storms, and because she is usually so docile, I ought to warn the grooms. My presence is generally enough to calm her." He pushed his betrothed gently towards the door.

"Don't be long," she called. He lifted a hand and hurried

around the side of the main house heading for the stables. About to go inside, Lucy was halted by Elspeth, who appeared in front of her.

"I love storms." She grinned. "And I think this one will be quite fearsome. Watch it with me?"

Lucy, who bore a healthy antipathy towards extremes of weather, swallowed her aversion, and stood with her sister watching nature's light show. The inky blackness was riven by never-ending flashes, celestial fingers of luminescence flaring out like hundreds of ribbons as far as the eye could see. The storm was moving fast now, and the temperature plummeted as the first drops of rain began to pelt the ground. The wind howled around the building and the roar of thunder was almost deafening. It was a sight to behold.

Awed by the untameable power of nature, the two women were spellbound, moving into the shelter of the massive doorway to avoid getting soaked. Lucy caught movement out of the corner of her eye, and assuming it was William, turned her head and smiled.

Anything she was about to say died on her lips when she saw it was a man on a horse, and he was less than ten feet away. Lucy frowned, puzzled as to who would be foolish enough to come visiting at this time of night and in such awful weather. Although, she reasoned with herself, he must have been nearly at the estate when the storm struck, maybe he'd come to beg shelter until it passed. The horse was rearing, clearly terrified of the cacophony raging around it. The man slid off and released his grip on the reins, of which the horse took full advantage, neighing loudly and galloping off in the direction of the stables. *Clever horse,* thought Lucy, subconsciously registering that the creature knew where to go, still staring at the newcomer, his identity masked by the downpour.

The man stood motionless for several seconds; buffeted by the wind and drenched by the rain. Then he strode towards them and Lucy's heart leapt into her throat.

It was James.

Her stomach tying itself in big, huge, enormous knots, Lucy risked a glance at her sister, who was gaping at James in shock, and she knew they were both thinking the same thing. *How was he here? He was supposed to be under lock and key. Would they **ever** be rid of this maniac?*

Lucy seized Elspeth's hand, and slowly they began to edge backwards. The door was inches behind them, but it was heavy and opened with excruciating slowness. Could they risk it?

"Do not move." His barked order reinforced by the pistol he was pointing at them.

Confounded — *where the devil did he get a **gun**?* — Lucy's momentary bewilderment, that not only had he escaped Lucas' custody, but also that he must have stolen a gun, flared into outrage at the amount of distress this man had caused.

"How dare you point that weapon at us?" she spat, her temper bubbling and, aware she had a tendency to be reckless when angry, did her best to quash it.

"You should be dead," he snarled. "If madam here had not overreacted, you probably would be. I will not make the mistake of trusting her again."

"Overreacted? Managed to escape you mean? How is your manhood by the way?" Lucy quipped with saccharine sweetness. She felt Elspeth trembling through their joined hands and prayed she could distract James long enough that someone would come and find them.

"Mind your business and cease your yapping, harpy. You are naught but a parvenu, who should have stayed in the slums where you belong. Come, Elspeth, we have a boat to meet." He stretched out his hand towards Elspeth, who shook her head, her lips clamped together to hide the fact her teeth were chattering, from cold and fear.

"Harpy? Did you just call me a harpy?" Lucy shrieked, and the two began to argue.

Insults flew, their voices battling with the storm and, for once, James was out of his league. He might know a few choice slurs but, while she was growing up and despite Cecilia's best efforts, Lucy had overheard and stored away a spectacular variety of profanities. Releasing Elspeth's hand, she stalked towards the deranged man, unleashing a barrage of expletives which, under normal circumstances, would cause a lesser man to quail, and ought to have made Elspeth blush — in fact they would have probably made the dockhands at Rotherhithe blush — but Elspeth was too scared to register the actual words, and although James took several steps backwards, he did not pause in his vitriol, neither did he lower the gun.

None at the centre of the scene noticed three more people enter the frame.

Something, and he never knew what, prompted William to circle back around to the front of the house after settling Gipsy. Rodney, wondering where Elspeth had vanished to, poked his head out of the front door. Lucas Withers, who rode from the coaching inn like a man possessed and who had dismounted out of sight in the shrubbery, materialised from the gloom, alongside William, positioning himself as close behind James as he dared.

Well versed in diffusing tense stand-offs, Lucas made eye contact with William and Rodney who nodded their acknowledgement. They would wait for his signal before acting.

Fear for her sister outweighed her own fright and, heedless of the deluge, Elspeth dashed over to where Lucy and James were trading obscenities.

"James," she entreated. "Why are you doing this? You are, you were, my friend. I trusted you and you betrayed me. How did it come to this?" She pointed to the gun which he was waving dangerously close to Lucy. A child of the nobility, Elspeth's status and sheltered upbringing protected her from the harsh world beyond her privileged doorstep. This meant she always saw the good in people, and to concede anyone, let alone a person she considered family, would deliberately cause her or anyone she loved harm was beyond her comprehension. Thus, even after everything she had endured, not to mention a surfeit of indisputable evidence, Elspeth was still not absolutely convinced of James' guilt.

James gave a cruel smile. "*Friend? **Friend**!* I was never your *friend,* Elspeth. You are naught but a means to an end. The woman whose status will provide the influence I will need when we arrive, whose presence will open doors, previously slammed in my face because I am not of the *ton*. That you are passably pretty and have an affection for me is merely a bonus."

"*You* were the one calling me your love, not the other way around." Elspeth was dumbfounded, unable to equate this volatile man to the James she thought she knew. "Why me? Of all the eligible women, why me?" she could not help but ask.

"You were there," he sneered. Elspeth blanched, prompting him to add. "I hoped you might come to love me, it would make our life together somewhat easier, and I presumed a few endearments would sweeten the pot, but no matter." He jabbed the gun towards her. "Do you know, my cousin turns her nose up at us… my cousin." His voice rising, contempt hardening his features. "Have you any idea what that feels like? Of course not, you are far too pampered to care about those beneath you. People falling over themselves to do your bidding, with little or no recompense. You talk of betrayal. After everything I've done for you, arranged for you, 'tis *you* who betrayed *me*. You think I am prepared to accede my claim to Westbrook, a more inept man I have yet to meet. Elspeth, you are mine, you have been mine since first I laid eyes on you. You owe me. Come now, 'tis time."

During James' speech, Elspeth remained motionless, stunned at his rationale, or lack thereof. If he had not been waving a loaded pistol she might have laughed at the absurdity of his words. When he made his final demand, however, the last vestiges of belief in the man she had trusted with her very life, fell away.

"*Yours?* How *dare* you? I am no one's possession. Pray tell me, how on earth did you plan to drag an unwilling woman onto a ship? More drugs? The intimation I was mad and therefore needed subduing? Was your intent to pay the captain handsomely to marry us even though I was *insensible*? James, I cared for you as a friend, but friendship is not enough to build a life together. You just wanted me for your own selfish aspirations."

In the middle of a maelstrom, looking more than a little bedraggled, Elspeth straightened her shoulders and emptied her face of all expression. Then, with as much dignity as she could muster, spun on her heel and began to walk back to the house.

"Goodbye, James."

"**NO**," he bellowed. Elspeth's hollow dismissal shattered the last of his dwindling sanity. "You will *not* walk away from me again."

Through the din, Lucy heard a click.

James raised his arm and pointed the gun at Elspeth.

Guessing his intent, unadulterated horror sent shards of ice along Lucy's veins, and she began to move. Everything slowed down, the intermittent streaks of lightning giving James and Elspeth a ghostly aspect, and she prayed it was not a portent. The racket from the storm faded and all she could hear was her heartbeat. It seemed as though she was wading through quicksand. She wouldn't reach Elspeth in time. Barely a hair's breadth from her sister, Lucy saw a flash, and the report of a gun being discharged, reverberated around them. Screaming, she flung herself at Elspeth, shoving her with brute force. The sisters crashed to the ground. Landing hard on the gravel, the air knocked out of her, Lucy registered an excruciating pain pierce her side. As a grey mist blurred the edges of her vision, she was astonished to see a gaping hole appear in James' forehead, blood arcing from the wound. He dropped like a stone, his lifeblood merging with the unceasing rain.

She could see three pairs of boots, then became aware of hands moving over her. The pain was spreading.

"***Lucy***!" She heard William bawl, and then he was lifting her off the sodden ground. "Lucy, don't you dare die on me. You promised me forever and I refuse to let you renege on the deal."

"Elspeth?" Lucy croaked. Fighting the blackness that seemed determined to claim her.

"Is fine. Rodney has her."

"Hard to breathe. Side hurts," she whimpered.

"You have been shot my love, but please keep breathing."

"William…" she felt his lips on her cheek.

"Yes, my darling."

"I think I might be going to faint again. Please don't let go." The last thing she heard was,

"Never!"

Chapter Thirty Six

The storm finally blew itself out in the early hours of the following morning. Lucy had not regained consciousness. Lucas Withers, who possessed a rudimentary knowledge of wound care, had tended to her injury. The bullet, thankfully, only grazed her side, missing anything vital, but she lost quite a lot of blood. This, according to the family doctor — when he came at Lady Rycote's urgent behest to examine Lucy at his *earliest* convenience — on top of her recent ordeal in the icehouse, accounted for her prolonged insensibility.

James' body had been removed, all traces of blood washed away by the relentless rain. When dawn broke, on a perfect summer's day, not even the smallest hint of what transpired scant hours earlier, remained — for which everyone was truly grateful. At first light, Lucas set off for London. He offered to deal with all matters pertaining to the unexpected death of James Garrick, including the bizarre circumstances leading up to and surrounding it.

Seeing a crazed lunatic aiming a gun at Elspeth, galvanised Rodney into action, and he petitioned Lord Rycote to approve his suit. The couple, officially affianced, were already behaving in the giddiest fashion, prompting Christopher to propose they marry with all haste.

Confined to bed, Edward had no idea of what happened during the storm, his bedchamber being at the back of the house. Appalled when apprised of the details, he questioned how James had managed to abscond from under Lucas' nose, something everyone wanted to know. It was later revealed, James had bribed the man — whom Lucas paid handsomely to guard his prisoner while he organised a meal — with an even larger sum. Lucas was away from the room for less than fifteen minutes, but it was all James needed. Patrons of the coaching inn were far too trusting, leaving their belongings within easy reach, allowing James to steal a gun *and* a horse, before hightailing it back to Gillingham Park.

The rest they knew.

Although saddened at James' demise, his perfidy had already broken the bonds once shared, and perhaps death was the lesser retribution for his actions. Thus, although the reason behind his behaviour would never be completely clear, it was over and, at least this way, his family would not suffer for his treachery.

William refused to leave Lucy, her second brush with death in as many days, making him consider that never letting her out of his sight again would be too soon. Back at Harcourt House, an important document lay safely tucked away in his desk and he hoped Lucy might be agreeable to its contents.

The sun was already on its slow descent, sparkling on the rain-washed leaves and enveloping Gillingham Park in mellow radiance, when Lucy finally awoke. In the chair by her bedside, William was dozing, his hand entwined in hers. Puzzled, the picture was so familiar, Lucy ruminated whether the storm had been a figment of her overactive imagination. Then she tried to move, unable to prevent a groan at the pain ratchetting through her and realised it was no dream.

William aroused at her agonised moan. "Lucy."

"William…? I… oooof, that hurts." Her breath catching.

"Just rest my love, you were shot."

"It was real then? Not a nightmare?"

William smiled his lopsided smile. "I am sorry, it was real."

"James?"

"Is dead."

"Elspeth?"

"Is floating around the house in betrothed rapture."

"She and Rodney are betrothed?" Lucy squealed and without thinking, threw back the covers. The sudden movement made her head spin and sent another bolt of pain through her side. She hissed. "Bloody hell. What did he shoot me with, a cannon?"

"Nice to see you have woken," a deep voice spoke from the doorway. Christopher Gillingham walked over to the bed and stared down at her. Lucy flushed, feeling like a child caught stealing fresh biscuits from the kitchen. "If you might indulge a father's ageing heart and refrain from confronting deranged madmen for a while, I should be most grateful."

"Sorry, Papa," she muttered, her tones *almost* contrite. "In my defence, I did not arrange for him to escape his guard and come back here," she protested, holding the hawk-like gaze of the earl. Christopher grinned and reaching over the bed, patted her hand.

"I am glad you are still with me, my daughter. Although I suspect I am about to lose both my children in the not too distant future. Two betrothals. Mayhap I can persuade Elspeth and Rodney to stay on at Rycote House, 'tis large enough for a newly-wed couple to have some privacy." The earl chatted a little longer, then seeing Lucy's eyes drooping, took his leave.

"I cannot keep my eyes open," she murmured, sliding down the pillows.

"Then sleep," William coaxed.

"Lie with me," repeating her plea of forty-eight hours previously.

"I do not want to jar you.

"Lie here," indicating her uninjured side. Gingerly, William lowered himself onto the bed, taking care not to jostle Lucy. She reached for his hand and brought it to her lips.

"I love you."

"I love you too, now sleep."

*****

During the next week or so, Lucy slept more than she was awake but, blessed with a natural resilience and healthy constitution, her recovery — while not as fast as she would have liked, patience being a virtue which had bypassed Lucy — was not protracted. The doctor recommended she travel back to London by carriage, riding a horse not the most conducive exercise for a healing gunshot wound. The violent storm, which wreaked havoc across the county, left days of uninterrupted sunshine in its wake. Lucy, who had grown to love Gillingham Park, in spite of everything that had happened, took full advantage of the balmy weather and the restrictions imposed by the doctor, enjoying daily constitutionals around the estate, or relaxing in the shade of one of the many sprawling trees; the restful, ever-changing scenery soothing.

William rarely left her side and she relished his attentiveness. Aware he worried about her being out of his sight, however, did feel it fair to warn him that she would have a thing or two to say should he become over-protective once they were back in London.

"If we are together all the time, we will have nothing to discuss at day's end. Moreover, if you are working for Lucas how can you also be with me?" she pointed out one afternoon about three weeks later — quite reasonably she thought.

"I know, my love, and you are correct. In truth, I have no desire to clip your wings, I love your free spirit and independence. All I ask is that you humour me for a little longer — at the moment the memory of that night is too close."

"Maybe this will assuage your fears…" Glad they were far

from prying eyes, Lucy kissed William with a fervour that turned his head to soup. Minutes ticked by, then, lifting her head, she held his gaze — subdued storm-cloud on glittering sky-blue. "I never..." she kissed his scarred cheek, "break..." his jawline, "my promises," recapturing his lips, while her hands tugged at his shirt — the day was hot and he had removed his waistcoat and jacket earlier, both of which hung over the edge of the bench they were sitting on.

Cool fingers sought the hardened planes of his chest, and she felt William's heart rate soar. Just as suddenly she withdrew and leaned away to study his beloved features. His expression was comical. "You see," she grinned impishly. "I am very much alive."

"Lucy Truscott, you cannot do that to a man. Have you any idea...?" he trailed off, his voice raspy.

"Show me."

"Beg pardon?"

"Show me what it does to a man."

... and in the dappled light under a majestic copper beech tree, on a country estate in the middle of nowhere, William did just that.

Epilogue

It was mild for the time of year, the harsh winter quickly forgotten now the trees were beginning to sprout new growth. Lucy Harcourt, Marchioness of Blackthorne — a title that never failed to amuse her — was leaning against the frame of the open French doors leading from the library to the terrace. She was reminded it was a year to the day since she met William, grinning to herself in memory of that less than auspicious encounter. Who could have guessed it would lead to such happiness?

The months since she was shot had flown by. Upon their return to London, William mentioned with studied casualness that he had obtained a special licence, permitting their nuptials as soon as they could be arranged should she be amenable. *Should she be amenable? As though he had to ask!* Her grin becoming a chuckle when she recalled her response.

They were married a week later. The ceremony, organised by William with the help of Christopher, took place in the park at the edge of the daffodil garden. Of course, there were no daffodils flowering in June, but by some miracle, William had managed to nurture a bowl-full, which stood proudly on the small table carried down for the occasion. Surrounded by family, friends, and the staff from both their homes, William and Lucy pledged their lives to each other.

The year moved on, the seasons changed. William began his role within Lucas' organisation and Lucy resumed her days at The Wise Owl. The couple rarely attended Society functions, content among their tight-knit circle, which now included those with whom William worked — people from every walk of life. William no longer hid his scars. If being with Lucy had taught him anything, it was that if others were not able to face him, on their head be it. He could not change what had happened and, although there was once a time, he wished he could — no more. To be loved as unconditionally as Lucy loved him, was a gift few were fortunate to be granted.

Smiling, in recollection, Lucy stepped out onto the stone flagged terrace, breathing in the velvety air. So early in the year, the light faded rapidly; above her, the sky was darkening to purple as the sun slowly disappeared behind the houses. There was just enough time. Hugging her blue woollen wrap around her shoulders, Lucy meandered through the garden and out into the park. As ever, her path led her to the daffodil garden, which was full to bursting with blooms — their bright yellow heads bobbing in the breeze still reminded her of gossiping women at the market. Lost in contemplation, she did not hear her name being called, or the steady approach of footsteps. Nothing until a voice spoke close to her ear.

"Lucy…"

Startled, she spun to face him. "William, how marvellous. You are home early."

"'Tis a special day, and I wanted to spend as much of it as possible with my wife. I guessed you would be here."

Lucy could not prevent the broad grin from curving her lips. "I was not sure whether you would remember."

"Forget the day I met the woman who changed my life? Never." He stood behind her, drawing her flush with his body and bringing his cloak around both of them, as they admired the flourishing garden in the waning daylight.

"I think this might be my favourite corner in the whole world," Lucy murmured, delighting in his embrace.

"Lucy," he repeated.

"Hmmm…"

"I have a mind to kiss you."

"Why, my lord, do you really?"

"I do."

Lucy moved away from him and twirled her skirts, grinning. William thought he detected a wicked gleam in their blue-grey depths. "I have a mind to let you…" William took one step, "…but you'll have to catch me first." Before he could blink, Lucy had hitched her gown and fled across the park.

"Why you…" his jaw dropped and for several seconds he stood, gaping like a stranded codfish. A burst of laughter drifted back to him and, as though released from a spell, he chased after her. She had a decent head start and was fleet of foot, but his loping stride closed the gap rapidly and it wasn't long before he seized her around her waist and swung her over his shoulder.

"Hey," she panted, "what are you doing?" Trying to wriggle around. "William?" He held her fast and she had to make do with beating her fists on his back. Barely contained mirth rumbled in William's chest while he strode back to the daffodil garden. Loosening his grip, he stood her down gently and waited for her to berate him.

Hands on hips, she glared at him, but he did not give her chance to speak. Whisking her into his arms, he kissed her into silence. When their mouths met, and righteously indignant, Lucy tried to hold herself rigid, but he knew when she melted against him with a sigh, he was forgiven. They sank onto the grass, fingers searching, finding, and unfastening, buttons and ribbons. Cloak, jacket, cravat, waistcoat, and wrap were flung haphazardly across the ground with careless abandon. Lucy's gown yielding to William's persistence, his 'I shall never know why you women need so many buttons', making her giggle. She pulled his shirt over his head, as always marvelling at his toned physique, taking the time to trace knotty scars, following her fingers with her lips.

"William…" she sucked in a breath when his relentless fingers removed her chemise, the cool air only partially the reason for the tingles running over her skin.

Grabbing his cloak and placing it on the grass beneath his wife, William played her with the consummate skill of a maestro tuning a treasured instrument, until her whole body strummed with desire. The exquisite torment he was inflicting had Lucy writhing under him, the crescendo she was climbing staying just out of reach.

"William…" her voice caught.

He paused and lifted his head, her eyes mesmerised him, and her skin had taken on an ethereal glow in the encroaching twilight. "Do you have any idea how beautiful you are?" he murmured against her ear.

"Show me," she whispered, her chest rising and falling as she strove to steady her erratic breathing. He leaned back a little further and raked his eyes over her face. "Show me," she repeated, tugging at the fall of his trousers.

"I wanted tonight to be extra special." William managed to croak, as inquisitive fingers encircled him.

"Do you not think this is special? Among our daffodils and under the stars?"

There was a moment's silence while he held her gaze, then he smiled his tender, achingly sweet, and irresistibly quirky smile.

"I think, while we are likely to get rather damp, it is absolutely perfect," he said, tucking an errant strand of hair behind her ear before lowering his head to kiss her.

Dusk gave way to night, and as the veil of stars gradually winked into existence, preparing to light the moon's path across an obsidian sky, William, with intoxicating tenderness, demonstrated to his wife — his heart, his soul and his redemption — just how beautiful she was.

Scars are not always visible, and some are never revealed, but if you are lucky enough to meet that one person who loves you, not only in spite of them but also *because* of them — never let them go.

*****

Thank you for buying and reading this book - I hope you enjoyed it.

If you would like to check out my other novels, they are listed below.

Other Books by Rosie Chapel

Historical Fiction
The Hannah's Heirloom Sequence
The Pomegranate Tree - Hannah's Heirloom - Book One
Echoes of Stone and Fire - Hannah's Heirloom - Book Two
Embers of Destiny - Hannah's Heirloom - Book Three
Etched in Starlight - Hannah's Heirloom - Prequel
Hannah's Heirloom Trilogy - Compilation – e-book only

Prelude to Fate

Regency Romances
Once Upon An Earl - Linen and Lace - Book One
To Unlock Her Heart - Linen and Lace - Book Two
Love on a Winter's Tide - Linen and Lace - Book Three
A Love Unquenchable - Linen and Lace - Book Four
A Hidden Rose - Linen and Lace - Book Five

His Fiery Hoyden - A Regency Novella
A Regency Duet
A Regency Christmas Double

Contemporary Romances
Of Ruins and Romance
All At Once It's You

Anthologies
The Lady's Wager - For Melissa
Love Kindled - Building Love
Winning Emma - With Love From London - Voyages of the Heart:

Chasing Bluebells - Wicked Spawns - A Legacy of Evil - release date
TBA
A Guardian Unexpected - Unconditional - ASPCA Anthology TBR
Oct 2019

The Pomegranate Tree
Hannah's Heirloom - Book One

Hoping to trace the origins of an ancient ruby clasp, a gift from her long dead grandmother, Hannah Wilson travels to the fortress of Masada with her best friend, Max. Strange dreams concerning a rebel ambush begin to haunt Hannah and following a tragic accident, she slips into the world of Ancient Masada.

A woman out of time, Hannah must rely on her instincts and her knowledge of what will befall this citadel to survive. Will she escape, or is she doomed to die along with hundreds of others as Masada falls — and what does any of this have to do with an ancient ruby clasp?

Echoes of Stone and Fire
Hannah's Heirloom - Book Two

Pompeii - a vibrant city lost in time following the AD79 eruption of Vesuvius. Now rediscovered, archaeologists yearn for an opportunity to uncover the town's past. Some things however, are best left alone - revealing the secrets hidden beneath the stones could prove perilous. Hannah and Max are brought to Pompeii by a surprise invitation to join an excavation team who are trying to uncover the city's long history.

After entering an excavated house that bears a Hebrew inscription, Hannah's two worlds collide, and she falls back through time to ancient Pompeii. A place where her ancestor is a physician to gladiators engaged in mortal combat, where riotous mobs run amok and where a ghost from the past returns to haunt her.

Will Hannah and her loved ones manage to escape the devastation she knows is coming, before the town is engulfed in volcanic ash? Will she ever find her way back to Max the love of her life, waiting not so patiently millennia away? Or will echoes be all that remain?

Embers of Destiny
Hannah's Heirloom - Book Three

AD80 - Hannah and Maxentius must embark on a new journey to Northern Britannia. This harsh frontier is far from the comforts of Rome and danger lurks where least expected; a garrison of soldiers, some unhappy with their isolated posting; local tribes, outwardly accepting of their Roman occupier, but who may still resent the seizure of their lands.

Millennia away, Hannah Vallier finds a familiar item while working in a museum near Hadrian's Wall. It is the pomegranate; carved by Maxentius on Masada. Before Hannah can discuss it with Max, disaster strikes! Believing her husband has been killed, Hannah retreats into the past, her soul melding with that of her ancestor, but with little idea of what they could face. Is the risk from the conquered tribes, or much closer to home?

As rebellion threatens to shatter a fragile peace, Hannah's heart whispers that just maybe Max isn't dead and that he is calling her home. Can she trust her heart or will she remain caught out of time, her destiny floating away like embers on a breeze?

Etched in Starlight
Hannah's Heirloom - Prequel

Maxentius - a Roman soldier fresh from the battlefields of
Armenia, arrives to take command of the military outpost of
Masada, Herod's isolated citadel in the Judaean desert. A
seemingly mundane posting after years of warfare, Maxentius
finds it more challenging to maintain a focused garrison than to
face the wrath of the Parthians across a disputed frontier.

Hannah - a young Hebrew physician spends her days dealing
with injuries from street brawls, deprivation, disease and loss. As
her beloved Jerusalem plunges into chaos; her brother — who
belongs to a band of rebels determined to drive out their Roman
occupiers — tells her of their plans to storm a desert fortress and
steal the weapons stored there, persuading his reluctant sister to
go with him.

Masada - following the ambush, Hannah finds and treats
three badly wounded Roman soldiers. In the aftermath and
against impossible odds, Hannah and Maxentius realise that
they are more than healer and captive, their fate already etched
in starlight.

Prelude to Fate

For Lucia, staring into the jaws of an horrific death, escape seems impossible.

Rufius Atellus, a veteran Roman soldier, is appalled when he recognises one of the victims about to be executed. Surely this is a ghastly mistake?

A ferocious she-wolf, anticipating a tasty meal, suddenly finds herself under a human's control.

In an unexpected twist, and as danger threatens, the lives of all three become inextricably entwined.

Was it chance brought them together in that theatre of bloodshed, or simply a prelude to fate?

Once Upon An Earl
A Regency Romance
Linen and Lace - Book One

When Fate saw fit to intervene in the life of Giles Trevallier, the very respectable Earl of Winchester, by dropping a female — soaked to the skin and with no memory of who she is or how she came to be there — literally at his feet, no one could have predicted the outcome.

While uncovering her identity, Giles realises he is falling hopelessly in love with his mystery guest, who unbeknownst to him, is succumbing to similar emotions; but, when the heart is involved, a thoughtless word or gesture can thwart even Fate's best-laid plans.

Faced with misunderstandings, whispers of scandal, secret documents and foreign agents, their chance at a happy ever after seems elusive, but fairy tales often happen when least expected, and love — however inconvenient — usually finds a way to conquer all.

To Unlock Her Heart
A Regency Romance
Linen and Lace - Book Two

Abused by a duke, and shunned by Society, relief seems at hand when Grace Aldeburgh is bequeathed a house in a small village, far from malicious gossips.

Once there, a tentative friendship blooms between Grace and Theo Elliott, the local doctor, who has already resolved to be the man to unlock her heart.

Just when happiness appears to be within her grasp, her erstwhile tormentor once again stalks Grace. After a failed kidnap attempt, the duke's quest culminates in an acrimonious confrontation, and the reason for his venal pursuit becomes agonisingly clear.

Love on a Winter's Tide
A Regency Romance
Linen and Lace - Book Three

Every day, Helena disappears into a world few acknowledge, helping the poor, downtrodden, and abused. A husband is the last thing she can be bothered with.

Busy managing his shipping line, Hugh Drummond sees no need for a wife, whose only joy is dancing and frivolity. If — and it was a huge if — he ever married, it would be to a woman as capable as he, not some giddy society Miss.

Then, Hugh meets Helena and despite their resolve, fate, it seems, has other ideas. As their attraction deepens however, treachery threatens to tear them apart. Will they uncover the perpetrator in time or will their love be swept away, lost forever on a winter's tide?

A Love Unquenchable
A Regency Romance
Linen and Lace - Book Four

Jessica Drummond, a bright and cheerful young woman, rarely gives romance, let alone love, a thought. Long hours working in her brother's shipping office affords little chance of her ever meeting an eligible bachelor.

Duncan Barrington, veteran of the Napoleonic Wars, believes himself wounded in both body and soul. He has no intention of inflicting his demons on anyone, certainly not a beautiful and, in his opinion, irresponsible city lady.

One cold and snowy morning, the plight of a bedraggled puppy throws Jessica and Duncan together and, as a spark of something indefinable yet wholly unquenchable begins to burn, it is unclear who rescued whom.

A Hidden Rose
A Regency Romance
Linen and Lace - Book Five

After witnessing his mother's grief at the loss of his father, Nick Drummond resolved never to cause someone he loved such distress. Even the happiness of his siblings would not sway him – until he met Rose.

Rose Archer was almost content assisting her doctor father in a tiny fishing village in the north of Yorkshire. To experience the world beyond, a tantalising dream – until she met Nick.

Unexpectedly, the impossible becomes possible, and the renounced – desired above all things, but the shipwreck that brought them together, may yet tear them apart. Will Nick learn to trust his heart, or will his love for Rose remain forever hidden?

His Fiery Hoyden
A Regency Novella

Please inform your master, Sasha is perfectly happy here with me and there is more chance of hell freezing over, than of my brother dancing attendance on his Grace."

A plea for help ignored. A child left to bring up her baby brother.

Livvy has no respect for the nobility; they let her down when she most needed them. Why should she accede to their demands now?

Philip, Lord Harrington, is stunned to discover the young heir to the dukedom lives a stone's throw away in a ramshackle cottage, and resolves to restore the child to his birthright.

They meet in a clash of wills, but just when it seems Livvy might surrender, the victory Philip desires, may not taste all that sweet.

A Regency Duet

Luck be a Pirate
(first published in the Kiss My Luck Anthology)

Luck wasn't something retired pirate Kennet Alexson believed in – good or bad. However, even he had to concede that landing a job at Trentams shipyard, and meeting Lynette Collins, was more than coincidence.

Fortune it seemed, was smiling on him for once.

As Kennet adjusts to life on dry land, his friendship with Lynette deepens into something far more enduring, and what once seemed elusive now becomes possible.

Unfortunately, fate has other plans, and Kennet's good luck is about to run out.

The Highwayman's Kiss
(first published in the Once Upon a Love anthology)

Nothing exciting had ever happened to Juliette St Clair. Her days were spent assisting her father or calling on friends, wandering art galleries, taking constitutionals or, and more preferably, escaping into her books. Her evenings her evenings — an endless round of balls, where she preferred to remain invisible.

Until the day she was robbed by a highwayman.

A Regency Christmas Double

Heart Rescued
(originally published in the Tales for the Season Anthology)

Four years since Jasper lost the woman he was hoping to marry. Four years since he closed his heart and withdrew from Society. He has no idea his reclusive existence is about to be shattered.

Enter his sister's best friend, Harriet, a flame haired beauty, who needs his help.

Reluctantly he agrees and as they spend time together, it is clear their feelings run deep. Although Harriet affects Jasper in a way no woman ever has, he believes her to be out of his league ~ but it's Christmas and she might just be the one to melt his frozen heart

Catch a Snowflake

Romance often blossoms in the most unlikely of places - but in a ward full of wounded soldiers - surely not?

When Lucas Withers comes face to face with Jemima Parsons - a young woman who blames him for her brother's injury - falling in love is the last thing on their minds. What neither of them anticipated, was the magic of snowflakes.

Of Ruins and Romance

While escorting a group of tourists around the ancient Roman port of Ostia, Kassandra Winters bumps into someone she first met in less than auspicious circumstances two years previously. The encounter leads to a job offer - to be the assistant guide for a three-week tour of ancient sites in and around Rome. Unable to resist such an opportunity, Kassie agrees.

Kassie has intrigued Gabriel St Germain since he accidentally knocked her flying outside her university professor's office. Her face haunts his dreams, yet he never expected to see her again. So, he is surprised when she appears, as though destined to do so, in the middle of a ruin, and he concocts a plan to win her heart.

Gabriel's old-fashioned courtship touches something deep inside Kassie and, although struggling to believe someone as handsome as Gabriel could possibly be interested in her, she soon realises she has fallen irrevocably in love with him. However, just as Kassie shares everything of herself with Gabriel, her world comes crashing down. Can their romance survive or will it fall in ruins, like the relics of antiquity that brought them together?

All At Once It's You

When Alex arrives in the small village of Rosedale Abbey, to take up a position as a research assistant for a renowned archaeologist, the last thing she is looking for, or expects to find, is love.

Jake was perfectly happy with the status quo. When it came to relationships, he didn't do committed or long term. He called the shots, and if his current flame didn't like it, she knew what to do. A philosophy, which served him well - until he met Alex.

Romance blooms, but even as the untamed wilderness of the North Yorkshire moors weaves its spell, a long-buried secret might yet jeopardise their happily ever after.

CPSIA information can be obtained
at www.ICGtesting.com
Printed in the USA
BVHW041424120419
545366BV00009B/56/P